I0735897

CLAIM

LUNA MASON

CLAIM

Copyright © 2025 by Luna Mason.

All rights reserved. No part of this book may be reproduced in any form or by any electronic or

mechanical means, including information storage and retrieval systems, without written

permission from the author, except for the use of brief quotations in a book review. This is a

work of fiction. Names, characters, events, and incidents are the products of the author's

imagination. Any resemblance to actual persons, living or dead, or actual events is purely

coincidental.

Cover Design: Coffin Print Designs

Photographer: Michelle Lancaster

Formatting: Peachy Keen Author Services

This is for all my good girls who use books to live out their own spicy dreams.
*Here's to making your man drop to his knees and **bark for you.***
To those of you who will fold for a masked mafia boss chasing you through the woods… or getting you off with his gun.
Enjoy adding more fantasies to your research list.
Mikhail is ready to take you now.

PLAYLIST

Listen to it as you read here: https://bit.ly/ClaimPlaylist

- Bad Blood, Asking Alexandria
- Watch me burn, Atreyu
- Psycho, Asking Alexandria
- Dead To Me, From Ashes to New
- Dead Inside, Future Palace
- PLEASE, Ex Habit, Omido
- Body Bag, I Prevail
- Hurricane, I Prevail
- Nail Polish, Holywatr
- Kingdom of Cards, Bad Omens
- Dancing Under Red Skies, Dermot Kennedy
- Soulmate, Chanin
- Empire (Let Them Sing), Bring Me The Horizon
- Glass Houses, Bad Omens
- Afterlife, Holding Absence
- Self-Destruction, I Prevail
- Over my dead body, Ex Habit
- On your knees, Ex Habit

- Too Late To Love You, Ex Habit
- Like That, Sleep Token
- Chokehold, Sleep Token
- Rain, Sleep Token
- WOOF, FKA Rayne
- Never Know, Bad Omens
- Jaws, Sleep Token
- OFPP, Conscience
- FEEL, Beneld, BURY
- Euclid, Sleep Token
- Eyes On You, SWIM
- Devil Eyes, Luke Muzzic
- Hymm To Virgil, Hozier
- Two Black Sheep, Diggy Graves
- Feel Me Now, If Not For ME
- Toxic, Omido, Rick Jansen
- Baby, Elvis Drew, Avivian
- When he holds u close, Omido
- Do I Wanna Know? Arctic Monkeys
- Give, Sleep Token
- Bad decisions, Bad Omens
- Dangerous, Royal Deluxe
- Welcome to the Chaos, Fame on Fire, Ice Nine Kills
- Me and the Devil, Soap & Skin
- How Villains are Made, Madalen Duke
- Atlantic, Sleep Token
- Who Do You Want, Ex Habit
- Do you really want to hurt me? Nessa Barret
- Heavenly Bodies, Arankai

AUTHOR'S NOTE

CLAIM is a dark, stand-alone mafia romance. It is the last book in the Beneath The Secrets Series.

It does contain content and situations that could be triggering to some readers. This book is explicit and has explicit sexual content, intended for readers 18+.

There is NO cheating in this book. However, there is OWD. Trust the process, I am about to give you a satisfying ending to this situation.

A full list of triggers and information can be found on my website: Claim Trigger Warning

STAY UP TO DATE

You can stay up to date on all things in the Beneath Universe in Luna's FB page: https://facebook.com/groups/614207510510756/

PROLOGUE

MIKHAIL

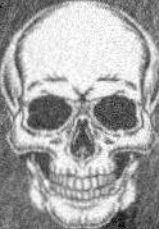

Six Years Ago...
Song- How Villains Are Made, Madalen Duke

"WHAT DO you mean that motherfucker has her locked up?" I cover my mother's shaking palm with mine and watch her expression.

She has always carried an air of calm composure, but as she's aged, she can't hide the subtle tightening around her eyes that is a giveaway to the turmoil inside of her.

"The last I've heard, your father has her in the west wing under guard. They were married two months ago." She takes a deep breath and lets it out slowly. "I'm not sure I have as much sway there as I used to."

"I've heard she's barely eighteen." The words twist in my mouth.

My fucking father.

Ivan has a type, apparently. He likes them young, naive, and weak.

I'm glad my mother figured out how to escape from him. But only after he forced three children out of her.

She nods slowly, stealing a glance over her shoulder to her new husband, Sergy.

It makes me happy to see the gentle smile she gives him.

"My sources say they can get her out tonight. They'll bring her here before we can route her to a safe house." He slips his arms around my mother's waist and pulls her tightly to him. "Are you sure you want to do this?" His dark curly hair drapes over his eyes after she nods.

"No one deserves a life with him. He's a monster." Her hands clasp until her knuckles turn white. "I want to." Her chin raises with her firm statement.

"What can I do?" I'm just finding out about her plans, but I'll do anything to get back at Ivan for what he's done to us.

Cruelty has guided every decision he's made.

We all have the scars to prove it, even if they can't all be seen. I've watched Lara wither from a single look from him, proving that there's damage there I'll never fully understand.

"The best thing you can do is to get everyone away from him. Honey, what was your plan?" She flicks her gaze between me and her husband.

"I have an idea." He leans over the counter and flips a brochure at me. "See that guy? That's my oldest, Jax. He's an up and coming boxer and just had his first fight in Las Vegas, United States."

The glossy photo shows a younger version of the man in front of me. Same curly dark hair.

It must run strong in his family since Katerina has the same.

Nikolai has mentioned more than once how much he loves it, and is thrilled that their daughter has it too.

"Okay, what about him?" I admit, he looks like a tough kid, but not sure how this helps.

"He told me the one thing he noticed most about Vegas is

how easy it is to get lost there. Blend in." He taps his temple. "Disappear."

"Noted. When is she supposed to be here?" I know that stealing away my father's bride will be a declaration of war. I need to make sure the rest of my family is safe.

"Soon. Less than an hour." Sergy presses his lips to my mother's cheek before leaving through the hall.

She leans forward and grasps my hand. "Go, get Niki and the rest out of here. You're the only one who can save them."

"What about you?" I know she's fallen victim to my father's wrath too often in the past.

She waves her thin fingers idly. "He doesn't scare me anymore."

When I head into the living room, Nikolai and his wife, along with Lara and Alexei are all reclining.

Clapping my hands, I gain their attention. "It's time to go. Mother has some new guests arriving soon, and we need to go pack."

Lara raises one eyebrow. "What, we're getting kicked out? Who's so important?"

I scowl at her. "It's none of your business. When I say we leave, we leave." The less they know, the better.

Alexei stands and stretches, ruffling his own hair before reaching for Lara. "Let's go. He's the boss."

Nikolai also rises, but leans close. "What's going on?" he whispers.

I shake my head and let my lips thin. "We'll talk about it another time."

"You aren't in charge of me," Lara huffs, but she moves to Alexei's side.

She doesn't know it, but I'm going to need her help in America.

I'll save that conversation for another day.

"I'm going to say goodbye to Papa." Katerina wraps her fingers around Nikolai's wrist before disappearing down the hall.

Nikolai scoops up baby Elena, cradling her to his chest he turns to me. "Are they in danger?" he growls low enough no one else can hear him.

"Not if everyone leaves in time," I hiss.

He can be the one to help me, and has learned long ago that I'll fill him in when the time is right.

Just not now.

He nods, and uses his body to herd Lara towards the main door.

A thump echoes through the house from the back.

"Go!" I bellow towards my siblings before turning on my heel.

Sergy joins me in the hall as we both race towards the kitchen.

A young woman, barely eighteen, stands huddled in the utility area, clutching a dark silk shawl around her head.

I can only hope Nikolai got everyone out.

"Are you Sergy?" the girl asks as she turns, but when she sees me, her eyes widen. "You look like *him*."

"I know. I'm Mikhail. I'm going to get you to safety." When I step closer, she pulls away.

Sergy charges in directly, flicking his gaze between the two of us. "I'm Sergy. There's a safe area here in the back where you can stay until the transport gets here. Mikhail is the one who will be traveling with you."

Her large brown eyes work slowly up and down me before she rolls her red bottom lip between her teeth. "Okay."

Sergy glances to me. "I'll let your mother know she's early."

Holding out my hand, I offer it to Zoya. "Come with me, I swear I'll keep you safe."

Her dainty fingers spread over my palm before she hesitantly follows me the back way past the foyer.

I hope like hell no one else sees her.

The level of hell my father will rain down on anyone who knows she's here will be ungodly.

But I can see why he chose her. Hair the color of a raven smoothing around her olive skin gives a striking look.

We make it to the far wing of the house without seeing anyone.

The faint sound of yelling filters through the walls.

Fuck.

"Stay here, don't move." I point at her before latching the door.

It blends with the bricks making it nearly invisible.

Clever.

Striding through the corridor, I almost collide with Nikolai and his baby.

"Mikhail! What the fuck is going on?" He grabs my arm, stopping me from moving past him.

"You need to get the hell out. *Now.*" I grimace as his grip tightens.

I need to work out more, he's getting too much stronger than me.

"Katerina…" He looks around at the empty room. "I have to find her."

Lights flicker through the windows, glaring along the far wall.

Shit.

"If you want your baby to survive this, you *have* to go. That's Ivan." My finger stabs towards the glimmer of SUVs moving through the yard. "He's surrounding us. You know as well as I do what happens when he's angry."

Nikolai pales, letting me go. "My wife?" He looks like he's not sure which direction to go.

"I'll get her. Trust me." I hope I don't regret those words.

His teeth grit before he turns on his heel, ducking quickly past the plate glass wall.

I run down the adjoining wing towards where I know Sergy went to find my mother.

Sergy flings open his door before I get a chance to knock.

"What's the plan? Fighting back or running?" I look from him to where my mother sits perched on a stool near her desk. Katerina stands behind her, her knuckles white as she grips Mother's shoulder.

Sergy shakes his head, his dark curls bouncing across his forehead. "We'd need an army to take him on."

Holding out his hand, he shoves a piece of paper at me. "Take this. The man is an up and comer. He'll be able to help you hide Zoya."

I unfurl the note and memorize the name.

Enzo Testa.

Pulling out my cigar lighter, it disappears into smoke.

"Do you trust him?" I grunt, unsure what to do next.

Sergy nods. "With my life. He fought with me and the Butcher after Vanyos's daughter was kidnapped. He knows Zoya and will keep her safe." He grabs my arm where Nikolai had, deepening the bruises. "Go get her, we'll escape through the passage from my suite."

He shuts the door, leaving me standing in the hall.

The yelling is louder, I can begin to understand my father's words.

"Bring her out!" he repeats.

Time to go.

Skirting down the far side of the house, I manage to just reach the hidden entry when an explosion rocks the building, throwing me forward with the blast.

Shit.

Rubble nearly blocks the door from swinging open.

Zoya is huddled in the corner, her wide eyes rimmed with tears. That full lower lip trembles as I reach out to her.

"Come on. We need to hurry." I can hear Ivan's voice calling through the house.

He's inside.

Waving my palm, I try to beckon her to take it.

This isn't the circumstance to freeze.

"I'll carry you if you can't walk," I growl, barely able to keep the impatience out of my voice.

Fuck it.

Grabbing her, I toss her over my shoulder like a sack of fermenting potatoes and begin to trot towards Sergy's end.

"Mikhail. How did I know you'd be a part of this betrayal?" My father stands, silhouetted by the bright lights of the vehicles outside, a wave of smoke surrounding him makes him look like the devil himself stepping from the gates of hell. Flames lick the fractured beams that litter the ground, flickering ominous orange on his enraged features.

Shit. I'm trapped.

I let Zoya slide down my body, and push her behind me so I'm between her and my father.

"Give her to me." Ivan unsheathes a long knife and stalks towards me.

"Fuck you. She's practically a child, and you're a monster." I wish I had a weapon.

A twisted piece of rebar sticks out of a broken piece of

concrete. With a hard jerk, I'm able to free the gnarled metal and hold it in front of me.

It isn't perfect, but it'll work.

"That's my wife." He points with the tip of the blade. "Return her at once."

"Over my dead body," I grunt, squaring off.

"Such a simple demand," he yells as he rushes me.

He's fast for being so old, nearly overtaking me before I swing catching him in a glancing blow to the hip.

With a trained pivot, his arm rotates around and the edge of his knife scores me down my side.

Pain rips through my ribs when he tears a ragged line through my flesh.

Staggering away from him, I lash out with the rebar to keep him at bay. When he dives forward for another stab, I swing and connect with his thigh just above the knee.

With a roar, the knife tumbles from his hand and bounces on a piece of rubble. "You good for nothing piece of shit," he grumbles, rolling over the debris scattered floor.

Now's my chance. Lunging, I raise my bar over my head to drop it on him.

But he twists, holding a burning chunk of beam as a club, he fends me off and continues the thrust until it skewers me in the face.

Agony swallows me as the smell of charred skin and the taste of cinder forces itself into my mouth.

Stumbling, I crash to the ground, frantically pulling the hot embers from my jaw and cheek.

He climbs to his feet, looming over me, and raises the smoldering chunk of wood over his head.

This is it, my last moment.

Death by my own father's hand.

As he swings down the final blow, arms grapple him from behind, shoving him over in a tangle of limbs.

Sergy raises his head over Ivan's back and turns to me. "Run! Get the fuck out!"

My father bucks up, tossing Sergy off, elbowing him in the chest as they roll.

Shit.

The fire in my face screams at me, but the drive to get away is stronger. I manage to get my legs under me just as another explosion rocks the building, sending me crashing forward.

Concrete and wood plummet from the ceiling, pummeling me where I lie.

Strong hands clutch my jacket. Sergy flips me towards him, then collapses against a chunk of brick.

"Where's Ivan?" I ask him hoarsely, choking on the thick air.

It's only then I see the shiv of metal sticking out of Sergy's chest.

"He ran," he coughs, blood tinging his spit that gathers on the corner of his mouth.

That isn't good.

"Get Zoya out of here." His fingers claw at my arm. "And Mikhail, there's one more thing." He draws a ragged breath. "Ivan will be back for revenge. He knows about my youngest daughter, Anastasia. You have to keep her safe, too."

"Ana, who?" I don't know if I can handle any more obligations. I already feel as if I have the weight of the world on my shoulders.

"Please. She's my baby girl—" Spasms wracks his body and a bubble of dark fluid spills from his lips. "—Katerina doesn't know. Neither does your mother. Please, for me?" His hand falls limp away from me before his eyes unfocus.

Fuck.

He saved my life. Gave my mother a love she never had. Accepted Nikolai as a son.

God damn it.

"I'll do it. I'll keep her safe." My palm brushes over his eyes, closing them.

Zoya moves in the corner of my vision, climbing out from under the table she was hiding under.

"Is he, I mean did he…?" Her question trails off as her eyes chase the trail where my father disappeared to.

"We have to go." Roughly, I grab her hand and begin to lead her towards the main suite where I know Mother and Katerina are waiting.

But a wall of jumbled rubble blocks every access.

"Shit," I whisper, turning to lead her away.

We'll have to do this the old fashioned way.

"How fast can you run?" I ask.

She's already almost jogging to keep up with my brisk strides.

"Not as fast as I used to. The baby makes it harder." Her admission almost goes over me.

Stopping, I grab her shoulders. "Baby? Does Ivan know?" My nose is so close to her, I can feel her gasping breath over my skin.

Her wide dark eyes flick between mine and the burning wound on my face. Biting her lip, she shakes her head. "That's why I had to run now. Any longer and he'd find out."

"Fuck. Okay. Let's go." I practically drag her out the door on the far side from where my father's men are, then sneak out through the woods, circling the estate.

It's only then I get a clear view of the house.

Or, what's left of it.

The kitchen and living room where I fought Ivan is the only section standing.

Sergy's wing, where my mother and Katerina were, is flattened.

Hollow misery overtakes me.

I've gotten Zoya out, but at what price?

CHAPTER 1

MIKHAIL

Present Day

I DON'T NEED to look at the date to know it's been six years since our lives were ripped apart. I have the reminder every fucking day on my face.

Every year that goes past turns another part of me to stone, the evil inside me roots a bit deeper.

"Enzo, now is not a good time." I wave him away from my desk in the hopes I have just a few more minutes to finish double checking the scheduled events at my casino.

Who knew the life of organized crime meant actually doing real work to keep up the facade?

"Mikhail. This can't wait." He tosses his laptop down in front of me and flips it around to face me.

There's a black and white still image, but I have no idea what it is.

Raising my eyebrows seems to trigger him into action.

"Watch." He reaches over the screen and hits a button.

At first, it's just a grainy shot of a snowy alley.

But then a car skids in, slamming on its brakes as two big guys jump out and run off screen.

"Enzo—"

"Just. Watch," he grits, his fingers nervously tapping on the oak.

He isn't the type to get worked up, so I know this has to be big.

A moment later, the original two men, with another behind them, comes into view.

"What the fuck is he carrying?" I squint and lean closer, trying to figure out what the hefty sack is he has over his shoulder.

"Wait for it." Enzo shifts so he's standing next to me, his hand poised over the keyboard.

"There!" With a slam, he pauses the feed.

My lungs stop working, trapping the air in them as I recognize what I'm seeing. "Is that…?" I don't want to put a name to the scene that I'm watching. But the curly dark hair framing her face is unmistakable.

Enzo closes the top and nods grimly. "Door cam caught the motion and triggered me. But this is the only clear shot we got. Looks like it was a break in and grab. They knew right where they were going."

My fist bounces off the oak of my desk. "We need to get her back. What do you know about who took her?"

He sighs, pulling his computer to rest under his arm. "The worst possible option. Ivan."

"Fuck." It comes out in a long exhale.

Of course it was.

"I promised her father, and I failed. I've done my best to keep an eye on Jax, but…" My knuckles crack when I squeeze my fingers tightly.

I just can't keep the people closest to me safe.

Niki, Lara, and now even Alexei have all been captured under my watch.

We haven't found any sign of him for weeks.

My sister is a wreck.

It's like as soon as I get one back, another one disappears.

And I know why.

That monster of a father of mine.

I'm sick and tired of his bullshit.

The low buzz in my pocket is the last thing I need right now.

Begrudgingly, I pull my phone out and press it to my ear.

Unknown number. Great.

"Speak."

"Mr. Volkov. My name is Drago. I think I have something you may be interested in." A deep voice with a heavy Russian accent croons over the speaker.

"I don't have time for games. What do you want?" I growl into my cell.

I've been told my balaclava can muffle my words, so I make sure to push the volume so there's no issue understanding me.

"I can get your friend, Alexei, back." He lets out a soft laugh. "I like dealing with a man who gets to the point. I know where he is. The question is, how badly do you want him?"

Hitting the speaker button, I toss the device where Enzo's laptop was just resting, and gesture for him to listen.

"How do I know you have Alexei?" I know he's been missing for weeks, it will take more than some stranger to get me excited.

"Find out the prisoner list for Kamen Gulag." There's a click and the line goes dead.

I glance at Enzo, but he's already pulling out his laptop

again.

After the silent room being filled with only the noise of his keystrokes, his olive skin goes pale. "He's there. But, look who else is." His finger shakes as he holds his manicured nail beneath a name I thought long gone.

Vanyos Pushkrov. The Butcher of Buresk.

My hands shake as I hit redial on Drago's number.

"Believe me now?" He doesn't wait for formalities.

"Why did you give him to me? What do you want?" There's always a catch in this line of work.

Drago's deep laugh makes the small hairs on the back of my neck stand up. "I simply ask that we keep the lines of communication open. Your Alexei has repaid his debt to Tatiana, but she never intended for him to leave. I'm offering him to you with the hope we may be able to rely on each other in the future."

I don't believe him. "Just give me a dollar amount. I do not handle being in the debt of favors."

It always ends in grief. My fingers find the scar beneath my balaclava, a sharp reminder of all the promises I've failed to uphold.

He clears his throat, and takes a long breath. "Let's just say, I have a feeling that feathers are soon to be ruffled here in Russia, and I want to keep as many options open as possible."

I glance up to Enzo.

His brows raise and he shrugs.

Fuck.

"Alright, Drago. What do I have to do?" I'm guessing he

already knows I'd do anything to get Alexei back.

I can't watch Lara withering away every day that he's gone.

For both of their sake, I need him here.

"I can arrange for him to get out of his cell. I need you to land your plane outside the gate." He pauses. "I'll make sure there's enough of a distraction that he can escape."

My mind churns.

Escape.

Free and clear.

Untethered, not owing anyone. Not being pursued.

It sounds appealing.

"Very well. I can do that much. I do have just one small favor in return." An idea brews in my head.

"Tell me." Drago's teeth grit.

"Once I've taken off, give me the count of four solid minutes to get to enough altitude, then I want you to shoot me down." I think this will work.

Enzo chokes. "What?" He mouths, his arms going away from his head.

"Please repeat that. I think our connection is bad." Drago makes a tapping sound through the speaker. "It sounded like you wanted me to fire on your plane?"

"Exactly. Aim for the engine. I don't want you to accidently hit Alexei. He's an expert skydiver, he'll be fine." I wave Enzo back who's violently trying to get my attention.

Drago takes a deep breath, his exhale making the cell static. "That was a short-lived friendship. I'll make sure Alexei knows I'm on his side."

The click when he hangs up is audible.

"What the fuck?" Enzo smacks my shoulder.

He never gets worked up, nor touches me.

"You're going to get yourself killed? What the hell is

going on?" He doesn't hide his concern, but jumps up to begin pacing the room.

"I need to get Anastasia back. I can't do that if Ivan is keeping tabs on me. The best way to fall off of his radar is to die." I shrug, clasping my fingers on the desk. "I'll stay in the safe house with Zoya until it's safe to come out. You already have encrypted communication there, it'll be a good base to work out of."

His dark eyes narrow and his lips thin. "You know this is a bad idea?"

I nod. "It's the only one I have."

He sighs, and pulls open his computer again. "Fine, I'll start getting a contact system set up and new identification papers." He stops typing and looks up. "Are you going to tell your family?"

Silence hangs heavy in the room.

"No. Keeping secrets is what kept them alive. If any of them had known the truth about Zoya, she would be dead, and my littlest sister would be back with my father." I lift the corner of my balaclava enough to down the bourbon as I pour it. "Any of them would be dead if they had known where she was. Ivan would have discarded them like an old newspaper once he gathered the information he needed."

"I agree. Knowledge is power." He resumes tapping on his keyboard.

He should know. I swear he lives on intel.

It's the entire purpose of all of his clubs, his business endeavors, his relationship with me, and even Frankie Falcone.

Contacts.

Enzo always knows more about what and who than anyone else alive.

And I'm going to need every ounce of it.

CHAPTER 2

ANASTASIA

I CAN HEAR movement and quiet talking echoing around me, but can't see a damn thing with this stinky ass bag over my head.

"Hey, assholes! I can hear you!" The heat from my breath bounces back against my eyes.

If only they'd loosen the ties on my wrists, my fingers are going numb.

There's a scuff of a foot, and maybe something like the scraping of a chair.

What the fuck?

"Come on! This sucks. I didn't see the way here. I forgot to brush my teeth before they took me. I'm dying of boredom. Can anyone like, just pull the edge up a little?" I make sure to add some extra whine to my voice.

I can play the role of the petulant teenager.

The cover is ripped off my head, flinging my curly dark hair all over, including into my face.

Blowing and wiggling my nose doesn't get it away, but at least I can breathe.

"Do you ever shut up?" A tired looking beefy guy holds the sack they used.

I remember him. He was one of the men at the car when they took me.

Was that yesterday? I have no idea.

"Only if you're nice to me." I roll my eyes at him. "Jerk."

He purposefully kicks the leg of the chair that I'm in, sending a hard jolt through me.

"I can be nice to you, my dear." Another voice sounds from behind me. This one is deeper, almost calming in its level tone.

"That must be your boss." I glower at the man who's walking away. "He's gonna be ticked when he finds out you left me sweating in there for hours."

I know he can't see me, but I make sure to stick out my tongue before he disappears out of the door.

I shouldn't have.

A hand snakes out from beside me and grabs it before I can slip it back into my mouth.

Old cigar and cologne taint my taste buds as a graying beard appears, attached to the vise-like hand.

"You shouldn't offer this, if you don't intend to use it, my dear." He lets me go, and takes the leather chair in front of me.

His dark eyes pinch to match his lips as he stares at me. Crossing his legs, the shine of his black shoes catches the reflection of the high lights in the cavernous room.

No wonder there was odd acoustics, this place is massive.

Like a mansion, or castle.

Nothing like the tiny house that my mom and I live in. If only she had listened to me and moved out.

But she kept saying it was a safe place, that it was paid for, that we were taken care of there.

It's all bullshit.

Now I'm here, being eye fucked by some creepy old guy in a designer suit.

"Do you know who I am?" He pulls a cigar from a silver gilded box near his elbow and clips the end.

When he leans forward and smiles, I can see the nicotine stains on his teeth.

I don't even try to hide the shudder of disgust that ripples through me. "No. I'm unimpressed. Can I go now?"

His gray beard twitches before his fingers snake out and grip my chin harshly, bruising my cheeks with his iron clasp.

"I'm Ivan Volkov. Your father took everything from me. So I'll do the same." His manicured nails dig into the skin before he releases me.

"You're going to kill me?" If that's the case, I guess I don't need to hush. "Then get it over so I don't have to look at you anymore."

For added effect, I coil up a wad of saliva and spit it towards his face.

It lands on his chest, but I'm sure he understands the intention.

"No, you petulant brat," he growls, red mottling his throat. "I'm claiming you as my own. I'm going to fuck an heir into you so Sergy rolls in his fucking grave."

Gross. The thought of him touching me makes me gag.

"I barely even knew him. He died like six years ago. What the hell is wrong with you?" I try and fail to twist around in the chair, but I'm tied too tightly.

The flame of his lighter flares in front of his face before the acrid smoke from his cigar billows over me. "Oh, you see, Sergy still lives on. And there are those who betrayed me that would be very upset to hear of our fruitful joining." He drops his hand to his black trousers and rubs his palm over the bulge in his crotch. "You're feisty. It will be a pleasure—" His fingers snake out and wrap around my throat, then he squeezes until the room starts to fade. "—to break you."

When he lets go, the burning air fills my lungs until I cough in his face.

"You're a monster," I croak, still sputtering.

"Hmm, so I've been told." He takes a long inhale before puffing small circles into the still room. "I can be quite a benevolent master, though. As long as you mind."

"So, if I disobey, you'll put me out of my misery?" I can see the writing on the wall.

I hate him already.

"Quite the contrary. I will bestow hell on earth and make you beg for death until the day I finally die." His grin is sinister and doesn't reach the dark pits of his eyes.

"That sounds lovely. Does that option mean you leave your shriveled little dick out of me?" If I'm gonna suffer, I'm at least going to earn it.

But he laughs.

And that's even worse.

"Oh, you young women thinking that making fun of what you don't know somehow makes it less scary? Don't worry, I'll have you begging for it before I'm done."

CHAPTER 3

MIKHAIL

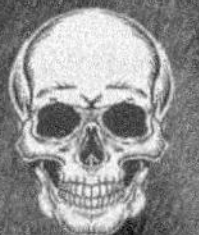

KEEPING all of the instruments off as I try to land my plane on an unfamiliar access road in the middle of the night isn't something I'd rank high on my odds to survive.

But, for Alexei, I'll take my chances.

"Two minutes." I pull off the headset after making my announcement to Drago.

I hope he heard me.

My wheels are almost touching down when a massive explosion goes off on the far side of the prison complex.

Orange and white flames rocket into the air before the concussive blast almost knocks me off course.

Fighting the cross force, I barely manage to control the Piper to a rolling stop.

Jumping out, I find the gap in the fence that Drago told me would be there.

At least he seems to be keeping up his end of the bargain. We've been over the plans a dozen times, yet there was still lingering doubt that he'd actually follow through.

The guard outfit I'm wearing doesn't allow for free movement, tightening uncomfortably across my chest and arms as I duck into the unlocked door at the end of the concrete building.

It takes my eyes a moment to adjust to the dim light after the bright blaze of fire that lit my way here.

Relax. I'm supposed to know what I'm doing so they think I'm one of them.

Taking a deep breath, I press on, taking the right that leads me to where Alexei is supposed to be hiding.

The ground shakes with another explosion, rocking me against the wall. Screams and sirens blare through the air as a wave of dust ripples through every space.

Coughing, I step around the corner to find three men, two are huge, huddled in a defensive position.

Peering through the visor on my helmet, I manage to spy Alexei between them. Flipping up the front, I take another hard look to make sure.

Who the hell are those guys?

"Alexei? It's me, Mikhail." When I reach for him, the two men try to step in front.

"Mikhail!" Alexei rushes towards me, wrapping me in a fast embrace.

"You're supposed to be alone." I try to keep my voice down.

He shakes his head. "They're coming with me. I'm not leaving without them."

Fuck.

"Fine, let's get the hell out." Turning, I retrace my steps, leading them towards the hole in the fence.

The bigger men grunt, struggling to get through.

Yea, it was tight as shit for me too. The heavy uniform helps to not get scratched up.

When I climb into the cockpit, I let off one quick light to signal to Drago, while Alexei gets his friends loaded.

"Who are you?" I yell back.

At this point, I don't really care, but I have to keep up charades.

"This is Ben, and his brother Sven." Alexei points to each. "They saved my life in there."

All their extra weight is going to make this a rough take off.

"Hold on!" I call, jamming down the throttle.

The small plane barely crests the trees when I hear the first ping of a bullet.

Right on time.

Then they start getting more rapid.

"Fuck! They're shooting at us!" Alexei shrieks.

Another shot hits something in the engine, sparking a sputtering fire that lights up the cabin.

But one comes up through the floor, hitting me in the side.

With a groan, I try to stem the blood through the thick jacket hiding my parachute.

I can hear Alexei talking to his buddies in a hurried tone.

They better know how to jump.

The propeller sputters with another hit.

It's time.

"Alexei? You gotta get out!" I need him out of here. I wish I could say goodbye. Knowing he'll be going home helps. Lara needs him.

Enzo is ready to pick him up.

He'll have to make sure they're safe.

Within seconds, they're all gone.

More bullets rip through the thin metal skin, one catching me in the shoulder.

Fucking hell, Drago, stop!

Fighting the yoke, I try to keep the altitude high enough that I'll have time to deploy.

Just a few more seconds.

Heat from the fire pours through the broken glass making my eyes cloud.

I can't hold it any longer.

Pushing out of the seat, I jump to the back, and let myself fall out the door. The rushing wind deafens me as I leap into the pitch black night.

One.

Two.

Pull!

My parachute is as dark as the sky in hopes that no one will see me.

Especially Alexei.

He needs to think I crashed.

It will be him telling everyone, I know it.

The silk has barely widened to full when I'm plummeting into the icy water of the lake. It's like hitting a wall of concrete with my legs.

Then the shock of the cold soaks into me.

It's only a split second before the thin emergency life preserver inflates, bobbing me to the surface.

Which direction is the land? I know this lake is big enough, I could swim for hours before finding the shore. I chose it for the size, but that long in the frigid water will kill me before I can get out.

A giant boom breaks through the dark, then a plume of fire from my crashing plane brightens the night.

There it is.

I think I can make it.

The cold works its way into my bones, but I force myself to keep going.

One more kick, one more stroke, then my toe drags across the rough bottom.

I can barely feel my feet they're so numb with the cold.

Each step is grueling until I can drag myself out of the heat-sucking lake.

Now to figure out where the hell I am. But first, I have to warm up before the heavy frost of the night turns my soaked clothes into icicles.

I don't even have my phone. I made sure to leave it with Enzo so I couldn't be tracked, nor could it be compromised for all of the information on it.

The small survival kit I had in my pocket seems inadequate in my frozen fingers.

Fuck. I should have strapped on some extra clothes, too.

At a certain point though, I can only carry a certain amount, knowing I still had to fight my way to Alexei.

I hope he's okay.

Won't matter if I don't get this damn fire going.

A few dry sticks, and the packet of tinder, and soon a tiny flame lights the dense forest around me.

Finally.

Shivering, it takes all of my patience to keep adding the kindling until it's grown enough to move to the larger sticks.

Bigger and bigger, I let the blaze go until my jacket is steaming and I'm starting to get some feeling back into my limbs.

That was close.

I hate to do it, but I strip down, hanging my wet layers as close as I dare to the heat. I need to dry them out.

Wincing, I peel off my base thermal top. At least the negative temperatures are good for something. It helped to stem the flow of blood.

I'm picking the dried bits of tissue from around the worst wound when I hear a droning sound.

As it gets louder, I look around frantically, but can't find the source of the noise.

"Mikhail." A tiny voice comes from the sky above me. "I have Drago heading to these coordinates." The drone drops to my field of vision, and Enzo's tone clears. "Are you hurt?"

"Not bad. I'll live," I grunt.

"I'm going to guide them in. Glad you survived the crash. The plane didn't." He doesn't give me a chance to respond before elevating into the darkness.

That's too bad, I liked that one.

If I can get Anastasia back, I'll buy a new one.

It isn't long before a heavier motor works through the trees.

A blacked out SUV appears, and a giant man with dark paint on his face climbs out.

"Mikhail? Drago." He beats his chest before coming up, holding out his hand. "Let me help you into the truck."

I'm still not sure if I should completely trust him, but he did get me Alexei.

If the worst that happens is he's turning me over to my father, I've prepared for that.

I won't be taken alive.

CHAPTER 4

ANASTASIA

I think the old freak is really going to go through with it.

The days start to run together. I can only keep track by the stilted formal dinners that Ivan insists I attend with him, and the haggard old woman who comes in to fit me into the most hideous wedding dress I've ever seen.

"How can you work for him, Stella?" I finally ask her as she makes the final adjustments. "He's making me do this against my will." Maybe if I find her heart, she'll help me.

"Hush, child," she admonishes me, the wrinkles on her face deepening into a frown. "Don't you know it's worse to be on his bad side? Ivan runs this region. You'll be the second most powerful woman here."

"All this bullshit to not be first?" When my arms wave she tries to tug them back down. "Who's above me? Does he have, like, another wife or something?"

Ow. She poked me with a pin.

I bet she did that on purpose.

Bitch.

"You need to wise up and learn to keep your mouth shut before he cuts your tongue out," she hisses.

"Oh, you're just jealous because you're too old for his taste." My chin rises with disdain.

I can tell.

She's hated me from the moment she saw me.

"Don't be an idiot. He's using you for a bigger game, and trying to hurt people I care about because of it." Her wrinkles deepen as she scowls. "You're too stupid to understand, and I don't have the patience to draw it out with crayons." She stands, poking the last of the pins into a small cushion on her wrist. "Take it off. I'll come back tomorrow for more alterations."

What is she talking about?

"Wait, tell me." I pull my arms from the fluted sleeves carefully so I don't get stabbed inadvertently. "Who?"

Stella shakes her head. "It doesn't matter. Ivan is using you as bait. You think you're the only young pussy in Russia? *Think about it.*" She drapes the white fabric over her arm before rapping hard enough on the door that the guard lets her out.

Great. Now I'm alone *and* confused all over again.

Maybe she's right. Because I really don't understand who would be hurt by me being Ivan's choice.

Is it the mystery man that's fed Momma money and food all this time? It's been over five years that she's been cared for by someone new, ever since Papa died.

A pang shoots through my chest.

I can't believe it's been that long already. I hadn't seen him much since I was little, but he was always reliable about visiting or staying in touch.

An even more painful squeeze tightens, making it difficult to breathe.

What about Momma?

I've been trying so hard not to think about her since I was taken. How she must be feeling.

But what if they hurt her when they took me?

Or killed her?

Fuck.

The thought sends me face down on the mattress, sobbing into my pillow.

I can't lose her. She's everything to me.

Maybe I can ask Ivan how she is? If I act like a lady, and not be cruel?

Yes, I might be able to pretend to tolerate him, if he can give me a tidbit of reassurance that she's safe.

I miss her so badly.

The need to blow my nose pushes me from the thick comforter to the ensuite where I catch a glimpse of my red eyes and messy curly dark hair.

It's just like Papa's.

I used to hate it, because it tangled so easily. Momma would spend so many days when I was younger brushing it out for me until it was smooth and shiny like hers.

Only for it to twist again the next time I got it wet.

I wish I could wince under her comb again while she quietly cursed at me to stay still. But she'd always follow with a gentle kiss and thank me for being patient while she straightened it.

Please be okay, Momma.

A splash of cold water helps the puffiness in my cheeks go down.

Perfect timing. The heavy knock on the door signals it's time for my appearance with Ivan.

One last shudder of disgust, then I pull my shoulders back and make sure my features are neutral before going down the grand staircase to the dining hall.

"My lovely fiancée, here to impress me with more derisive remarks?" Ivan is sitting at the far end, his lavish meal already laid across the ornate oak table.

The heady smell of meat and pastries makes my belly rumble.

It must be a new form of torture he's devised. All of that wonderful food sitting just a few feet away, and he feeds me nothing but a plain meal of salad and boiled chicken.

I want to scream and complain, throw my boring plate against the wall.

But I sit quietly. "Not tonight. I'm learning that this is my fate. It's been hard to wrap my head around it. I'm sorry it took so long." Stabbing a few leaves with my fork, I pretend it's going into his eye.

"Can you tell me some of the wedding plans? It might help me get more excited about it." I flash my best smile and chew the flavorless greens as if they're filet mignon.

I hate my life.

Ivan's gray eyebrows raise and his lips purse through his trimmed beard. "Interesting. I'm happy to see that your mood has lifted somewhat." He leans forward and takes a bite from a buttery roll. "It will make our wedding night much more enjoyable for you if you don't fight."

It's a struggle not to let my cheeks pale at the thought.

"Then again—" He sits back, chewing thoughtfully. "—I was quite looking forward to fucking you while you claw and scream." He chuckles watching me squirm, then lifts his glass of red wine to take a sip.

I bite the inside of my cheek hard enough that it keeps the tears at bay.

I have to stop letting him goad me into reacting.

"Are you expecting many guests?" The mushy chicken sticks to the roof of my mouth when I try to smile around it.

His dark dead eyes narrow. "The only one that counts is in the wind. Once I know where my son is, we'll have the ceremony."

I can't fathom this monster being a loving father. Any flesh and blood of his is probably just as awful as he is.

But I have to play nice.

"Who's your son?" My plate is nearly empty. All I want to do is find out about my mother, but I need to keep him talking.

Ivan pushes back and opens a wooden box near his elbow. Withdrawing one of his stinky cigars, he clips the end and circles his lips around it.

After the smoke wafts through the hollow room, he finally answers.

"You know him. He's kept you hidden and safe from me for years. My oldest boy's name is Mikhail." He draws a long inhale making the ember glow.

No. Not the man who gave Momma money all these years?

How can they be one and the same?

CHAPTER 5

MIKHAIL

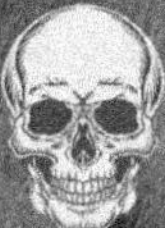

My stitches pull when I raise my arm to knock.

It only takes a moment for her to answer. She hasn't changed since the last time I saw her, except the fear in her dark eyes has been replaced with an eager shine.

"Hello, Mikhail. I didn't know if I'd ever see you again." She gives me a soft smile, then backs away to let me in.

"Zoya. You're the only place in Russia I know is safe. Thank you for agreeing to let me stay temporarily." Slinging my bag over my shoulder, I push past her into the living room.

I wouldn't call it exactly lavish, but certainly comfortable. It seems she's done incredibly well with the money I've sent.

"Where's Galena? I'd like to see my sister." I glance around, but don't see her.

Zoya's to the end of the hall, gesturing to the first room. "You can have this one. She's at the neighbor's house playing with the other children. I'll be leaving shortly to bring her back."

That riles me immediately. "Do you trust those people?" I growl, dropping my duffel next to an ornate dresser.

Her eyes widen and she steps back. "Of course. I've used the fake names since day one." Her fingers land at her collar. "Do you think I'd want to put my daughter in danger?" There's an edge to her voice.

"Sorry. Instinct. You've been buffered from the hell my father has brought down in search of you both." I slump onto the corner of the mattress. The weight of the past year suddenly feels very heavy.

"Oh. I can't even imagine." She crosses her arms over her belly. "Is that why you're here?" Chewing on her red bottom lip, her brows furrow as she watches me.

"Yes. He took someone important in retaliation. That's why I'm here, to get close enough to get her back."

Her head tilts, draping the side of her face with her long black hair. "Is she special to you?"

"No. I don't even know her, really. But, like you, I've been tasked to protect her." The burner phone that Drago got for me from Enzo vibrates in my pocket. "I have to take this."

Zoya doesn't move for a moment, but then backs out of the room. "Sorry."

"Enzo?" I keep my tone low.

The less anyone knows, including Zoya, the better.

"Word is, your father is taking Anastasia as his new bride." Enzo sighs into the speaker. "There isn't much that surprises me anymore, except Ivan."

"Wait, he took her to force her hand? Fuck." I have to get her out of there before that happens. "That bumps up the timeline. I have to go tomorrow. This will be the key to getting him to drop his guard. He got reckless when Zoya disappeared. This might be his tipping point that I can use to finally end him."

"Mikhail," Enzo grumbles. "I can't get you any backup though. Drago said he's played his hand and won't send men."

"Then I guess I'll have to just do it myself. Hopefully the crash diversion worked. Drago is the only one on this end who knows I'm alive, and he works for Tatiana." I put all my trust in him, I hope it doesn't bite me in the ass.

"Did you see her?" Enzo's voice raises.

"No. But I'm sure I will when it's time for debts to be called in. Even though Drago said I don't owe him, I have my doubts." And I know how cruel her payments can be.

Alexei spent months in the Russian gulag to fulfill one of them.

Movement catches my focus when Zoya reappears holding a steaming cup.

Soundlessly, she sets it on the table nearby.

When I pick it up, the heady smell of coffee and liqueur warms me before I even have a sip.

"Thank you." I mouth, holding my cell away from my ear.

She smiles, then leaves.

I feel bad for her, trapped in isolation and fear of Ivan for all of these years. No wonder she always tries to extend any call with me or Enzo.

"What are you going to do?" Enzo brings me back to the conversation.

"Fuck. The only thing I can, kidnap her back."

CHAPTER 6

ANASTASIA

MAYBE I SHOULDN'T HAVE PLAYED SO nice.

It's been three days of me pretending to tolerate the old freak, but now he's starting to act like I *really* like him.

Eww.

What is he, forty years older than me? Just, why?

Tonight he has me sitting closer. Maybe he might start letting me eat better?

Except now I'm able to smell his cloying cologne with the stench of stagnant cigar smoke tainting it.

Everything about him is repulsive. But it's also because he *kidnapped me*.

That's hard to look past.

"Come, dear. Sit next to me." He grabs the leg of my chair and screeches it over the marble floor so that my knee brushes his under the table.

"Let's see how nice you really are. Will you bite the hand that feeds you?" He picks up a piece of rich meat and holds the morsel in front of my lips. "Open wide, *malyshka*."

My spine stiffens. I am *not* his baby girl.

But I have to be.

Obediently, I let my jaw drop slack for his thick fingers to push the dripping bit into my mouth.

Oh fuck, it tastes so good, I can't stop the moan that escapes.

Weeks of nothing but lettuce and bland ass chicken makes this divine tidbit resemble heaven on my tongue.

Ivan leans closer and wipes a drip from my chin that he licks off of his own thumb. "See how good I can treat you? You'll be making that noise for me every night."

I'm going to puke.

"So—" I might as well before he pushes any further. "—do you think my mom will make it to the wedding?" My breath catches in my chest when he leans away.

A knot forms in my throat that I can't swallow around.

I wish he would just answer me!

Instead, he pulls a dollop of mashed potatoes onto the tip of his nicotine stained finger and holds it in front of me.

"Show me how badly you want to know the answer." His lecherous grin bares his teeth as he stares at my mouth.

Why won't he tell me?

If I don't do what he asks, will I ever know?

I'll find out at the ceremony, but there's no way I'm going to survive until then. My only choice is to escape or die trying.

My tongue darts over my lips nervously with indecision.

No, I can't do this.

Shaking my head, I try to back away from his hand.

But his other snakes out and grabs my jaw, forcing it open.

"You're going to take everything I give you." His hot breath festers over my skin before I feel the wet lick up my cheek.

Then his finger drives into my mouth, far enough that I begin to gag.

"That's it. Get used to choking on me." He smears the mush into the back of my throat.

Jerking my head away, my palms push against the table until I can gain the leverage to bite his intruding digit.

Grabbing my knife, I swing around and lash the tines across his face.

He yanks himself from me, stemming the sudden flow of blood.

"You fucking bitch," he growls, pressing a linen napkin against his jowls.

I don't want to wait for him to lash out.

Kicking my chair out, I run upstairs to my room as fast as I can.

CHAPTER 7

MIKHAIL

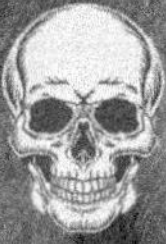

HER BIG BROWN eyes match her mother's as she stares at me, clinging to Zoya's side.

I can see my father in her nose and jaw.

Galena reminds me of Lara, showing that Volkov spunk.

"She might be less intimidated if you took that mask off, Mikhail." Zoya pats Galena's head, smoothing her dark hair.

"Believe me, it's best I keep it on." Ever since the fight with Ivan those years ago, the scars on my face are too unsettling to show.

It's just been easier to keep them covered than constantly see the unnerved reaction of anyone who sees them.

"I remember you being handsome." Zoya gives me a wide smile. "You were my hero, and have been since."

My teeth grit. "I'm a villain, remember that. I'm only rescuing this girl to try and get Ivan out of his hole."

"Are you really my brother?" Galena says from behind Zoya's leg. "But you're a bad guy?"

I squat so I'm level with her. "I am your brother. And you'll want to learn early that things aren't black and white. Sometimes the worst men can do the most good."

It's always been hard for me to talk to kids, even those that are my own flesh and blood.

Nikolai's daughter has always seen past the mask, accepting that it's just a part of who I am.

But my littlest sister doesn't know me.

She'd be wise to stay as far away from our family as possible, it's safer.

Except she pulls away from Zoya and steps closer to me, her small face moving within inches of mine. Her tiny hands rest on my knees as she peers into my eyes.

"I think you're nicer than you pretend to be." Her cheeks widen in a grin. "I've always wanted a brother. Now I know that Wilhem won't mess with me on the playground if you're there."

That draws a chuckle out of me. "If I ever see him being mean to you, I'll make sure he never does it again."

"Do you, um…" Zoya chews on her lower lip. "Will you come back?"

I shrug as I stand. "Depends on Ivan. This has to end."

"Well, it would be nice to see you more than once every five years." Zoya glances down to her daughter. "At least for her sake."

She's right. I'll protect my sister as long as there's breath in my body.

"I'll see what I can do." Hefting my heavy bag over my shoulder, I move outside where the truck Enzo arranged for me sits.

It should be fully decked out with all of the weapons I need to break into Ivan's compound.

Watching Zoya stand with Galena watching me leave makes a pang of guilt go through my chest.

I should have spent more time getting to know them. There's a very real chance I may not survive today.

But I'm tired of Ivan always having the upper hand. I need to rescue Anastasia, and once I know she's safe, I'll be able to finish him.

There's a small rocky outcropping just a mile or so from his estate that I know I can hide my rig by. No one will see it parked there, but will be handy for when I'm ready to escape.

I just need to find out where they're keeping her.

Creeping slowly through the thick woods, I only stop when I hear the crunch of leaves betraying someone else's presence.

Shit.

This will either be my downfall, or the chance to find out where she is.

I squat low behind the trunk, and wait.

Holding my breath to keep the steam low, I can hear them turn closer.

Perfect.

A dark shadow solidifies into the silhouette of a man with a rifle.

He moves at a steady pace, not pausing nearly as often as he should on patrol.

Amateur.

His mistake is going to cost him.

I take a long inhale, and hold it when he passes. I give him a full stride away before I make my move.

Grabbing him by the back of his jacket, I snatch the strap of his gun, pinning it to his chest, and whip him around so he's pressed against the tree.

"Fuck," he gasps.

"That's right. You are fucked. But you have a choice." My forearm tightens against the back of his neck. "You can tell me what I want to know, and I make this quick. Or, fight me, and I make sure you die in agony without being able to scream."

His rapid panting makes a fog form around his head.

"I'll talk," he whines as his fingers dig into the bark.

"You're smarter than you look. Where is the girl that Ivan kidnapped?" I pull out my knife and let the tip trace down his jaw.

His nostrils flare and he shows the whites of his eyes as he looks back wildly. "You mean the brat? I'll lead you to that little bitch's quarters myself."

"What did you do to her?" I growl.

"Are you kidding? You must not know Ivan. He'd fucking kill me worse than anything you can dream up." A smirk forms on his lips.

He thinks he's being cute.

My hand on his throat squeezes him silent while I take my blade and push it into the back of his ear, sliding it beneath the skin of his cheek until it imbeds into the tree.

His muffled cry doesn't make it far.

"Are you done? Do you want me to cut tiny ribbons from your face and hang them like garland on this pine? Tell me you'll cooperate, or you'll have a very merry Christmas." I pull out the blade and keep him quiet until he stops struggling.

He nods against my palm, and I uncover his mouth.

"Now, where is she?" I ask hoarsely. "Or do you want to speak out of *both* sides of your mouth?"

"He has her in the east wing." His words are garbled from blood.

I had a feeling that's where he was keeping her. The same place he kept my mother near the end of her marriage. Someplace close enough that he can keep tabs, but also where she can be locked away.

I don't give him warning, just tilt the edge of my knife enough I can bury it into his throat.

He doesn't make a sound as he slumps to the dirt.

Now I just have to work my way to the other end of the compound.

The moon gives off enough light I can make my way silently past the next two guard posts without being seen.

Its glare reflects from the white marbled tiles that accent every window.

But what really catches my eye is the black drain pipe that runs along them to the roof.

I bet if I climbed up there, I could break into that top room, then work my way down. Ivan's men would never expect me coming from above.

I'm just about to break from the cover of the trees when the very glass I'm aiming for swings out.

What the hell?

CHAPTER 8

ANASTASIA

THE DOOR SLAMS shut with a heavy thud and the lock clicks firmly. A sigh of relief escapes my lips. That was close. The ghost of his touch lingers on my skin, even as I run my hands over my neck. It's inevitable, he'll make me pay for that sooner or later.

I'm not sure how many times I can fight him and win. He might be old, but he's sharp. He's bigger than me. And he has a whole mansion full of bodyguards who will probably be happy to rip my head from my shoulders.

Looking down, I'm met with the gruesome reality of blood caking my palms. It makes me sick. He deserves to die, not just have a slash on his face.

I wish I drove it through his fucking heart.

On shaky legs, I make my way to the bathroom and turn on the faucet. The crimson swirls down the sink as I scrub my hands.

I don't care who he thinks he is, or how powerful he might be in this fucked up world. He doesn't have the right to my body. I won't let him. I've kept myself for this long, waiting for the right guy to come along.

Saving myself, when actually, it is about to be ripped from me by an old ugly monster. I feel the hot sting of tears on my face, and with a trembling hand, I wipe them away, hoping to stop the flow of emotion. I can deal with this another time, I'm sure I won't be walking out of here the same woman I came in.

But I won't go down without a fight. I know I did damage to the old bastard with that knife, so I have a small window of opportunity to try to get the fuck out of here.

If I'm going to die here, I might as well go making some kind of escape. Pacing the room, I run my fingers through my hair and pull. I want to scream. Making my way over to the window, I rest my hands on the cold, damp ledge. The icy breeze blowing through the gap and sending shivers down my arms. I look into the darkness, and the moonlight casts long shadows across the ground, making the scene look pretty. Surely there has to be a way off this estate. I just have to keep running.

Pushing myself up on my tiptoes, I look down. Shit. I'm so high up. Can I? What's worse? Falling to my death or being raped for years?

I'll take death.

Pushing myself further out of the window, I spot a black drain pipe to my left. I think that's my only option. I race around the room, grabbing my sneakers first and throwing on a black sweater. Rubbing my hands on my leggings, I try to wipe away some of the nervous sweat on my palms.

The muffled, deep voices in Russian outside my door sent a jolt of fear through me, urging me to the window. With trembling hands, I silently slide it open as wide as it would go, creating a narrow escape route. The air is thin, and the wind bites at my skin as I sit on the ledge, legs dangling, eyes closed, and taking a deep breath to gather my courage. It doesn't help. The frantic rhythm of my pounding heart echoes in my ears.

Scooting my way to the left, I lean out slightly, the coolness of the drain's metal pressing against my palm. Okay, it's not wet, that's something. Fueled by pure adrenaline, I slam my foot against it, reaching over and gripping with both hands. Muscles straining, I twist my body, shoving my toes into the narrow space between the bricks.

With a deep breath, I cling to the pipe, my arms straining with the effort.

Don't look down, Ana. Jesus. How the hell is this my life? Slowly and carefully, I move down. Why does it feel like only an inch at a time?

Keeping my eyes solely on my sneakers, working out roughly where each foot should go as I work my way down, the light from my bedroom and the moon is just about enough to see.

Time seems to stretch out endlessly during the descent, and as I peek over the edge, the ground is startlingly close. Just a few more moves and I'll be free. Even if I let go now, I won't die. A small smile tugs at my lips. That was badass.

Deciding the coast is clear, I push back from the wall, crashing onto the grass, the impact jarring my whole body.

"Ouch," I hiss.

I lean back on my hands, looking up at the stars in the night sky.

My heart pounds against my ribs as the sound of rustling leaves to my left is followed by a heavy footstep.

My mouth drops open as I see his outline. He's fucking enormous. I squint trying to get a better view. I can't see his face. Is it covered?

I'm rooted to the spot, and I can only shuffle back on my ass before I jump to my feet, but even then they don't budge.

His shadow looms larger and larger, my body frozen in place as he closes in. I can see his eyes, deep pools of brown that seem to hold secrets.

Evil yet captivating.

The black balaclava conceals his mouth, so he presses his index finger to the fabric, a silent request for quiet.

What fresh hell have I just landed in?

CHAPTER 9

MIKHAIL

Song- Welcome To The Chaos, Ice Nine Kills

With my finger pressed against my lips, I frown, each step echoing in the silent space as I draw closer. My plan was to climb the drainpipe and snatch her from her room. She beat me to it. Which makes me think she isn't as innocent as I naively thought. She is Sergy's daughter, after all.

She fell right into my trap and now she's like a statue. Just waiting to be grabbed. It's like I'm under a spell, unable to tear my eyes from her as I scrutinize every detail. The platinum blonde curls around her face seemed to glow against the backdrop of her obsidian hair. Her pale blue eyes, like shards of ice, seemed to cut through the darkness, locking onto mine.

A single scream from her would be like a siren's call to Ivan's army, and we'll be caught in the crossfire. And I think she knows that.

She's trying to assess what kind of threat I am. She's bright and absolutely drop dead gorgeous. I've never taken much notice of the intel we have on her over the years. That wasn't my priority. She was safe. That was my promise kept.

It's a good thing. Because if I had taken notice of her, I would have become addicted.

Those blue eyes stare into my soul. I can feel it in my chest, this tightening. Clenching my fist, to try to knock myself back into the real world.

Maybe it was watching her scale out of a four story building in nothing but sneakers and her wits. Or the little proud smile she had when she got to the end. It shows the guts she has.

She just ran from the most dangerous man in Russia. Straight into the path of another.

Except I am a different kind of monster compared to my father. I save women from him, not harm them.

Her fingers twitch by her side, her piercing blue eyes that once stared into mine, glance to my right.

She's about to bolt. A smile tugs on my lips. Not that she can see my amusement. It's one of the benefits of this mask. I clear my throat and her eyes go wide.

She flinches, taking a small step back, her body reacting instinctively, as if a force beyond her control is pushing her away. To her credit, she hasn't run from me yet. Grown men have fled quicker than her. But they know who they are dealing with. My gut is telling me she is going to be a ball of fire in my life.

I glance between her face and her left foot twitching against the leaves.

"I dare you to run. Let's see who enjoys it more when I catch you."

Do I want to scare her? A little. I need her to submit as easily as possible to save ourselves. I'm not ready for an all out war yet.

I need my brothers. My army. My fingers press against the mask, feeling the uneven texture of my scars, and my anger rises like a tide. The asshole that did this to me is behind those walls. I'm so close to my revenge, it's tempting to brush past her to seek him out.

My anger blinds me for a moment. Seeing me turn, she pivots and sprints towards the tree line, triggering the security lights that cast a harsh glare across the field.

"Fuck it," I mutter, breaking out after her.

It's not a bad view watching her perky ass run from me. In fact, my cock is almost twitching at the sight. I catch up with her in no time. My arm circles her waist and I lift her up and press her hard against my chest, squeezing her tight. I quickly cover her mouth with my palm, stifling her scream before it can escape.

Her breathing is frantic. She wants to fight. I can feel her tense. But this clever little thing doesn't struggle. Well, not yet anyway.

"I'm saving you. Now keep your mouth shut before you get us both killed. Can you do that for me?" I whisper harshly into her ear.

She nods slowly. I half expect her to bite me, but she doesn't. I carefully remove my hand, my first test of trust with her.

"Who are you?" Her voice shakes.

"A toss up between your knight in shining armor and your worst nightmare. That's all based on your choices, Princess."

"Don't fucking call me that." She shivers against me.

Hmm.

I slide her slim frame down mine back onto her feet, then lace our fingers together. She turns to face me, glancing between my eyes and our interlocked hands. Did she feel that spark run up her veins too?

"We will talk in the car when it's safe. Now, keep hold, and stay behind me. Got it?"

"Yes, big man," she says, raising one eyebrow.

I squeeze her tight, not realizing my own strength. I need her to believe I'm not the bad guy, just to get us out of here. Then she can see the real Mikhail.

Or, the one I need her to believe exists.

I lead the way, staying close to the treeline, until I count five trees from the gate. Before I can turn left onto the gravel road leading to my car, I catch a glimpse of a man emerging from the double doors, bathed in the harsh glare of the security light.

I turn back to Anastasia and fix her with a steady, unwavering stare.

"Not a fucking word. Don't even breathe."

She sucks in a deep breath, dramatically puffing out her cheeks.

Fucking hell, this woman. Enzo didn't warn me about the attitude that came with her. Although, as Jax's sister, what did I expect?

Feeling the weight of danger, I guide her deeper into the treeline, forcing her against a massive tree trunk as I draw my gun from its holster. Ideally, I don't wanna kill this guy. But Ivan thinks I'm dead and it has to stay that way.

You can get away with a lot when the world believes you're a ghost.

As I step back, the sound of a twig snapping under my boot echoes through the silent woods, making me flinch and close my eyes.

"Motherfucker," I whisper.

The guard's head whips up in our direction. Kill or be killed, that's what my father always drilled into us.

"Be a statue again." I remove my hand from hers, and in that split second when our eyes lock, I see her worry and I almost want to comfort her.

I take a position in front of her. I have a vest on, I can protect her. I move to the tree directly in front and wait, watching his every step as he creeps closer to us.

When he finally catches up to me, I act quickly, seizing the collar of his white shirt and fire three bullets into his forehead without hesitation. I feel his body go slack in my grip, and I let him fall to the ground with a soft thud.

But when I turn around, she's gone.

I search frantically for Anastasia, my heart hammering in my chest.

She taps me on my right shoulder.

"What did I tell you?" I growl.

She shrugs, her movements light and quiet as she tiptoes past me to the body. She kneels gracefully on the ground, her knees sinking into the earth.

"Oh, Charles, what a shame. I guess that's karma for being such a dickhead."

I shake my head in disbelief. A sly smile plays on her lips as she meets my gaze.

This woman has me too stunned to even form words.

"Charles?" I tilt my head. I very much doubt that's his name. I know of no Russian men called that.

She nods.

"I dunno. I gave all of them silly names that didn't suit them. Helped pass the time. And pissed them off royally."

I want to chuckle. She's funny. But I can't let her see that side of me.

She presses two fingers against the dead guy's throat.

"What the hell are you doing?" I ask, hiding the amusement from my tone.

"Making sure he's dead, dead. You know. I think it might be worth shoving another couple of bullets in his chest, just to make sure." She looks back up at me, completely serious.

What the fuck went on in that house?

I clench my fists. If they've touched her, I swear to God, their deaths will be worse than I already planned. I'll burn this entire estate to the ground.

I shake my head, bending down and grabbing her wrist with a firm grip, pulling her up.

"We need to go. Now."

She salutes me, and that throws me off.

"Yes boss. You lead the way."

How is she this calm in my presence? She's smart. Fiery. Ruthless.

No. I don't trust her one bit.

I squat down and scoop her up in my arms, her small frame resting comfortably against my chest.

"This is not the time for games, *Anastasia.*" I emphasize the last word.

Yep. I thought that would keep her quiet. I'm not her savior.

The freezing air whips against my skin. She must be turning to ice. I make my way through the treeline, and aim towards my truck. I place her on her feet next to the vehicle and unlock it, opening up her door.

"You want me to get in there, I take it?" Her teeth chatter as she speaks, so I shrug off my jacket and place it over her shoulders. For a split moment, her face softens.

She gives me a curt nod and jumps up into her seat. Hopping in the driver's seat, I unholster my gun and rest it on my lap. This woman needs reminding who is in charge. I wait for her seatbelt to click and I turn on the engine, getting the fuck out of here as fast as I can.

I can feel her gaze burning into my side. In fact she radiates pure fire. I keep my eyes fixed on the road ahead and relax into the silence.

She clears her throat next to me and I glance over. Fuck. She's gorgeous. Full lips, a button nose and those eyes. Damn, those eyes could break a man. Not me though.

"I'm not some weak princess that needs saving from the monster."

I grip the steering wheel tighter. The way she speaks to me shouldn't turn me on as much as it irritates me at the same time.

CHAPTER 10

ANASTASIA

He chuckles menacingly, tapping his weapon against his thick thigh, and I swallow the lump in my throat. He's intimidating. Yet, something I can't quite put my finger on, is comforting about his presence.

"You've gone from one monster to another, iskorka. I was never there to save you. I was there to take you."

Why the hell is this man calling me spark? I'll take it over princess. God damn, his voice seems to rattle straight through my bones. So deep. So sexy.

Who the hell is he? And why do I want to keep pressing his buttons? He could kill me with one hand, yet, something about him is telling me he won't.

"You're an asshole. You know that right? Just take me back. I can probably end that old fucker myself. I already gave it a good go."

I wish I could see under his mask. The way the creases appear next to his eyes, it's almost like he's grinning even though he keeps his focus fixed on the road.

My leg bobs up and down. Fight or flight. "Wait."

He turns to me and his dark eyes burn through me. And

there it is. That spark. It's as if I've met him before, maybe in a previous life. That connection is real.

"What?"

"How did you know my name back there? Who the hell are you and what do you want?" I spit out.

I've had enough of men thinking they can claim me, taking what they want.

"If you behave for me, one day I might tell you."

My eyes roll as his hand unexpectedly shoots out, grasping my leg with a surprising strength. I let out a long breath trying to keep my cool and my thighs clench together. I might not have slept with a guy before, but I know enough about my body to know he's turning me on.

Which means I have to hide that from him.

"I don't behave," I say with a smirk.

This seems to be the best way to stay alive. I think he secretly likes this side of me. I bet women rarely push him like this, because he's scary as hell.

Scary, yet incredibly sexy. And if I'm going to die anyway, I might as well have fun with it.

CHAPTER 11

MIKHAIL

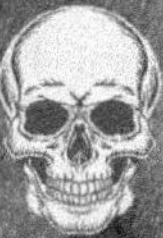

My god the mouth on this woman should not be turning me on.

I'm taking her to draw my father out.

She is merely a stepping stone in my revenge. That, and a promise to Jax's dad I made many years ago.

"And you're a mouthy brat. I suggest you keep it shut for the drive. You really won't like me when I'm angry."

She huffs and I remove my hand from her thigh and tighten my grip on the wheel. I can't keep touching her, it's flickering something within me that needs to be dulled out again. She is the perfect brat to be tamed. This could not be worse timing.

I can't let her see that she gets to me. I can't let her get those manicured claws into me.

Distractions are something I can't afford.

Even if the second our hands touched, electricity shot through me.

I felt something.

For the first time since the incident that plunged me into this dark hole, I came alive, burning from inside, *for her.*

"Are you going to kill me? I swear I have nothing to do with Ivan."

I hold my index finger up to my lips over my mask.

"No more talking. Keep going against me, I might have to."

Her fingers twitch by the seat belt. Taking the gun in my hand, I press it against her temple and her body shakes, her breathing erratically filling the car. I'd never hurt her, I just want to see how far I can push her.

"You run, I chase. But I promise you won't enjoy what happens when I catch you… I might though."

There is no *might* about it. I would enjoy every second of claiming her. She's such a firecracker, I imagine she's just as feisty in bed.

My eyes flick up and down her tiny frame. She's at least a foot smaller than me, with a petite, slender body.

No way she could handle me. Not to start with, anyway.

God, I'd have to gag her. Or would I? She would look perfect choking on my cock.

I need to stop thinking like this. Remember the plan. No time for bratty women to veer me off course.

CHAPTER 12

ANASTASIA

"I DON'T KNOW. I probably can run faster than you. All those muscles would slow you down." Sarcasm is my only option as he presses his gun against my head.

I don't think he'd hurt me. He would have if he wanted too.

He looks at me for a long moment, then reholsters his weapon. "You're either brave or stupid. And I don't think you're dumb at all."

"Did it hurt?" I try not to show my relief.

"What?" he grumbles, taking a turn fast enough to push me against the door.

I lift my chin, staring down my nose at him. "Giving me a compliment."

His fist tightens on the steering wheel. "Would you rather I called you a brat and bent you over my knee?" He shifts in his seat, adjusting his pistol.

Why did the thought of laying across those meaty thighs make my heart race?

I need to change the subject.

"Where are we going?" This isn't the way to my mom's

house. I watch the trees grow closer together, nothing like the apartment where I live.

"A safe place."

"Just take me back home. I'll tell you where to go." I don't even know who he is.

"No." His response is short, gruff.

My lips purse watching him. "Are you holding me for ransom? Shouldn't I be tied up or something?" I pull my knees under me so I can lean over the console, holding my wrists together.

His dark brows drop before he grabs both of my arms in one hand. "What the fuck are you doing?" He pushes me away so I sit back against my seat.

"Just trying to figure out what the hell is going on." My arms cross and I let my lower lip stick out.

I hate not knowing.

At least Ivan was clear from the beginning.

This guy is like talking to a rock.

A really sexy one.

"You know when you pout like that, it makes someone want to bite that lower lip off." His eyes crinkle again over his mask.

Is he messing with me?

"I'd like to know how my mom is. Can we at least stop by so I can tell her I'm alive?" It's been weeks since I've seen her.

He takes a deep breath, and reaches out to touch my leg again. "Ana, I'm sorry."

I shove it away. "Who are you to know? Huh? How in the fuck do you know who she is, much less me?" Tears sting in my eyes. Not because of who he may be, but I'm afraid that he's telling me the truth.

He whips the truck over to the side of the dirt road and

throws it into park. When he reaches for me again, I try to fight off his grasp.

If he stops me, he might tell me.

I don't want to know. Not if it's what I think it is.

"Don't touch me!" Struggling, I still lose, and I feel the walls I've built around my heart begin to shatter.

"Ana, it's me, Mikhail. I've been taking care of you and your mom for years. Enzo had your place checked the day you disappeared. He found her. She fought like hell for you." His touch is surprisingly gentle when he strokes my cheek, wiping away a tear that escapes. "She tried to do what I failed at. So I'm here to fix that. I'm going to protect you if it's the last thing I do."

"No," I whisper. "Please be lying." My chest aches and my chin trembles from the ripping pain running through me. "Say you hate me. That's why you're telling me this. Please?"

His dark eyes burn into me. I'm suddenly very conscious of how close he is.

And how good he smells.

"You know the worst part?" I finally manage to stammer.

"What?" His unforgiving grip heats through my skin, arcing through my body like I'm holding a live wire of electricity.

"I had a fight with her. It's why I left. I told her I wanted to leave, and she told me it wasn't safe." I knew I shouldn't have left.

She always warned me that I had a dangerous family. When Papa died, it was a big sign.

But I hated sitting at home all of the time.

His head tilts, and his eyes narrow. Yet they glint with a hint of mischievousness. "Let me guess, you didn't listen?"

That makes my nose wrinkle. "Asshole." It's hard to

dislike him knowing it's because of him that I've been taken care of for years.

He isn't so scary anymore.

"It's nice to meet you too." He pulls his grasp away, and shoves the truck into drive, then readjusts his holster again.

Maybe it doesn't fit right? It does look like it's sitting tightly against his bulging crotch—

Oh.

CHAPTER 13

MIKHAIL

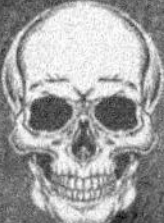

I HAVE NEVER FELT this conflicted around a woman before. I want to comfort her, spank her, fuck her, protect her.

All of it. None of it.

Maybe she isn't safe with *me*.

That's why we need to get the hell out of here.

I drag out my phone and pull up Enzo's number.

"Mikhail. Did you get her?" he asks before it even rings.

"I did. Is the plane ready?" I'm itching to get her to Vegas. Once she meets Jax, she'll have a safe place to stay with him. The brother she never knew.

"Should be. I had Drago get some backup. There's a yellow Cessna parked near the end for you." He clicks in the background. "Mikhail, the camera feed isn't working correctly, so be on your toes."

"Copy that." I click the call off and slide my cell back in my pocket.

"Be ready to run, princess." I smirk beneath my mask and glance at her.

I have to say anything to keep her at arm's length. If I let her close, who knows what I might do?

She grunts and wrinkles her nose at me. "I swear I'm going to kick you right in the shin, *after* we get out of here." She glances over and sticks out her tongue. "I can't have you slowing me down."

My jaw clenches. I want to put her in her place.

But getting her to Vegas and as far away from me is my priority.

"Fine. Watch me." I jab my finger towards her face. "And fucking *listen.*"

Her palms fly up. "Okay, sheesh. Don't get all excited, you might stroke out." Her lips twitch as she fights a smile. "I promise."

When she traces her breasts in an "X", I swear I'm almost coming in my pants.

With a growl, I throw myself out of the truck, then motion her to follow.

In a crouch, we cut through the trees and find ourselves on the back of a huge hangar.

Pulling out my binoculars, I make a slow sweep over the other buildings. I can't see anyone right away, but that certainly doesn't mean this place is empty.

"Can we go? I'm cold," Ana whines behind me.

Then her palm smacks my left ass cheek, making me jump.

"Jesus Christ." I almost stumble to catch myself. "What the fuck?"

She's grinning. Of course she is.

"You looked too serious." Her hand sits on my thigh as she squats next to me. "Where are we going?"

I can't even think with her so close.

"That yellow plane." I point to the next hangar.

There's a substantial amount of empty ground between us and it though.

"I'm trying to make sure we make it. Stop being a pain and focus." In a half run, I grab her hand and pull her with me.

Three quarters of the way from the next building, gunfire erupts around us sending me sprawling into the dirt, tugging Ana down with me.

Pockets of rocks and debris fly up with the frenzy of bullets.

I look up and see a group of men pouring from the tree line opposite of us.

Fuck.

"We have to go back!" Pushing up from the frozen earth, I don't give her a chance to argue but sprint towards the truck.

There's no way in hell I can make it to that plane where it sits in the open.

It's too exposed.

Gravel flies behind us as I slam on the gas, fishtailing the truck out of the parking lot.

"Shit. That was close." Her wide eyes stare between the seats behind us. "How did they know we were there?"

"Ivan owns all of this. He probably put out an order to lock down all the airports." My palm slams against the steering wheel. "Damn it!"

"So…what do we do now?" She pulls her knees up to sit cross legged in the seat.

"I have safe houses set up just in case. We lay low until we can fly out."

We drive in silence for the better part of an hour while Enzo preps the closest spot.

I don't want to show up with her, so we wait until I get the word the crew is gone.

A crazy thought drifts through me as I step around the truck to open her door.

What if, instead of just stealing her from my father, I claimed her as my own?

That really is insane.

"Inside," I growl, pointing to the small cabin nestled in the trees.

She climbs out and stops just inches from my chest, then looks up at me with those wicked blue eyes. "Is this where you take me to have your way with me?" A smile tickles along the seam of her full red lips before she turns on her heel and flounces away from me.

I have to adjust my holster again, my cock is so full it makes my pants uncomfortable.

My fingers tingle wanting to grab her throat and force her to her knees.

That takes a back seat to watching her ass move in those tight leggings up the stairs onto the porch.

She pauses before reaching for the handle.

"It's not locked." There's barely room for both of us on the narrow flat.

"You said it yourself, I'm also not stupid. Ivan will be looking for me." She waves her fingers in the direction of the house. "You're the big, strong, scary guy with the gun, you check it first." She smiles sweetly and tilts her chin up.

I twist the handle, opening the small living room to the cold evening air.

With only one bedroom, it takes seconds to sweep it and make sure it's clear.

"No boogeyman." I wave her in, then squat in front of the woodstove to start a fire. Winter in Russia is no joke.

Makes me miss the heat of Nevada, and the comforts of climate control.

She stands in the middle of the room with her arms wrapped around her like she doesn't know what to do.

"Make yourself comfortable. We'll be here for a few days. It's too dangerous to try and get to any airport right now." I drop my duffel next to the couch as the temperature begins to slowly climb from the warming stove.

Her icy blue eyes narrow as she stares at me. "Where are you taking me?"

"America. Las Vegas. I have someone there who would be very happy to meet you." I've been careful not to share her existence with Jax.

He's been through so much, I didn't want to tell him that he has family still alive, when I wasn't at liberty to share her location.

It's been easier to just keep the secret.

Except there isn't any hiding who her father is. Her dark curly hair leaves little doubt.

"Are you trying to set me up with one of your friends?" Her nose wrinkles. "I'm really not in the mood for any more matchmaking. Besides—" She flops backwards onto the cushions behind her. "—I'd rather stay with you. At least I know you're not going to kill me." She smacks one of the pillows making a cloud of dust rise through the last rays of the sun.

"The night is still young," I growl, moving into the kitchen. "Do you know how to cook?" The cupboards are stocked with everything we'd need to last for weeks.

Enzo is so thorough, I'm not sure what I'd do without him.

"Why, because I'm the woman, I'm supposed to know?" She tosses one of the smaller pillows, but it falls flat on the floor.

"I swear to fuck," I grumble under my breath. "No, because I'll be gone and I want to make sure you aren't going to starve to death, *princess.*"

"I told you not to call me that. Yes, I will be just fine here. All by myself." She gets up and retrieves her failed missile.

But when she moves closer, she doesn't even pause before pushing in front of me at the fridge to bend over and look inside.

Her ass presses against my leg, as if she's trying to move me out of her way.

Think again.

My hand falls to her hip, and I wrap my fingers around her, digging them into the soft curves.

With a jerk, I pull her tight against my thigh so my hard cock shoves to the top of her ass. Only the taut fabric of our pants keeps me from thrusting into her. "You want to fuck around? You're going to get burned, iskorka."

She flips her dark hair over her shoulder, and without moving turns to look up at me. Her pale eyes tighten with a smirk. "You think you're hot enough for me? I dare you to take that mask off and show me."

Reaching into the cold recesses of the refrigerator, she pulls out a long neck beer and a package of cheese with crackers. "Looky, big man," she says, standing and sauntering away. "I may survive to live another day."

She props the cap of the bottle against the sharp lip on the stove and pops the lid.

Sucking the neck into her mouth, she guzzles the foam, her gaze never wavering from mine.

My finger comes up to point directly at her face. "You're trouble. Stay here. I'll be back in a few hours."

Wait. She didn't listen last time.

"There are cameras. I don't let insolence go unpunished." I squat next to the stove and toss in another heavy log to keep the fire going while I'm gone.

"What are you going to do if I don't listen?" Ana sits

cross-legged on the couch and lets the tip of her pink tongue circle the rim of her bottle.

I may have to jack off in the woods after watching her mouth do gymnastics over the cold glass.

"Only one of us will enjoy it." Rising stiffly, I reach for my phone to send Enzo a text.

ME

She's a fucking handful.

ENZO

What did you expect with her being related to Jax?

ME

Not this.

ENZO

Is there something wrong with her?

That makes me stare at the screen. I steal a glance at her laying across the arm of the couch, thumbing through the stack of magazines.

Her round, tight ass poking up into the air makes it diffi-cult not wanting to grab it.

ME

No. That's the problem.

ENZO

Ahh, have fun!

And they say I'm the asshole.

"Look, we aren't far from Ivan's stronghold here. We made a wide loop so I can keep an eye on him. If you leave, there's a very real chance you could be caught." My fist squeezes as I try to keep my words level and my eyes locked onto hers.

I really shouldn't be letting my gaze wander down her toned body and tight fitting shirt. Nor the fact that her little leggings look like they've been painted on.

When she shrugs, I feel my blood pressure spike.

"You'd just rescue me again." She purses her lips and slides a piece of cheese slowly between them.

Torturous brat.

Fury bubbles in my chest until I find myself standing over her. "If my father catches you again, there's no hope of you ever escaping alive. He doesn't handle traitors lightly." I jerk my finger towards my mask, then stomp towards the door.

"Wait, he's your…father?" There's a tremor in her voice.

Grabbing the handle, I force myself to take a deep breath. "Yes. Always remember, I'm a Volkov, too."

I step out into the frigid night. Steam erupts from the edges of my balaclava with every angry exhale.

That fucking woman. She knows how to push my buttons.

I shouldn't let her. No one has cracked my armor, let alone a twenty-three year old.

My father's fiancée .

And my *step-sister*.

Every piece of this is wrong.

So why do I feel so close to saying "fuck it" to everything, and taking her like I own her?

CHAPTER 14

ANASTASIA

My stomach twists at the realization.

He's the son of that *monster*.

But what I've gathered from the whispers at the mansion, Ivan's children revolted and left years ago.

Does that mean Mikhail might not be like Ivan?

He certainly doesn't seem to be.

And Mikhail is the only person I've heard of that has outsmarted Ivan. Beat him at his own game several times.

Big, strong, with sexy brown eyes.

And that grip he had on my hip, grinding himself against me, I know he wants me.

Maybe I've found the perfect person to protect me after all? He's taken care of me for years, kept me and mom safe and comfortable.

The last few weeks of terror at Ivan's house were a hard lesson that there are truly evil men out there who will take anything they want, with no concern of who they hurt.

I don't want to be alone.

With Mom gone now…

Fuck. I'll regret my last words to her forever. I should

have listened and never snuck out. I didn't really understand the threat that she, and Mikhail, protected me from.

Papa trusted Mikhail.

I should too.

There's a piece of me that worries about him spying on Ivan. What if something happens to him? I believe Mikhail when he says that Ivan won't let me go without punishment next time.

A shiver runs through my body at the memory of Ivan's touch.

I don't want him to ever get close to me again.

Especially not *that* way.

The idea of that nasty old man being my first experience makes me want to vomit.

No. I'd die before that happens.

I just wish I knew what Mikhail's face looked like beneath that mask.

It makes me wonder if he's gorgeous, or hideous?

If he's ugly, will that change my mind? I think I should just go for it, get it over with before we leave for America.

Who is it that he wants me to meet in Vegas? Is he setting me up with someone else?

That idea scares the crap out of me. He could be sending me off to an even worse person than Ivan.

There's only one option. And it will probably hurt like hell.

Fuck it. I might die tomorrow.

I don't want to go out a virgin.

CHAPTER 15

MIKHAIL

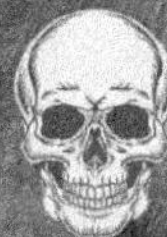

I'M BUMBLING through the woods like a drunken bear because all I can think about is the feel of her ass pressing against me, and how badly I want to throw her to her knees and make that bratty fucking mouth stretch around my cock.

So every fallen branch, hidden stone, and snow-covered hole seems to leap out of the dark woods and find me.

Crashing and cussing my way through the freezing night, I finally get to the hilltop vantage I was aiming for.

This is probably a waste of time.

Maybe I should go back and teach that little brat how to behave.

All of the blood in my sense of reasoning floods to my cock.

Yes, I really could just leave.

Resolved in my decision, I'm just starting to retrace my steps when I hear a vehicle.

I can wait.

The dark van pulls over in the clearing nearly in front of me, and a suited man climbs out. When he turns to face the rear tire and pulls his dick out, I can't resist my luck seeing the "V" tattoo just above his collar.

With only a few silent paces, I'm behind him and sliding the tip of my knife under his jaw. He doesn't make a sound as he slips to the ground, pulsing blood pooling around his slack features.

There's no one else in the vehicle, so I can load him in the back.

What else is in here?

Unzipping the garment bags reveals an ornate wedding dress and tuxedo.

Interesting.

I bet Ana would look absolutely stunning in this.

She should wear it for me.

Where that thought came from, I don't know. But now it plays on repeat through my head.

Doing a quick search of the glove box and console, I find the dead guy's phone lodged near a steaming cup of coffee.

Fucking thumb screen lock.

I go back to the rear and pull his arm out to open the cell.

The messages are the typical call to arms that I'd expect from my father. But there's one that stops me.

Ivan: I know Mikhail is here. Find him, bring me his head!

Well. Sounds like he's more in the loop than I realized.

Did Drago tell him?

Jumping into the driver's seat, I shift the van into drive and turn it down an abandoned looking road, then dump it behind thick trees so it won't be spotted from the highway.

I just need to grab those garment bags.

Sticking around when I know that Ivan is searching for me won't be a wise move. Getting Ana back to Vegas is the safest plan.

The heavy nylon crinkles in the cold air. I shouldn't have taken them, but I can't get the image of her wearing this gown out of my head.

When I make it back to the cabin, it's well into the early hours of morning. Frost gathers on my eyebrows and fringes on my mask as I stomp my feet to free the snow on them before stepping in.

The dark silence is almost deafening except for the slow crackle of the fire.

She must have put another log or two on after I left.

Good girl.

After I hang the clothes up, I make myself a stiff drink.

But I stare at the bourbon in my hand.

If I drink this, I may lose what last bit of control I'm clinging to.

With a groan, I unfold myself onto the short couch and let the heat of the flames lull me to sleep.

CHAPTER 16

ANASTASIA

I CAN SEE MY BREATH. Damn, I shouldn't have closed the door to the bedroom.

But I had to do something to keep myself from inviting him in.

Maybe I shouldn't stop myself.

I wonder if he's back yet?

If he isn't, I need to put more wood on the fire. And fuck it, I'm leaving the room open to let the heat in.

Deep snoring is radiating from the couch. I'm hit with a wall of warmth. I can't tell if it's the air, or if it's his presence that makes me feel like I'm burning up.

Tiptoeing closer, I can see him lying there in the light of the flickering flames.

There's two black shapes in the corner that startle me at first until I see that they're some sort of bags.

Lowering the zipper on the smaller one makes me almost gasp out loud.

I'd recognize that dress anywhere. I've spent hours in it already.

How did he get it? I hate that it's so beautiful, yet it is destined for Ivan.

Mikhail would be better. He'd look hot in a suit.

I kind of want to ask him.

Is he wearing his mask when he sleeps?

What the heck is up with that?

Can I sneak a peek?

My heart races and my pulse pounds in my ears as I extend a shaking hand slowly towards the swath of fabric over his nose.

He inhales, making it flex towards his mouth.

What if he's disfigured? Scars? Birth defect?

I don't care. I just want to know.

Gently pinching a crease, I try to move it down.

A dark line of stubble appears on the closest cheek, almost a shadow in the dim light.

But I can't see much yet.

The further I move it, the more my pulse jackhammers in my skull.

I almost have it low enough to see his top lip, when his eyes fly open.

With a growl, he grabs my wrist and yanks my fingers away, then drags me across his broad body.

His heaving chest rises and falls with me on it.

"What the fuck are you doing, iskorka?" he growls, his nose only inches from mine.

Shit.

"Why do you have my wedding dress?" I tilt my head and try to give him the most accusatory look.

Which is difficult considering I'm sprawled over his muscles, bathed in his musky scent, and my skin feels like it's on fire.

"Maybe I wanted to see you in it?" The edges of his eyes crinkle.

"If I put it on, will you take the mask off?" My lip rolls between my teeth.

It takes everything in me not to grind my hips against him. He's getting hard, his cock is digs into me.

He's so big he's going to break me.

"It's bad luck to see a bride in her dress before the wedding." His chuckle bounces me against the bulge in his pants.

He makes me crazy. Giddy. Like I could jump off a cliff and fly, if I was only brave enough.

I lower my mouth between my held arms until it brushes his ear. "Marry me then." Taking the lobe between my teeth, I bite down until he groans.

He rips me up, holding me away from him.

I can see the flush on his face and his temples clench when he grits his jaw.

Panting, he sets my feet down and backs away, shaking his head.

"You're something else, you know that? If I didn't know better, I'd say you're begging to be fucked." His thick fingers run through his rumpled black hair.

"Maybe I am." Pivoting on my heel, I aim for the bedroom. "But not now, you've broken the mood." I slam the door shut and fall against it.

Damn, it's a struggle to catch my breath.

Why does he hide himself?

The bigger question is, why did he stop himself? It's obvious I turn him on.

What if he's already married? Or has a girlfriend?

I fling the handle and stomp into the tiny living room.

He's on one knee tossing a log onto the fire.

"Do you already have a wife?" I stand over him with my hands on my hips.

He doesn't look up, but pokes the embers. "No."

"Girlfriend?"

He shakes his head.

"Boyfriend?"

"Ana…" he grumbles. "No, no one. I'm too busy for that shit."

"But you made time for me," I say softly, then move closer.

His eyes reflect the flames as he stares up at me. "Yes, I did." He finally relents.

That brings out my best smile.

I bend over and wrap my arms around his neck so my lips are near his cheek. "You're already on one knee. How badly do you want to see me in that dress?"

He tilts his nose up to rub it along the length of my neck, breathing me in deeply with the slow stroke. "You're putting it on in the morning. First light." The wood in his grip creaks with how fiercely he squeezes it.

Nervous energy courses through me. "Tomorrow?" I squeak.

I let go and step back. I didn't think he'd do it.

He nods and pushes the stove shut, then slides up onto the couch. "After that, you're mine, iskorka."

I can feel his eyes on me the whole way back to my room.

What did I do?

And why am I excited?

CHAPTER 17

MIKHAIL

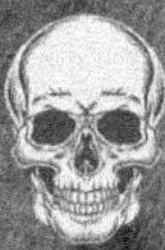

SHE WANTS TO PLAY A GAME? I always win.

I own a casino for fuck's sake. That's not by chance. I showed up in Vegas with only my family and what little money I smuggled from my father when we fled.

Everything else, I built from the ground up.

If she thinks I won't take what I want, she's sorely mistaken.

But taking her hand would be quite the devastation to Ivan.

Screw him.

"You have got to be joking." Enzo breaks into laughter on the other end. "You want to marry her? This morning?"

"Make it happen." I can't think about anything else but her. I might get tired of her later, but I *need* her like I've never wanted anyone before.

The drive within me to break her is worth the vows.

"Are you drunk? Did she drug you?" Enzo takes on a serious tone. "Put me on video."

"What the hell? No, she didn't." It takes me twice, but I click the camera on.

"Hold it up to your eyes, let me see them." His own get so close to the lens all I can see are his dark lashes.

"Jesus Christ, Enzo. I'm fine." I glower at him.

He smirks as he gets into view. "I thought that would be the only explanation. I can't wait to tell Frankie this shit."

"Leave him out of this. That's the last thing I need." I've had a good working relationship with Frankie Falcone for years.

But we're far from best friends. We both run our organizations with a hard line.

I do remember quite distinctly having to go to battle with him. And kidnapping his wife for him.

A grin pulls up my lip. Yea, I can imagine he'd get quite a kick out of this.

"Maybe I'll throw a party and invite everyone," Enzo snickers. "One big happy dysfunctional family."

"Sure. Later. What about this wedding though?" My cock throbs just thinking about her in that dress.

And ripping it off her.

"Give me twenty minutes. I'll email you the paperwork, and I'll get a hold of one of the officiants nearby. Oh—" Enzo leans back and turns the camera towards his computer screen. "—I don't know what you did to kick the wasp's nest. But you might want to consider moving to the next safehouse." He pans over the grainy black and white drone feed to show three cars and at least ten guys milling around the van I left hidden in the bushes.

Shit.

"I'll kick her in the ass. We'll leave right after." Not until I see that gown.

I'll fight all of Ivan's army for the privilege.

Stomping the snow off my feet, I push into the heat of the cabin.

And forget how to breathe.

The fire of the morning sun catches the glitter of fine diamonds that are sewn into the hems.

She's practically glowing. Her pale breasts push from the snug top, showing the long lines of her bare throat, slim waist, and hips that make me want to dig my fingers in until she begs for mercy.

"Well?" Ana has the audacity to raise her eyebrow while pursing her lips. "Where's my ring, big man?"

I knew she was going to ask.

Tugging at the chain around my neck, I pull out the one thing I salvaged from the night Ivan attacked.

The one that changed my life forever.

There's still a tinge of char around the edge, and a bit of the silver has melted off, but my mother's ring still holds the faint pink glimmer that I remember from my youth when she wore it.

"All I have is this. I think it might fit." Pulling the strand hard enough, it breaks apart, freeing the keepsake from its home against my heart.

"Oh." Her eyes brighten. "It's beautiful."

"I thought you might like that. Your father bought it." I hold it pinched between my fingers just long enough for her to get a long look, then slide it into my pocket.

She squints one eye with a scowl. "Why did Papa buy that for your mom?"

"When he married her." I smirk watching her features contort.

Holding up my other hand, I stop her before she melts down. "They met and married only seven years ago. Long after we were born." I can't stop the grin, even if she can't see it.

"They were unified with their mutual hatred of my

father." Grabbing her wrist, I drag her onto my lap then dial Enzo.

"I can see that. Funny, your dad is quite the matchmaker. Because of him, we met too." She wiggles on my thigh, pushing her breasts against my chest.

Fuck. What she does to me is criminal.

"Mikhail, always good to see the sliver of your face. Ana, you look well." Enzo smiles into the camera. He's flanked by his associate, Romeo, and a short gray haired man.

"I remember you. Mama said you were the go-to guy." Ana peers close to the screen. "Nice to meet you."

Enzo nods, and holds the camera further from his body. "Okay, there are two witnesses, and this is Pastor Harold. You have roughly eight minutes until Ivan's men make it to the cabin." He prods the old man in the elbow.

"Yes, hello. This is quite unconventional." His bushy eyebrows fill the frame momentarily. "I can't quite read these names—"

"Just ask for the 'I do's'," Enzo growls at him.

"What? That isn't—" Pastor Harold pulls out his spectacles.

"I do." I'll interrupt him. My hand finds Ana's hip to press her against my cock, grinding the slick silk skirt between our legs.

"Do you?" I ask her as my fingers press the fabric between her thighs.

Her cheeks flush pink and her chin drops into a pant. "Yes, I do." She manages to choke out when the tip of my index brushes the heat of her pussy through the gown.

"Good girl." My mask is the only thing separating my mouth from her skin.

I'm going to make her mine before she sees the monster she married.

"Enzo," I grunt. "How long?"

"You need to go." He jerks the phone image. "They're hot on you! I'll take care of the paperwork, congrats to the happy couple. Now get the fuck out of there!"

I just hear the pastor begin to protest when I end the call.

"Come on, wife. Let's find a safe place to rip that thing off of you." I pick her up and throw her over my shoulder, grab my bag, and spring towards the truck.

"This isn't very romantic." Her words are broken with the jostling of my run.

I'd rather have her disappointed than dead. Or worse if my father gets a hold of her.

"You're alive, aren't you?" I toss her in the passenger seat and throw my bag into the bed before leaping behind the wheel.

A spray of snow and gravel flies up behind me as I fishtail onto the dirt road leaving the cabin. It's a race to see if I can make it out of the driveway before Ivan's men arrive.

CHAPTER 18

ANASTASIA

I DID IT. I actually got married to someone who *isn't* Ivan.

But who is Mikhail?

I don't even know what he looks like. I just know how he makes me feel.

Safe. Protected. Wanted.

That's better than most of my life.

"Where are we going?" This dress isn't comfortable for sitting, I can barely breathe.

He pushes against the steering wheel and digs in his pants pocket. "Somewhere private and safe."

Using his knee to guide us, he turns and reaches out for my hand, then threads the ring onto my finger. "I thee wed." He winks one of his walnut colored eyes before taking control of the truck again.

I don't know why, but with the soft pink gem and silver ring, it makes the whole insane thing feel more real.

The vehicle slows, then he pulls it to a stop in a wide clearing. "I need to see if they're following us. It's too over-grown for the drone to get a good view."

"Wait." I hold up my palm as he climbs out. "How much

longer is the drive?" I don't think I can handle much more of this bumpy road in this gown. I feel like I'm suffocating.

His eyes narrow. "Two or three hours. Not long. Stay here. I'll be back."

"What? That's forever! Is there anywhere closer?" I stick out my lower lip. Maybe that will entice him to a better location.

Now that I'm a 'Mrs', I kinda want to see what he's hiding.

His finger comes to a sharp point. "Stay. Here."

"Fine." I slump against the seat. I just want to get to where we're going.

But I know he needs to make sure we're safe. It's both a turn on, and frustrating.

This dress is just so damn uncomfortable, and I have to pee.

The cab starts to cool, bringing goosebumps to my bare arms.

I hope he's okay?

Five more minutes.

Geez, where is he? I'm bouncing in the seat from a full bladder, running my palms over my shoulders.

No, screw this.

I jump out of the truck and dig into the back to see if there's anything I can use.

At least there's some paper towels and a few bottles of water so I can finally find some relief from all the coffee I drank this morning.

Sitting back in the chilly passenger's seat is boring. He's been gone forever.

Where the heck is he?

My fingers are getting cold. And, of course, he has the keys.

Maybe I can find him, get them to warm up?

Yes, I like that idea.

The frost hangs heavy on the trees, but it sparkles in the mid-morning sun. It's much nicer out here than the dreary apartment I lived in with Mom.

God, that hurts to think about her.

I should stay off the road, in case Ivan's men come through.

What was that noise?

Hurrying to a thick clump of bushes, I squat down to watch. It might be a deer.

Or a bear.

Oh shit, what if it's a bear?

I should get back to the car.

Just as I stand, a thick hand lashes out and grabs me roughly around the wrist.

Flipping on my heel, I'm caught staring up into my husband's masked face. His dark eyes are pinpricks as he glares at me.

"I thought—" He takes a deep breath. "—I told you to stay at the *fucking truck?*"

CHAPTER 19

MIKHAIL

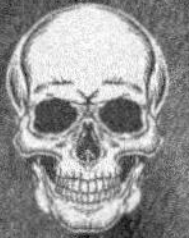

"Get in the truck, Anastasia," I growl, towering over her.

She rolls her bottom lip between her teeth, the gesture slow and deliberate, and it infuriates me further. My knuckles whiten as I clench my fist, my gaze darting past her to take in the surroundings. A tense silence hangs in the air. We're like sitting fucking ducks here. Her decision to follow me was reckless and put her in danger. She went against my direct orders.

And still, she won't listen. She continues defying me. To tease me. God, everyday living with her is a test. Her mischievous grin, her sass. Every single thing about her both riles me and turns me on. It sparks something in my chest I've never felt before.

Keeping her in my sight is all that matters, despite the sharp, physical pain her presence inflicts. Each shared breath is a stab. I crave the impossible.

She flinches as I pound the car roof, but defiantly crosses her arms and raises her chin.

"Do not make me repeat myself again. Get in the mother-fucking car before I drag you in there myself."

Her eyebrow arches, and one side of her mouth curves into a smirk.

"Take the mask off and I might think about it."

Fuck.

I swing open the passenger door and she takes a step back. I see that glint in her eye.

"Don't you dare," I warn.

As she steps away, I get a hold of the top of the door. I restrain myself from pursuing her, inhaling deeply to regain composure.

"What are you going to do about it, big man? I gave you my rules."

I chew on the inside of my mouth. It is taking every ounce of restraint I possess not to grab her by the throat and throw her on the hood and fuck this behavior right out of her.

That's all she needs. This brat needs taming.

I take large steps toward her, and she retreats, fear flick-ering in her eyes before being replaced by an expression of desire. That spark between us is real. It has been from the moment I grabbed her hand. A familiarity I can't put my finger on lies between us.

"You do not get to make the rules with me, Ana. I made a promise to protect you, yet again, you put yourself in harm's way. I do not accept this disobedience, and now I have no choice but to punish you."

That makes her stop. Her plump lips open and her eyes go wide.

"What is it that you want, iskorka? Why do you continue to push me? You want me to fuck the attitude out of you? Is that what it is? You want me to test your limits? You want to be punished and put in your place? Hmm?"

"I-I," she stammers, dropping another small step away. Her foot poises as if she's going to turn.

I take a final step, closing the distance between us. I can smell her desire for me. Her rising and falling chest, and the heat she radiates are palpable.

"Use your words. I know you're full of them." I press.

"You're an asshole. I'm not getting in that damn car until you treat me with respect. I'm your *wife* now. Is this how it's always going to be?"

I scratch at my jaw over my mask. I have an answer, yet that isn't necessarily the truth about why I can't ever let her go. But that isn't something I want to even admit to myself.

I grab her throat, yanking her upwards until she is on her toes. She gasps softly as I lean in, our noses touching.

"No one speaks to me that way," I snarl.

Her pulse hammers against my palm and my cock aches for her.

"Is this a game for you? You think I haven't worked you out and know exactly how to play to win?"

I tilt my head and study her reaction as she swallows. Releasing my hold, she stumbles away. I expect her to be furious.

"You think you can win my game, Mikhail? You don't know me or what I want," she snaps back.

I nod, my heart hammering in my chest. *So, so wrong, pretty girl.*

"I know you want to run. And I also know that you want me to chase you, catch you and throw you against a tree and have my wicked way with you."

Her eyes dart from left to right, weighing up her options. Her gaze settles on my crotch and I smirk. She gets to me, I can't help it.

"Run, pretty girl. I will catch you, and I am going to enjoy every second of ruining you when I get my hands on you."

CHAPTER 20

ANASTASIA

HOLY SHIT, what the hell am I doing?

Why can't I stop myself when it comes to winding him up? That look in his eyes, it was a warning.

An exciting one. His smouldering gaze lit me up like a damn firework.

He watches me, almost with amusement. I take a deep breath, the scent of pine filling my lungs as I kick off my heels.

With one final grin playing on my lips, I slowly retreat, the silence amplifying my every step.

"Looks like you better catch me then," I tell him before turning my back to him and take off in a sprint.

Grabbing a fistful of my dress, I yank it up to give me more space to run. The tree line is my only hope. Once I'm there, I can disappear among the brush and lose him. I can feel him gaining on me, but I'm faster. It may be my only chance to escape.

The icy ground sends a jolt through my foot each time they land making me wince, yet the adrenaline keeps me moving.

Maybe I've lost him? Slowing to a stop, I rest my hand on a trunk and try to catch my breath. It's so still. Eerily silent.

Just as I go to make a hard turn left, the world blurs as I crash, my face impacting his hard chest with a jarring thud.

His hands tighten around my waist, a possessive grip that both thrills and frightens me.

"Too easy, pretty girl," he drawls.

I push against him, but he holds me tighter, a low chuckle rumbling in his throat.

Okay. New plan.

"Mikhail. T-there's a guy behind you." I put as much fear in my voice as I can.

As predicted, with a swift, practiced movement, he sweeps me behind him, the leather of his holster creaking as his gun comes free.

I take the opportunity to slide away from his back, getting out of his grip.

"Anastasia," he growls.

Shit, that was hot. I let out a giggle. I can't help myself. Without looking back, I run.

"You best keep running, baby. For both of our sakes," he growls. "Don't let me catch you again. Remember, I'm a monster."

How am I both scared and incredibly turned on?

The rhythmic thud of my blood filled my ears, a deafening counterpoint to the ominous creak of branches as I fight my way through the endless line of trees.

My body trembles, a wave of fear washing over me as I try to take another step, but my feet remain rooted to the spot.

"Shit," I hiss. Looking down and seeing the white sparkly fabric of my dress tangled up against the branches. I pull as hard as I can, the sound of tearing echoing into the forest as I lose my balance and tumble forward.

"A bit stuck, pretty girl?" His low voice goes right through making me freeze.

Before I can inhale, his hand is around my throat, choking me as he lifts me. My back is pressed against the rough, unforgiving bark, where the splinters dig into my skin.

"Is this what you wanted, hmm?" His dark mask hovers in front of me with his lidded eyes raking up and down my body.

I fight for breath feeling the chilling touch of his fingers on my bare collarbone. It's a stark contrast to my racing pulse.

"Y-yes."

His thick thigh presses between my legs, while his grip tightens around my neck, making the blood pound in my ears.

"We cross this line and there is no going back. If you want this, that makes you mine. My wife in every sense of the damn word. Understand?"

My stomach churns with nervous anxiety, but I defiantly tip my chin up, the subtle metallic tang of fear in my mouth.

"Do it, big man. I. Dare. You." I utter those words with as much confidence as I can muster.

Is this how I thought I'd lose my virginity? No.

Do I want it? Yes. More than anything.

His eyes burn into mine, assessing me. I feel exposed like never before. His hand slowly releases my throat and moves up the back of my head, fingers threading through my hair and tugging gently on my scalp until it tips my chin up.

"You are fucking mine, Anastasia." His voice is so deep and gravelly, my pussy aches for him to be inside. That is more exciting than the fear dancing in my veins.

A yelp escapes my lips as he spins me, my face scraping against the coarse trunk.

The cold air whips around my legs as he shoves up my

dress around my waist. My legs shake, a silent vibration beneath me as I squeeze my eyes shut. I hug the rough bark of the tree, its coolness seeping into my skin, as I struggle desperately to keep my balance.

"Fuck I bet you taste so good, gorgeous."

He spreads my ass. I let out a yelp as he runs his finger along my pussy.

"Nice and wet for me, my naughty girl."

I scream out when his finger slides in.

"Jesus," he hisses behind me as he pushes inside.

It takes a moment to adjust to the feeling. I press my face against the bark. He yanks my head back by my hair and I can't help the moan that escapes my lips.

"Fuck, I could come just watching you like this."

I hear his zipper and the next thing I feel the tip of his dick pressed against me. How the fuck is that going to fit?

I take in a deep breath and bite down on my tongue as he thrusts inside me, his own groans distracting me from the stinging that consumes me as he shoves himself in, inch by inch.

Holy fuck, how big is he? It burns to the point tears spill down my cheeks.

I hold my breath, riding out the pain as his hips meet my ass.

"Damn, you feel so fucking good, iskorka. Made for me."

My chest tightens at his words, almost softening the pain. I knew the first time would not be an easy ride, especially not with a man like Mikhail.

He doesn't give me time to adjust before he pulls back and slams inside me. A scream tears from my throat, and then his hand is there, a suffocating weight over my mouth.

A wave of unfamiliar sensations—a strange blend of

agony and ecstasy—consumes me, overwhelming my mind, body, and soul. I forget that I'm in a forest, bare to the world.

I push aside the reality of his absent lips, the unscented air, and the complete void of romance.

No. This is better. It's raw. It's dark and dirty. It's very us.

Gasping for air, I feel the burning in my lungs before he releases my mouth and presses firmly between my shoulder blades, drawing my body closer to his as he intensifies his movements.

Until I see stars in my vision.

Holy fuck. Is this what I've been missing out on?

CHAPTER 21

MIKHAIL

Her cries echo in my ears, a beautiful sound. I hate that I have to press my palm over her mouth to muffle them. I'm so deep in her I can't have anyone turning up and ruining this moment. Fuck. I slam into her with everything I have. Over and over. Ruining her for any other man with each thrust. I'm just waiting to unleash inside her. To fill her up and make her mine.

My wife. I won't ever be letting her go.

I groan, my release about to explode. The moment her walls start to strangle my cock, I lose it.

Pulling my hand away from her mouth, I slide it up the back of her hair and tug from the roots. A feral scream rips from her lips.

I dig my fingers into her hips, clasping her in place as I fuck her to the point I spill inside her. Her name comes out as a groan. I slow the pace, making sure she milks every last drop from me and my cock is twitching inside her.

"Shit, iskorka. Your pussy is so fucking tight, almost feels like you've never been fucked by a real man before," I say almost breathlessly, and slap her ass.

"Jesus, Miki."

She rests the side of her face against the tree and her body sags.

Taking a few deep breaths, I stay where I am, enjoying her warmth as I get my heart rate back to a non deadly pace.

"That's because I haven't. Not by a real man. Not by any man. Just you."

My heart almost stops.

I blink rapidly, processing her words in my post orgasm state.

Just me? No. She has to be fucking with me. The woman is gorgeous.

She was begging for me. She wanted this out here. She made me chase her.

"Don't lie to me, Ana."

"I-I'm not," she says softly, with almost a hint of guilt lacing her words.

No, no, no. I shake my head. Speechless, I don't have words.

I slowly pull myself out of her and look down at the streaks of crimson coating my cock.

"Fuck. Ana." I hiss, rubbing my hand over my face.

Part of me is turned on, knowing I claimed her virginity. That I'm the only man who will ever get to feel how perfect she is. The only one for the rest of her life that will get to feel her.

The other part of me is horrified. She deserves better. This is not how her first time should be. She's worth so much more.

Fuck.

I clench my fists. I don't want to scare her by punching a hole in the tree.

Shoving my dick back in my boxers, I swallow the lump in my throat.

She hasn't moved. This isn't like my little sassy queen. I pull down her dress to cover her red ass and lightly wrap my fingers around her neck and pull her up, spinning her to face me.

Her perfectly flushed cheeks, the graze on her face, a tiny scrape from the tree bark, catches my eye. I see the faintest trickle of blood.

"Shit," I groan, wiping the blood away.

I'm a fucking monster.

This is the first time in as long as I can remember where I truly feel remorse. Yet she's staring at me like I'm some sort of savior with a twinkle in her eyes.

I open my mouth to speak, but no words come out. I run the back of my hand along her freezing cheek and shake my head. Shrugging off my coat, I place it over her shoulders.

"It's cold, baby. Let's go home."

My dick throbs against my pants, looking at the way she's admiring me with those big blue eyes.

With her wrapped under my arm, tight against my chest, I lead her back to the truck, scanning the area with every step. Opening up the passenger door, I help her up. She grabs my hand as I go to shut it.

"Thank you, Miki." She smiles sweetly at me and I nod.

I'm pissed off at myself, completely dumbfounded and more obsessed with this woman than I have been with anyone in my lifetime.

"You should have told me. I would have done it differently. Are you okay? I'll look after you when we're back."

"I guess I'm sore. Not too bad. Maybe soft and slow next time, big man." That naughty grin of hers tugs at her lips and I bite the inside of my mouth.

Pulling myself up using the roof of the car, I press my nose to hers. Her hot breath beating against my mask.

"You'll have exactly what I give you, pretty girl. Your sass might work outside the bedroom, inside there, you will be mine to tame, when I decide you're ready for me."

I rub my nose gently against hers and she closes her eyes, letting out a satisfied sigh.

I need to make this right, and then I can open her entire world up.

CHAPTER 22

MIKHAIL

"IT'S NOT A GOOD IDEA. She's in a safe house too. Ivan is not above torture to try and learn locations. Stay here, I'll be back soon." I hate leaving Ana, but at the same time, I promised Zoya I'd see my littlest sister one more time before heading back to Vegas.

"I don't want to stay here by myself." Ana pushes a dark curl behind her ear and sticks out that lower lip.

Fuck, I hate what it does to my cock. It's distracting.

"I'll be back soon. Stay here, or I can promise you will *not* enjoy the damn spanking." I check my pistol and put it in the holster before walking towards the door.

"Fine, I'll just stay here and enjoy my *own* company." Ana leans back onto the small couch and props up one knee before sliding her palm down the front of her leggings.

Jesus Christ.

"I have to go." When I slam the door shut, it takes me a minute to catch my breath.

That woman is going to be the best kind of death of me.

I send Enzo a quick text to let me know if she leaves.

Why do I need extra eyes on my own wife to keep her safe from herself?

Getting back to America should help, being on my own turf. At least I know that danger isn't lurking around every corner there.

The drive to Zoya's feels much longer since I'm staring at my phone most of the trip, dreading a notification from Enzo that Ana did something wild.

Maybe I should put a GPS tracker on her?

"Mikhail, I'm so glad you're here!" Zoya answers the door with a beaming smile in a snug bright blue dress.

I nod, stepping into the foyer. "I promised I'd say goodbye before I leave Russia."

Her face drops. "Oh. You're leaving so soon? I was hoping you'd be able to spend more time here, with Galena."

Glancing around the room, I don't see any signs of her. "Where is she?"

Zoya waves her hand idly, making her flowing sleeve fall to her elbow. "She's at a friend's house. I tried to talk her into staying here for a little while longer, but she insisted."

Rubbing my temple doesn't make the forming headache fade. "Zoya. She's six. And I don't have time for this." All I can think of is Ana waiting for me.

"She'll be back soon. Let's have a drink while we wait?" Her knee shows through a waist high slit in her skirt with every step towards the kitchen.

There's already two glasses set out with a full bottle of bourbon between them.

"Zoya, I have to leave today. I'm heading back to Vegas. Tell Galena I'll call to talk once I'm home." My palm lands on the handle.

"Back to your big fancy casino?" She tosses her hair over her shoulder and begins to pour.

"Yea. I miss my Corvette." This truck I've been driving bounces so hard I swear my kidneys are bruised. "Once you get used to the finer things, it's hard to step down."

"See? I knew you'd understand. I feel the exact same way." She pushes one of the tumblers into my hand. "That's why I'd love to leave this hovel." Her nose wrinkles.

With her father being the Butcher, she did enjoy the lavish life.

"You're safe here, Zoya." I stare at the glass.

I'm not here to drink.

She leans close enough I can see down her low cut dress. "Take me with you?" Her fingers dance over my wrist.

Gently, I peel them off and put my full tumbler into her hand. "This is a good place for you. Ivan would be looking for you in Vegas. He's already tortured two of my family trying to find you. He has men everywhere."

Her dark eyes widen. "See? That's why I need to be there, where you can watch over me." She smiles, biting her bright red bottom lip.

I can see where this is going.

"I have to go. I'll have Enzo check in on you." I'm outside before she can touch me again.

The thought of any other woman besides my wife makes my skin crawl.

Ana is everything I need, or want.

Zoya steps out, her long black hair whipping in the cold wind. "Wait, Mikhail! I don't want to be stuck here. Please, I want to leave." She wraps her arms around her waist, hemming in the thin fabric of her dress.

"I'm sorry, there isn't any other choice." I crawl behind the steering wheel, leaving her watching me until she disappears in the rearview mirror.

Fuck, I wish there was a better option.

CHAPTER 23

ANASTASIA

Song- Sleeptoken Rain

I TAP my fingers on the wooden table, listening to the rain pelt against the single glazed window. The sound is almost comforting, but not enough to distract me from my thoughts.

Why won't he touch me? He basically ran out of the door earlier.

Last night, he barely said a word to me.

I got what I wanted, I guess. He took my virginity before it could be robbed from me. I shouldn't want more, not with him. I shouldn't crave to be touched by my husband like that again.

Except, I am. Desperately. I'm not delusional enough to think he's going to rush in and sweep me up into his arms, declaring his undying love for me.

But there is something there. I can see the fire in his eyes, he feels our connection. He wants to fuck me again.

He's already been gone an hour and I'm bored of missing his company. With my mind spiralling, I head to the kitchen and start jabbing some buttons on this old ass radio on the counter.

"Perfect," I mutter when some faint music comes through the speaker. I twist the knob to turn the volume up slightly. What Mikhail doesn't know won't hurt him.

Hmm. It's kinda got me in the mood for a glass of wine. I know we have none of that, but there might be more booze stashed somewhere.

Searching through the cupboards, I do a little dance when my hand connects with a dusty bottle of vodka.

"Oh well, what's the worst that can happen? It's vodka. I'm Russian. I'll be fine," I mutter to myself.

Taking a glass out, I pour a double measure. I don't want to get completely wasted, just something to take this edge off.

Sitting back, letting this disgusting liquid burn my insides, I hold back a cough.

The door clicks shut and I down the rest of the contents. I need some courage to ask him what's going on.

His heavy footsteps get closer and I straighten my spine. He stops at the edge of the table and rests his ring covered fingers on the wood.

"Want some?" I ask, holding up the half empty bottle.

"No thank you."

Ugh. So polite.

He drags a seat out and sits down next to me.

Why does he have to be so distractingly hot?

"Wanna dance?" I ask, holding back a smirk.

He raises an eyebrow.

"I don't dance, pretty girl."

The nickname makes my heart race. His dark eyes burn into mine and I nudge my chair in closer.

"Come on. How can you live life being so serious all the

time, when in reality, how much can you actually control? Hmm?"

I rest my palm on his massive bicep and squeeze it, feeling him tense under my touch.

"I can control enough. I have you here don't I? I have a plan. I have an empire."

I shouldn't push his buttons, he appears to be in a sour mood. But I can't help myself.

"Yet you're still hiding from your father? What does one night off do to mess with your plans really? When's the last time you turned that damn brain off of fight mode and just took a second to enjoy something… or someone?"

I lean back into my chair and face him, trying to gauge a reaction. It's hard to decipher through that damn mask.

"It's been a long time. I have too many people's lives relying on me. Including yours, iskorka."

I nod, leaning over to grab the vodka from in front of me. He catches my wrist before I can get it.

"Oh, am I not allowed?" I pin him with a stare.

When I yank my arm out of his grip, he sighs. What is up with him? I stand up and tuck my chair in, then go to the back exit and slide my sneakers on.

"Where are you going? It's pouring rain and it isn't safe."

I turn and smile at him, tucking my hair behind my ear.

"Just wanna go dance in the rain." I shrug, pulling open the door.

Before I can step outside, his hand connects with my hip and he spins me to face him, pressing me into the wall.

"You'll freeze to death."

My heart races and I take a deep breath, him being this close… pressed up against me. I want him.

"I won't. Don't be dramatic, big man."

As I go to move, he blocks me in, pinning his hand up against the wall next to my head.

"Don't ignore me." He almost growls, and holy hell that's hot.

"What you going to do about it? Leave me here and not tell me where you're going again? Or chase me through the woods?"

His eyes darken and he shakes his head. It's almost like he's sad. And I hate that.

"Come on, big man, dance in the rain with me." I tap his chest.

He tips my chin up to him and studies me.

"Don't make me beg. Let me show you the world won't end if you're happy for just a few minutes."

He looks down at my lips and back to my eyes. God, I could get lost staring into his, the window to his soul.

"You think you know what would make me happy?"

"You think you're so mysterious, don't you? I see you, Mikhail. I can see straight through you. You might be used to people being scared of you. I'm not. Now dance with me."

I wanna kick him out of whatever mood he's in.

"Nobody really sees the real me. They see the person I choose to be for them." His voice drops.

Interesting.

"That might work on everyone else. Trouble is, Miki... you can't hide your soul from me. No matter how hard you try. See, I believe we were meant to find each other..."

I stroke my hand along his mask and for a split second he tilts his face into my touch.

"Soul mates don't exist. It's a fantasy. People are scared of me for good reason. You should be, too."

I can't help but laugh and shake my head. I am not scared

of him. Quite the opposite. He's the first person to ever make me feel truly safe.

"If it's bullshit, then explain why your heart races when you see me."

I place my hand on his chest.

"Why, even when we're in the same room, your eyes are constantly searching for me? Tell me why you are letting me speak to you like this? And tell me why you are about to go outside in the pouring rain and dance with me, it's because you know it will make me smile, isnt it? And finally, tell me you didn't feel it the first time you grabbed my hand. You are many things, Mikhail, but you aren't a liar. Tell me I'm wrong, I dare you. Deny it all you like, it doesnt change the truth."

I'm almost out of breath letting that all out.

"Are you always trying to romanticise your life? Is that what this is? You found a monster and you want to fix him? I am beyond fixing, iskorka."

I roll my eyes and he grips my chin.

"Are you always so damn negative? Oh, so broken, so unworthy. I've told you before, I'm not anyone's princess and you certainly aren't the prince either. That isn't what a soul mate is. I've seen your demons and I wanna play with them."

I duck under his arm, muttering under my breath. I wish he would just listen, and see what I see. And stop treating me like I'm delicate.

"I'll dance with you, pretty girl," he says, almost as a whisper as I go to step out the door.

I stop and turn to face him, not hiding the smile lighting up my face.

"Careful, big man. You might fall in love with me." I hold out my hand to him.

His eyes go wide as he looks at my open palm. Oh fuck. I shouldn't have dropped the 'L' word.

"Vozmozhno ya uzhe. *Perhaps I already am,*" he says under his breath.

A wave of emotion washed over me, causing my eyes to fill with tears. Validation that he feels whatever the hell this is between us.

He entwines his fingers with mine and I lead him outside.

The rain batters down on us, a deluge of icy water, and he spins me to face him, placing his hands on my waist, his touch warm through my soaked clothes, as I lay my palms on him. And we sway in silence, his body keeping me warm. I don't know how long we stay in this perfect little bubble.

"It's dark out, iskorka. The rain has stopped. Let's get you inside to dry off."

"But look…" I point up at the sky, "you can see the stars in the dark."

"That is usually how it works." He chuckles and I bat his chest.

"They're always there, you know? No matter how dark it is, no matter what the weather, they are there whether you can see them or not," I say, almost in awe as I look at the beautiful sparkles in the sky.

"Hmm." I can feel his gaze burning into me, so I look back at him.

"Sometimes you don't have to look up at the dark skies to see the bright light in your life. Not when it's right in front of your eyes."

CHAPTER 24

MIKHAIL

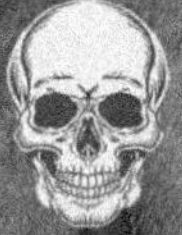

Song- Give Sleep token

As she snuggles against me, all I can think about is how I fucked up.

I took her virginity against a damn tree and then carried her ass back to a truck.

I had no idea. But I should have done better. That wasn't the way I should have taken my wife for the first time. She just riles me up something special, that woman.

And I wouldn't have it any other way.

With my eyes closed, I gently press a kiss through my mask onto the top of her head.

"I want to make it up to you," I whisper.

With a slow tilt of her head, she looks up at me, her gaze curious and questioning.

"Make what up?" She frowns, and I can almost hear her mind spinning.

"I want to make up for the way I took your virginity."

I swallow the lump in my throat. She's more than that to me. She needs to see it, to feel it.

147

"I wanted it, Miki. I enjoyed myself. Stop worrying."

I grasp her face, my hands warm against the cool of her cheeks.

"No, iskorka. You deserve better. Hell of a lot better than being fucked in the woods like some animal."

A slow smirk, a hint of something wicked, curves her lips.

"Oh, well, I was about to ask you if you'd chase me again?"

I chuckle and shake my head.

"Another day I'll chase you anywhere you want. But today, I want a do over. Please let me show you how you should be treated. I just need your trust for one night and I'll make this right."

"I really don't need— "

I cut her off before she can continue.

"You were made for me, pretty girl. Let me prove I'm worthy of you."

I tilt her chin up with my thumb and stare into those bright blue eyes that melt away a little more ice around my heart.

"You? Worthy of me? Don't be ridiculous. It's the other way round."

That adorable frown makes me smile.

"One day, you'll see the real man you're dealing with."

And I fear that day will be the day I lose her. When she sees what's under that mask, the scars, the evil in my life, she will run a fucking mile and I won't be able to stop her.

I can't trap her with a monster.

But for now, while she's mine, I want to show her what she means to me.

Without realizing, this little spark has brought some life back into me.

The cold breeze picks up and she shivers, so I pull her

closer, stroking her hair away from her face, feeling the damp strands.

"You're my wife. I claimed you as mine. I want to explore every inch of you. I want to take you to new heights. Figure out what makes you shake, what makes you scream. I want my wife to be a constant mix of sexually frustrated and freshly fucked. You're a firecracker that needs taming."

I have a good idea what she needs.

My little brat.

She is mine to explore.

"And I want to learn how to please my husband."

I rub my thumb along her wet bottom lip.

"Trust me, anything you do will send me feral. I know you'll be my perfect submissive and a spectacular brat. I'm never going to deny the fact I enjoy both sides of you. Just always keep being you, keep creating fires even in the rain, pretty girl."

Her beautiful eyes glaze over, losing their sparkle, and I gently cup her cheek, feeling the coolness of her skin.

"Don't cry on me, baby," I whisper.

A small sniffle escapes her, and a sharp, physical pain shoots through my chest.

"No one has ever seen me. Not properly. That's why I never gave myself to anyone. But you, I knew from that first second when I looked into your eyes that you were special. That you saw straight through me."

I'm thinking she was right about the whole soulmate thing. There is no other explanation that in the first instance I wanted her. That I felt like I'd known her my entire life.

It felt right making her my wife. The thought of losing her is as painful as losing a limb.

It's made my entire life before her seem meaningless. It

only started the moment I met her. It's now I start living with her and for her.

"Show me. Give me the do-over."

I press my forehead against hers. Damn this mask. I want to press my lips to hers, to consume her absolutely and steal her breath.

She deserves to be kissed in the rain and feel how truly crazy I am about her.

I wish I could give her all of me. If there's one person on this planet who could get me to take this mask off, it's her.

"I've got you, iskorka. Always."

She slides her small palms up my t-shirt and rests them on my pecs.

That single touch ignites a wildfire of sensation, scorching its way through my veins.

"I know. I trust you. Make me yours, and rock my world, big man."

I bend down, gently scoop her into my arms, and carry her back to the cabin. Once inside, I slam the door shut with a resounding thud, then kick off my muddy boots before heading to the bedroom.

I want to ravish her and I'm not sure how I am going to stop myself, she makes me wild just looking at her.

Laying her softly down on the mattress, she runs her hands through her wet hair.

"I'll warm you back up, baby. Don't worry about that." I wink at her and she blushes.

With a groan, she pushes herself up, and I reach out, taking her calves in my hands, pulling her towards me to the edge of her bed.

I run my fingers along the bottom of her top as she raises her arms, allowing me to remove the damp fabric from her skin.

"Fuck. So gorgeous." I tell her and she bites on her lip.

"I want to run my tongue along every inch of you. Does that sound like a good start?" I whisper as I lean in and unclasp her bra with one hand. I tear it from her and toss it away, then run my lips along her shoulder.

"Be a good girl and lift those hips for me."

She does as I command, and I peel those sexy black leggings off to reveal her toned legs.

"I can't take my eyes off you. So beautiful and all mine."

She smiles at me. She's quiet, almost nervous, which is unusual for my girl. As she goes to cover her breasts, I shake my head. I don't want her hiding any part from me.

I guess I'm a fine one to talk.

"Hands above your head. One lesson you'll learn quickly is, in here, you listen to my every command. Everything I do is for your pleasure, or it acts as a lesson in submission. I will learn your body, mind, and boundaries. This requires trust and communication. Is that okay, baby?"

She nods and her eyes go wide, flicking around the room.

Between her spread legs, I crawl closer, and my hand tightens around her jaw.

"Eyes on me and use your words. Is that what you want?"

I stroke her hair away from her face, and she studies me.

Shit, my growing cock is pressing against her hot pussy.

"Yes. I want that. I want to be a good wife for you in every way."

"That's my good girl."

Siting on my heels, I rip my T-shirt over my head and unbuckle my belt. I need to do this right, which means I need my mask off.

I need her on my tongue.

"Arms above your head, iskorka."

I work my palms up her sides and cup her breasts,

pinching her erect nipples between my fingers. That touch alone has her back arching off the bed and a little moan escaping her.

Fuck, that brings my cock to full attention.

"So sensitive, aren't you, baby? Perfect for me to play with."

With her hands raised, I grab the belt beside me, swiftly looping it twice around her wrists and fastening it securely to the headboard to prevent any movement.

I don't want her to see my face but I also can't have her touching it.

I can't lose her, not yet.

Rifling through the drawer, I grab one of my black T-shirts and fold it up lengthways. As I climb back on the bed, I can't help admire her, cuffed and spread for me.

Her mouth makes a perfect "O" as I give her the gentlest of touches along the seam of her pussy through her little black lace panties.

"I don't want you to think. I just want you to focus on how good I make you feel."

Sliding my hand under her head, I gently tug on her hair at the scalp, and she looks up and grins at me.

"Keep your head like this for me."

I tie the tee around her eyes and secure it in place, then gently rest her back on the mattress.

"What can you see?" I ask.

She laughs.

"Absolutely fucking nothing, Miki. I want to see you, watch you enjoy me." She pouts.

"One day. For now, just lie there and really feel what I'm doing. It will heighten everything else."

I do feel bad. I hate that this is part of my life.

"Okay, big man. I'm ready for you."

She bites down on her lip so I lean in and suck on it.

"I'm not sure you're the one giving the orders around here. After today, talk like that and you'll get punished. This is your first and only free card."

"Oh, punished?"

"Hmm, mmm, however I see fit."

I sit up and study her. The way her chest rises and falls in anticipation. The goosebumps running up her arms.

"I'm not giving you a safe word."

"It's fine. I trust you won't hurt me."

Do I trust myself with her?

"No. We will start with colors. Red means stop. Yellow, you need me to calm down, green is carry the fuck on. Got it?"

"Do you, er, do this a lot with women?" she asks quietly.

"I have a past. But recently, no."

Before my face got fucked up, that was a lifestyle. No emotions, no girlfriends, just an outlet.

"Hmm. Okay. And yes, colors work fine for me."

"Such a good girl."

"Fuck," I mutter, trailing my hand down her chest. I grab her breast and squeeze.

"These are mine."

I untie my mask and toss it to one side of the bed. It's a relief. A step closer to showing her the real me.

Dipping my head in, I take her rosy bud in my mouth and suck. She pulls in a sharp breath and pushes her chest out.

I move between her breasts and lick her soft skin all the way down to the hem of her panties. My mouth almost salivating at the thought of tasting her.

Peeling her panties over her legs, I debate putting them in her mouth, but I don't want her to be quiet. I want to hear every noise that escapes her.

I push her legs further apart, I hold them down as I line my face up with her pussy. Pressing kisses on the inside of her thigh, I alternate between each leg, getting closer to her glistening cunt.

"So fucking wet for me, gorgeous," I say and kiss her there.

"Oh." She almost sounds surprised.

So I do it again, this time, I suck after.

Spreading her open with two fingers, I lick her from her clit to her entrance.

"You taste divine."

When I look up, a blush is spreading up her neck and she's biting on her lip, with her fists clenched above her head.

"Color?"

She flattens her knees into the mattress and pushes her hips up and I slowly circle her clit with the tip of my tongue.

I know the answer.

"Green. So fucking green. More."

I swipe my tongue all the way along her slit.

"More, what?"

"Please, Mikhail."

I groan at the way my name rolls off her tongue in her subtle Russian accent. It's sexy. But it's the desperation in her voice that has my cock twitching against my boxers.

"Good girl."

Her hips buck as I feast, her thighs closing around my head so I push them back down flat and hold her still.

"Legs stay like this and I'll let you come on my face. Got it?"

She rolls her hips. "Mmm, hmm."

"Words, baby."

"Yes, sir."

Fuck.

I slide my fingers along her dripping pussy and press two gently inside her, letting her adjust to them, at the same time licking her until her entire body is quivering around me.

"You taste so good. Your pussy is perfect. I could sit and eat you all day." I start pumping my fingers in and out, feeling her walls clamp around them.

Maybe I'll spend twenty-four hours eating my wife out.

"Fuck, Miki," she says breathlessly.

The faster I fuck her with my fingers, her breathing becomes more shallow, those quivers turn to shakes.

Pressing my left hand down on her lower stomach, I curl them inside her to hit her G-spot and I lick up every drop of her.

"Oh my god," she chants.

"Come on my face, pretty girl. Don't hold back, I want all of it."

Her screams echo through the room and I swear I nearly come in my boxers. I hold her still, letting her ride her climax out all over my face. Fuck, this has to be the most erotic view of my life.

Just as her body sags into the mattress and she tries to catch her breath, I climb over her, resting my weight on my forearm and run my wet fingers along her lips.

"Taste yourself, taste what I do to you."

"That's hot."

I grin and slam my lips over hers, our first proper kiss with no mask. Fuck, hers are so soft. Sliding my tongue in her mouth, she moans and her legs wrap around me, pressing my hard cock against her soaking pussy.

I let out a groan as she grinds her hips against me, and I deepen our kiss, with my hand wrapping around her slender neck, her pulse going wild against my palm.

"You want your husband's dick inside you now? Is that why you're desperately grinding on me?"

I don't want her to stop.

"I want you," she manages to say.

"I really fucking want you too, Anastasia. I want to feel that tight pussy take every inch of me and then I'm going to fuck you, nice and slow to start with and then I'll push your limits to see how much my good girl can take. Then, I'll fill you up until my come is sliding out of you."

CHAPTER 25

ANASTASIA

Song- FEEL, Beneld, BURY

Jesus. Fucking. Christ.

This man.

I'm glad I waited for him. I could lay here for hours and let him eat me out. I'm still buzzed from that. But feeling his enormous dick pressing against my throbbing pussy, I don't know how much more I can take.

"Fuck me, Miki. Please." I exaggerate the "please" hoping it will get him to act faster.

"You're learning. I love it when you beg for my cock."

My cheeks burn from his praise. I want to be good enough for him. I know I can be. The more time I spend with him, the more that makes me want to stay by his side and in his bed.

His fingers tighten around my throat, and I suck in a breath. It's still loose enough to inhale. Everything is extreme. Every slight touch sends my heart racing.

I feel the head of his cock push against my entrance, and I squeeze my eyes shut and hold my breath.

"Baby, breathe. You've taken all of me before. I'll go nice and slow to start. I won't hurt you."

He starts kissing along my cheek and I tilt my head to the side, allowing him to work along my jaw and down my neck.

I let out a moan as he slides inside. The pressure he's putting on my clit distracts away from the slight burn as I adjust to the size of him.

"Fuck," I pant out.

"Almost there, baby. You're doing such a good job. Your pussy is taking me just perfectly. God, you're so tight." He lets out a groan and his hips slam against mine. I can't help but scream.

He leans back over me and presses his lips against mine. They're soft. He tastes like mint and me. That's sexy as hell.

"I bet any pussy feels tight when you've got a dick that fucking huge, Mikhail."

He chuckles against my lips.

"Don't make me spank you. My hand is itching to make that fine ass red."

I swallow hard, and his hand tightens around my neck.

He pulls out slowly and then pushes back inside me. Each time, I get closer to the edge of release. As he ups the pace, he keeps circling my clit and kissing me. Every unfamiliar sensation is consuming every part of me.

The harder he thrusts, his fingers tight around my neck and his lips over mine.

I can't fucking breathe.

Blood pounds in my ears, all I can focus on is him fucking me, the way he's grunting in my ear. It's all too much. I'm ready to explode.

"Color?"

I can't even reply.

Is he squeezing my throat on purpose? Is it to shut me up

or kill me? Because I probably shouldn't want to come all over his dick while he's doing it?

But he'd never hurt me, I don't think…

He releases his grip and stops, keeping his dick inside me.

"Color." His stern voice snaps me back into reality.

I open my mouth.

I want him to keep going.

I suck in a deep breath, and it's like a relief having air in my lungs.

"Yellow? My head went a little fuzzy. I thought I was going to explode, but it felt really good?" I whisper, almost embarrassed.

"Fuck. I'm sorry, baby." He presses a kiss to my throat.

"Did you like it?" he asks.

I nod. "I did, I just shocked myself I think. I got scared I might run out of air."

"Okay. Do you want to try it again? This time I'll talk you through it, I'll tell you when to breathe, when I'm loosening my grip and you tell me when you're about to come. I will never let anything bad happen to you, I promise you."

"I'd like that."

He runs the tip of his fingers along my sides. It tickles and I giggle.

This time, when he grabs my throat, I relax into his touch.

"Okay, you good to go again?" he whispers against my lips, stroking my cheek.

"Green. Go."

"I'm gonna spank you so hard next time."

I cry out when he thrusts inside me. He keeps his fingers lighter around my neck and his stubble grazes my ear.

"Such a good fucking wife."

My back arches, and he sucks on my throat, tightening his fingers.

"You're close aren't you, baby? I can feel you on my cock. Fuck, it's amazing."

"Y-yes."

"Take a breath for me, iskorka, and then let go. Come over my dick and let me feel it. I'll keep the pressure on your neck about the same."

Stars fill my dark vision. With a few last thrusts, I hear him swearing, his fingers pressing beneath my ears, and I can't hold back anymore. A violent orgasm rips through me. I shake uncontrollably, my toes curling as an unfamiliar sensation washes over me.

"Fuck!" I cry out and he presses his lips to mine, releasing my throat.

As he continues pumping into me, his pace slows down, and he gently intertwines our fingers above my head while I ride him.

"Good girl, give me all of it," he grits.

Instead of pulling out, his hands snake around my waist and he rolls me on top of him, cradling my head into his neck and he holds me tight.

I close my eyes and sink into his warm touch, listening to his strong heartbeat through his ribs.

His hand trails down my back and I let out a satisfied moan, feeling his cock twitching inside of me. A little yelp escapes when his hand slaps my ass.

"Told you I'd spank you."

I laugh and press a kiss to his neck.

"How was that for you?" he asks.

"Amazing. I wanna go again."

His chest vibrates beneath me.

"Oh, we will be going again, many times. That was just our warm up. First, let me clean you up."

My back bounces on the mattress as he lies me down and spreads my legs.

I wish I could see him. I bet he has a handsome face.

"Oh, shit." I gasp out as his fingers push inside me.

"Making sure you keep it all in there, baby. Your pussy looks incredible filled with my come."

When he sucks on my clit, my hips buck against his face.

"Green," I cry out.

After a few circles with his tongue, I sigh as he moves away. The next thing I feel a warm damp cloth on the inside of my thighs and then my wrists are free.

I blink a few times, adjusting to the harsh light of the bedroom when my blindfold is removed. Disappointment washes over me when I stare into Mikhail's dark eyes and his mask is back on.

No more kisses.

I sit up on my elbows and he lays down next to me, sliding his arm under my head and I cuddle into his side, while his hand gently rubs my ass. I look down at his chiseled body and his cock is standing to attention.

"You need me to clean that up for you?" I ask, biting my lip.

"You can suck my cock any minute of the day, pretty girl. I'd love to see those lips wrapped around it."

I grin at him, my pussy throbbing at his words. Mine. He is mine.

But he's absolutely fucking huge and I'm not sure how the hell it's going to fit in my mouth.

"Breathe through your nose and take as much as you can. I'll go easy on you this time." He strokes my hair away from my face.

"Can I ride you after? I wanna see how that feels."

His eyes crease as I wrap my fingers around his dick.

"Oh, now you want to experiment on me?" he says and I nod.

"Yep. I wanna learn all the ways to ride my husband's dick and make him come inside me."

"Sounds perfect to me, wife." He taps my ass, and I quickly get into position between his thick thighs.

He keeps one hand with his fingers threaded through my hair. I start by licking the tip. I've watched some porn. I'm not completely dumb.

I take him in my mouth, just the tip to start and run my tongue around it, making it as wet as I can.

"Holy fuck," He grunts.

I think I'm doing a good job.

His fingers tighten in my hair and he pushes my head down. I take more of him and he stops. So I bob lower, sucking him off the best I can. And by the noises coming from him, he likes it.

"So fucking good."

I don't have time to register what's happening. His hands grab me under my arms and I'm spun round. With my legs on each side of his head, I use my hand to guide his dick back in my mouth.

"Shit." I hiss as his tongue connects to my pussy and his fingers dig into my ass.

"I need your cunt on my face. Fucking soak me while you suck my dick."

His words spur me to take him deeper, as far as I can and I try not to gag and I let my fingers explore his balls at the same time.

"I'm obsessed with you."

His words make my heart flutter and my pussy ache. I'm so close.

The more my own climax builds, I take him deeper, almost choking.

"Can I come in your mouth, baby?" he asks.

"Mmhmm," I reply with a mouth full of his cock.

"Good fucking girl. Fuck."

His hips thrust up, and he spills down my throat. I close my eyes and focus on swallowing every last drop, sucking him clean like a lollipop.

"Come on then, pretty girl. Come on my tongue like a good girl. Push back, fucking smother me. I don't care, just come on my fucking face."

When he slides his fingers inside me, I do just that. I push myself back, smothering his face just like he asked, and I scream out his name, letting this orgasm light me on fire.

By the time I come crashing down to earth, I struggle to catch my breath. This time, he lifts me up and carries me in his arms and turns the shower on.

When he puts me on my shaky feet, he guides my face up to his and strokes all the way down the side of my face.

"You are incredible, Anastasia."

I close my eyes as he kisses me through the mask on my forehead.

"So are you, big man," I whisper back.

CHAPTER 26

MIKHAIL

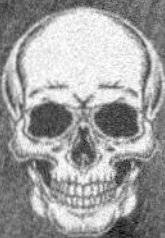

Song- Baby, Elvis Drew

THANK FUCK I'm getting rid of this truck and leaving this hellhole.

Enzo has a jet arranged, one more hour and we are out of here. I can't wait to show Ana her new life in Vegas.

She's going to thrive in America. She's bright and hungry to live. An asset to me in every way.

Or she can stay home and let me make babies with her. Anything she wants.

I could regret that though. She's wrapped me around her little finger. I want to give her not just the world, but the stars, the moon, the universe, if I could.

Anything to see that beautiful smile, the one that could light up a room and make the world seem brighter.

Ana's dainty hand reaches across and grabs my thigh.

"You okay, pretty girl?"

"I was thinking…" She trails off, biting her lip. That

means I will probably like her train of thought. That's her *"I want to be naughty"* face.

"Thinking what?"

"These woods are looking awfully pretty, especially with the snow setting on the branches."

"Hmmm,"

I know where this is heading.

"You want to try out run me again?" I ask in amusement.

"Hey! You only caught me last time because I was in a damn wedding dress and I got caught in branches. I want a redo. I can beat you."

The chuckle that escapes me is a low rumble, shaking my chest.

"I will always catch you, no doubt about it." I squeeze her hand on my thigh.

There isn't a corner of this earth I wouldn't go to find her if I had to.

"Prove it, big man."

God. This woman. Created to keep me constantly turned on and on my toes, and I am loving every second.

"We don't have time, Ana." I look at the digital clock on the dash.

"Baby. You scared you'll lose against little old me?" She teases. "I bet I could catch you easy."

Oh, a challenge.

Eyes glued to the pull off ahead, I quickly swerve, the tires screaming as I slam on the brakes, and we lurch forward with a jolt.

"You catch me, you can do whatever you want to me," I tell her, gripping her chin.

The corners of her mouth curl up into a mischievous grin, a glint of playfulness in her eyes.

"When I do, I'm climbing you like a tree, big man. Be ready."

Well shit. I want to be caught now.

"Close your eyes. A kiss for luck." I lean in for a kiss. As she obeys, the sound of my belt buckle and the heavy thud of the door echo in the stillness before I run into the forest. With each crunch of snow under my boots, I maintained a steady pace, hoping she spots me.

I aim for the thicker row of trees to my left, their leaves a dense, almost impenetrable wall, dodging branches as I enter the darker depths where the air grows cooler.

A frozen lake stands still, its glassy surface reflecting the stark winter sky, utterly silent save for the occasional snap of ice. The silence is heavy, broken only by the sound of her quick footsteps behind me.

She is fast.

The sound of her approaching quickens my pace, and I break into a jog around the lake, my heart beating in time with her steps. I've not broken a sweat yet.

I look behind and glimpse her red face and I speed up, heading towards the birch trees. I dart through the gaps as best I can, the winter sun beating down through the trees.

"Come on, pretty girl. I thought you could catch me?" I taunt, slowing my pace, allowing her to gain on me.

Making a sharp right, I head back towards the lake.

I can't hear her.

As I jog towards the edge of the ice, I skid in my tracks, coming face to face with her. She runs towards me and I don't fight it.

I let her get as close as possible before I turn on my heel and sprint.

"Not so fast."

I flinch as her nails dig into my neck. It burns from the scratch.

"Damn." I run my hand on my skin, slowing up.

In that time, she leaps onto my back, her arms tight around my throat, legs bracing on either side, her breath warm against my ear.

I spin round, trying to shake her off. I lose my balance, my fingers scraping against the bark of a tree as she tightens her deadly grip around my neck.

"Told you I'd catch you, big man."

"Couldn't resist the lake, could you? You like shiny things."

A low growl rumbles in my chest as I reach around, yanking her off me by her puffy, snow-dusted coat. She falls to her ass and I grin, towering over her.

She shuffles back on her butt until she bashes into the tree behind.

"Who is winning now, pretty girl?"

I lean down, fingers tightening around her throat, yanking her to her feet, and slamming her roughly against the tree.

Her breath hitches, nostrils flaring, betraying her emotions in wide, startled eyes. Every single time. She always says she can read me by my eyes, and I can with her too.

My naughty princess is hungry for more.

"Nothing to say, iskorka?"

I firmly grasp her thigh and guide it upward, positioning myself between her legs. She claws at my jacket, fumbling for the zipper. I watch her with amusement as she yanks it down.

"Fuck. Me," she pants out. "Take me, make me yours."

How I want to rip my mask off and crash my lips over hers.

Letting go of her throat, I run my hand up her body and tear open her coat as she leans in, sinking her teeth into my neck.

"Fuck," I groan.

My cock aches to be inside her.

The trickle of warm blood down my collar is accompanied by a metallic scent that fills my nostrils. I swipe it away from my neck and look at the crimson coating my fingers.

With a smirk, I push her mouth open and shove them in.

"Clean up your mess."

Her nose wrinkles, but she does as she's told, sucking them clean.

She grins at me as I remove them, her white teeth now stained red.

"Your blood tastes good. Did I forget to mention I'm a vampire?" She winks.

I hold in my laugh. Fucking hell, this woman's sass.

Leaning in, I lower my voice.

"Does it make me one too, if I eat your pretty little cunt out when you're on your period?"

"Jesus," she hisses.

I push her back against the tree and hold her still, shoving my hands down her leggings and panties.

"So wet, baby."

I slide two fingers in easily and her breathing gets shallow. God, those raspy moans in my ear are making me feral.

Inserting in a third finger, she cries out, stretching around me. I love the fact that I'm the one to explore her and take her new heights.

Withdrawing my hand, I release my grip and step back.

Her eyes meet mine with confusion. As she opens her mouth, I press my finger against her lips.

Those blue pools stare into my soul. I bring my nose to meet hers and whisper one simple word.

"Run."

She blinks and processes my command. Taking a deep breath, she turns and sprints between the trees, straight towards the lake. Readjusting my mask over my nose, I give her five more seconds before I break out into a ground eating jog.

I need to be inside her.

She skirts around the edge of the water. I keep my gaze fixed on her toned ass as she runs. With each step, I close the distance. Taking a deep breath, as soon as I can reach her, I shoot my hand out, grab her by the waist and throw myself on the ground, making sure she lands on top of me.

Quickly rolling over, I hook her legs over my shoulder and pull her leggings over her ass, whip out my dick and thrust into her.

"Fuuuuck."

Grabbing her by the neck, I push us forward, her long hair a dark curtain against the bright white of the frozen lake below.

She looks to her left, realizing her head is over the ledge as I continue to fuck her. Keeping her in place by digging my fingers into her hip, because I'd never let anything happen to her. The way her heart is racing against my palm just pushes me to go harder.

"Is." *Thrust.* "This." *Thrust.* "What." *Thrust.* "You wanted?"

"Yes!" she cries.

I pound into her so hard she moans in rhythm. Pulling her back up, I sit back on my heels and let her straddle me.

Nuzzling her face into my collar, the little demon bites

down again and I groan, holding her down by the shoulders and pushing my dick deep into her.

"Such a dirty girl for me, aren't you?" I tell her.

"Y-yes."

"Fuck, I love it when your pussy squeezes me like that."

She throws her head back, revealing her slender neck. I want to sink my teeth in, mark her.

One day I will show her my true self. I have to. There is no way I can live my life not having my mouth everywhere on her.

"Miki, I-I."

Her head falls onto my chest, but I hold her tight.

"Come for me, pretty girl," I whisper in her ear with my release on the cusp.

Tangling my fingers in her hair, I unleash everything I have on her.

She screams out my name. It rips through the air and that ruins me. Hearing my name on her lips, fuck.

I coat her insides with my come. She takes every single drop. My lungs burn, but I don't want to leave this moment.

Pulling her face to mine, I press my forehead to hers.

"Is that what you needed, sweetheart?" I whisper, trying to catch my breath.

"You know it was. You seem to know exactly what I need."

I nod.

Because we were meant to be. She was right and now she's mine.

CHAPTER 27

ANASTASIA

I‌t feels so good to be finally leaving the frozen wasteland of Russia.

Even better to be nestled in the warm embrace of my burly husband as we land in Las Vegas.

I can't contain my excitement seeing the wide tarmac and buildings come into view.

"Which one is yours?" I ask with my nose pressing against the glass.

He lowers his face next to my cheek and points at a clump of imposing towers. "That one, my office sits in the center. And they're 'ours', not just mine any longer." He sits back, dropping his palm to squeeze my thigh.

I set mine over his knuckles. It's like a third the size of his. The pink diamond of my ring shines in the midday sun streaking into the plane.

"When do I get to meet the rest of your family? I hope they're nicer than your dad." I give him a broad smile.

"Cute. We'll get settled first, then you'll get to meet all of yours." The muscle in his temple clenches. "Even ones you didn't expect."

"What does that mean? Is that this 'mystery' person you keep talking about?" I wish he'd just open up.

I get that he has secrets. There can't be anyone in his position without any.

Like who that woman was he had to meet up with yesterday. He wouldn't tell me anything about her, or why he had to see her before we left.

He has a whole past I know nothing about.

But I'll figure it out.

He carries our bags and stuffs them into the tiny trunk of his matte black sports car.

Opening the passenger door with a flourish, he stands back and takes my hand. "Let me take you to your new home. Then I'll introduce you to everyone. They don't even know I'm alive yet."

"Wait, what do you mean?" The black seat is hot as hell sitting in the sun.

But it only takes a few moments before the air conditioner blows a cold breeze over me.

I get lost trying to pay attention to the turns and roads he takes before he pulls into a long driveway leading to a huge white house.

"Welcome home, my little iskorka. There's someone you get to meet right away." His eyes crinkle in the corners before he helps me out. "Let's hope he likes you. He doesn't generally take to strangers."

He chuckles as he punches in a code near the entrance.

A bellowing bark echoes through the house that gets louder when Mikhail pushes into the dark, cool interior.

"Hades!"

I'm not sure who's scarier, Mikhail or the terrifying sound of a giant dog galloping closer.

A massive black head followed by a body the size of a

horse rockets over the white tile and skids to a stop when it sees me.

Huge jowls pull back to show teeth that seem as long as my fingers when it hunches with a low growl.

"Enough," Mikhail snaps.

The enormous black dog falls onto his haunches and pants, looking up at his master.

"Ana, meet Hades." Mikhail reaches out and scratches between the short ears.

"Is he friendly?" I'm not so sure about this. His jaw looks big enough to take off one of my legs in a single bite.

"He is to me. But he won't bite unless I give him the command. You're safe." Mikhail lifts our bags onto his shoulder and steps past Hades.

Who then fixes his eyes on me.

His nose flexes and he stands, inching closer hesitantly.

I am a statue. I'm not sure if I should even move.

"Are you a good puppy? You aren't going to eat me, are you?" I flatten my palm and hold up so he can sniff me.

Hades pushes at it, leaving a cold wet smear on my knuckles when he pushes his head into my reach.

"You want petting? I can give good scratches." My nails dig lightly through his short fur over his neck.

Then his tail starts wagging, then his body.

Before I know it, I have a nearly two hundred pound dog flipping onto his back with his tongue lolling as I scratch his chest.

"Traitor." Mikhail laughs when he reappears. "I suppose that means you're friends. He generally doesn't let anyone touch him."

"Everyone loves a good belly rub." I smile as I stand, then chase after Mikhail, wrapping my arms around him to run my fingers over his tight abs.

"I think you're right." He pauses mid stride, then grasps my wrist to push my hand lower to where his cock is hardening in his pants.

I let out a shriek when he whips around and tosses me over his shoulder.

"Let me show you where the master suite is, and where I have an itch you can scratch."

CHAPTER 28

MIKHAIL

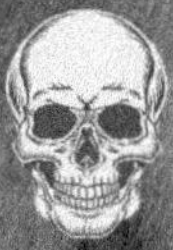

I'M NOT SURE WHY, but I'm more nervous than she is.

Probably because my family still thinks that I'm dead.

Enzo has arranged for everyone to meet in my office with the express purpose of sharing news about my whereabouts.

"Expect some reactions," I whisper to Ana as we step off the elevator. "They don't know I'm alive."

She stops in the middle of the hall and clutches my sleeve. "What? Why? How could you not tell them?"

I grip her cheeks between my palms and make her look up at me. "I died to save you. I had to disappear." Curling my hand behind her neck, I pull her to my chest. "But you've made me feel more alive than I have in years. This will make things quite…interesting. Don't mind my sister, she hates being out of the loop."

"Oh my god, this is gonna suck." Ana's face pales as she walks next to me.

We're both somber when I push my office door open.

A sea of wide eyes stares back before an explosion of noise crashes over us.

"You're alive!" Nikolai is the loudest, nearly overshadowed by Alexei's cackle from the back of the room.

"Mikhail!" Lara clutches her fingers to her mouth, her eyes flicking between me and Ana. "Who is this?"

"Everyone, I'd like you to meet my wife, Ana." I search until I find Jax standing to the side. "Her father is Sergy."

Nikolai is the first to pause. "Wait. As in, Katerina's father?"

I watch his face run through the gambit of emotions. Mila places her palm on his shoulder.

"I didn't know she had a sister," he says quietly, then holds his hand out to Ana. "Welcome to the family you didn't know you had. Your older sister was my wife, Elena, my daughter, is your niece. I'll bring her by to meet you."

Ana's head turns quickly to me before a flood of tears bursts over her cheeks. "I had a sister? I have a niece?"

"I'll do you one better," Jax says hoarsely as he pushes his way forward. "I'm your brother." His tongue bar clicks behind his teeth while he stands awkwardly.

Lara slumps to the cushions with Alexei sitting next to her. "This is all so much!" A wild smile flickers across her lips.

Sofia gasps watching Jax and Ana hug, then claps happily. Her own face has a broad grin while she wipes her cheeks.

Nikolai comes and pats me roughly on the arm. "You're gonna have to fill me in one of these days."

Enzo pushes closer. "Mikhail. I need to talk to you." He glances at the rest of the room. "Alone."

I nod, and squeeze Ana's hand before letting her go.

She has a lot to get caught up on.

Enzo leads me into Lara's office next door.

"I had to make a call while you were settling in." He

calmly folds his hands. "Zoya reached out yesterday while you were in the air. Ivan's men have rooted her out, and she needed an emergency evac."

I can feel my face twist beneath my mask.

Why do I have my doubts? The timing is just too coincidental.

"Where did you put her? Is Galena safe?" My fingers tighten into fists.

Zoya is a frustration I fear I'll never be rid of.

First it was the requests for more money. Then begging to leave.

Now this?

"Yea, they're fine. They should be getting settled in their rooms here as we speak." His dark eyes narrow. "She's making a fuss about not being comfortable here, though. She keeps saying she needs to see you."

Fucking Zoya is pulling me away from Ana's biggest moment in our family.

"She can wait." I set my shoulders and head back to my office.

I haven't seen my siblings in weeks. I'll deal with Zoya tomorrow.

CHAPTER 29

ANASTASIA

I'm so overwhelmed, I can't stop myself from crying.

I thought when my mom died, so did the last of my family. But now I have a brother, and a niece, that I never knew existed.

"I guess our dad liked to sow his oats, huh?" Jax pushes his curly dark hair back and gives me a lopsided grin.

There's no denying he looks exactly like Papa, just twenty years younger.

It makes my chest ache missing him.

Yet, at the same time, my heart is suddenly so full I feel like it might explode.

"I have so many questions." My voice is hoarse.

"Don't worry, there's plenty of time for all of them." Lara looks up at me, then pats the chair near her. "Come here and tell me how you two met."

I chew on my bottom lip as I sit.

"Well, I guess he's been taking care of me for years. Ever since the night that Papa died." I glance up to see Nikolai wince.

"So, when Ivan took me—"

Lara inhales sharply. "Ivan, our father?"

I nod.

Nikolai curses under his breath as Mila takes his hand.

"Ivan has caused a lot of pain." Her lips thin. "I'm so glad Mikhail rescued you. Did Ivan want you to get him information? Or did you already have it…"

"Well—" I twist my dress between my fingers. "—he wanted me. He was trying to make me marry him."

"Jesus fucking Christ." Jax shakes his head and bunches up his fists. "You guys gotta let me beat that asshole to death."

Alexei giggles, showing a silver tooth. "I think everyone here has dibs on him. That's pretty messed up Ivan was planning that. How did you get away?"

"I stabbed him in the face and then jumped out of the window." I still can't believe I did that.

"Holy shit," he says with a broad grin. "You're a badass." He wraps his arm around Lara, then leans over and kisses a faint scar on her cheek. "She'll definitely fit in this crazy family."

Lara smiles at me, and pats my knee. "You're lucky to have gotten away."

By the time Mikhail returns, I feel as if I've been amongst them my whole life.

Nikolai still seems a little reserved, he gets a pained expression every time he looks at me.

"Ana, we have to go. I have a meeting and I want you

there with me." Mikhail holds out his hand until I grasp it, then he tugs me against his side.

"So soon? I was having fun." I let my lip stick out in a pout, but follow him out the door.

Once we're in the solitude of the elevator, I thread my arm around his waist and set my chin on his wide chest. "Where are we going?"

I can see his jaw work under his balaclava.

"One more sister to meet, along with my father's last wife." He pulls me tightly against him.

"There's a lot of you. My head is spinning." I give him a big smile. "I can't believe I have a brother. All these years I just thought I was an only child. I always wished I had a big family."

His dark eyes find mine as he brushes a hair back from my cheek. "I can give you that."

Stepping out of the double doors, instead of turning left to go towards the parking garage, we turn right towards the huge maze of rooms attached to the casino.

"She lives here?" I trail behind him as we stop in front of an executive suite.

"Apparently she does now. That's who I went to visit before we left Russia." Mikhail takes a deep breath, then drops his knuckles against the door.

When it opens, a gorgeous woman is standing there with a long flowing black dress, raven colored hair, and bright red lips.

They drop into a frown when she sees me.

"Oh, Mikhail. I'm so happy you're here! Did Enzo tell you about the frightful time we had?" Her gaze drops to run up and down my body. "Did you bring a babysitter so we can have some time together?"

A *what?*

"Hey, I'm not the—"

Mikhail squeezes my hand, quieting me. "She's not the help. Zoya, I'd like to introduce my wife, Anastasia Volkov."

Zoya's mouth opens and closes soundlessly, but her dark eyes narrow. "I see. I didn't know you were married." She gives me a wane smile. "You're so young…newlyweds?"

I nod. "Last week. It was kind of a whirlwind. You see, after Ivan kidnapped me, Mikhail—"

He jerks on my elbow, silencing me again.

"I'm glad you're settled. You'll be safe here. We can schedule a meeting with the rest of the family later this week once you're comfortable." He slides his palm down my arm and wraps his thick fingers around my wrist. "We'll be going. I'll have Enzo check on you in the morning."

As he pulls me down the hall, I hear her scoff and click her room shut.

"We didn't get to see your sister," I protest.

"There'll be plenty of time for that later. I've had enough time with family for today. I'd rather spend the rest with you."

He jabs the button to call the elevator, and as the door slides open he grabs my wrist and drags me in, hitting the parking lot button. Before the doors can close, his hand is around my neck and his lips over mine.

The heat of my cheeks burns as he pulls back and hits the red stop button, making the floor shake beneath my feet.

"On your knees."

I look around the open glass, searching for cameras. I don't know. What the hell is he doing?

"Do not make me ask again."

He frees his cock from his pants and without thinking, I

drop to my knees in front of him. Smirking down at me, he taps my lips with the tip of his cock.

"Open that sassy mouth of yours."

I do as he says and almost gag when he thrusts in my mouth, hitting the back of my throat.

"Good girl. Now I'm going fuck it and teach you a lesson in staying quiet."

His fingers tangle in my hair, holding me firmly in place.

"Your mouth is sinful. And so fucking bratty," he groans above me, sending shockwaves to my pussy.

I take it I said too much back there, maybe I shouldn't have mentioned the details to her about how we got married.

But if this is punishment, I'm not sure it's having the right impact on me because I am horny as hell.

"You're going to be a good girl now and let me come down your throat."

I nod, he pushes me back against the metal wall of the elevator and my scalp burns as he pulls my hair, relentlessly fucking my face.

Tears stream down my cheeks, but I do my best to take him. As I look up at him through my glassy eyes, he throws his head back. The way my name rolls off his tongue in that deep Russian accent makes me burn for him.

With a few more thrusts, he eases up and finishes in my mouth, still rocking his hips gently.

His eyes lock with mine as he finishes. My god, that was so hot to watch him fall apart.

I suck him clean and swallow the warm, salty liquid. As he pulls out, he swipes his finger across my swollen lips.

"The sounds you make when you gag are incredible, pretty girl."

He pulls me up to my feet and presses his lips to mine.

"So you like my mouth sometimes," I tease.

He raises an eyebrow at me and tugs me against his side, leaning us against the railings.

"I like your mouth all the time really. It makes you, you. I think you enjoy the punishments as much as I do."

He slides his hand under my dress and he runs his finger along my soaking pussy.

"Yep. Feels like you do. I'll clean up your mess when we get home."

I let out a sigh of frustration. Home feels like forever away.

"Tease," I pout.

His dark chocolate eyes pin me with a glare and I snap my lips shut. The last thing I need is a worse form of punishment.

He presses the elevator button and we start to descend again and he helps me into the passenger seat of his matte black Corvette, then gets behind the wheel.

It makes warmth spread through me knowing he wants to be with me, especially after seeing just how stunning that Zoya woman is.

"So, for her daughter to be your sister. That means Ivan…?" I let my meaning hang in the air between us.

Mikhail nods. "Helping Zoya escape is how Katerina, my mother, and your father all died."

"And that gave you the scars you still hide from me," I say quietly. "What will they think that you're still covering your face from your own wife?"

A rumble comes from somewhere deep in his chest. "We talked about this, Ana. Is it so wrong that I want you to like me before you see the monster?"

I turn in the seat to face him. "Mikhail," I say with a completely straight face. "I've had your dick in me. We're married. Don't you think that counts at least *somewhere* on the scale of 'like'?"

His eyes crinkle at the corners in what I've learned is a smile.

"It's a hard habit to break." He reaches out and grips my thigh. "I promise, I'll be ready soon."

CHAPTER 30

MIKHAIL

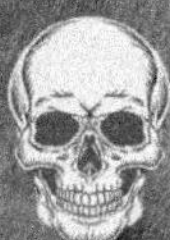

I'M QUESTIONING MYSELF NOW.

It's almost gone on too long, keeping the truth of what I look like from her. I should have shown her in the beginning so she could go ahead and run in fear.

I couldn't stand the looks of disgust I received after Ivan scarred me.

The mask is just easier. And for a man in my position, it's added to the mystery.

If my enemies don't know what I look like, they can't pinpoint me. Cameras have a harder time tracking me. Many people wear masks nowadays, so it's almost easier to blend in.

There have been some advantages.

My damn phone has been buzzing with messages since we left the casino. I'm sure most of them are my siblings, each wanting the full story of where I've been and what happened over the last few weeks.

There will be time.

It's only when it rings that I dig it out.

"Hello, Enzo. It's been at least—" I roll my arm to check my Rolex. "—thirty entire minutes since I've seen you last."

"Well, I didn't get a chance to tell you about the big event I have planned. Now that you're back on the surface, I want you to be one of the headliner guests." His voice takes on a pained tone. "I think it will pull Ivan and Tatiana out of hiding."

"That's a good idea. It's time to finish this shit. Do you think we'll find their moles? Someone has to be feeding them info." How else would my father know that I was in Russia?

"I have Romeo looking harder into Drago. I still wonder if he turned you in." Enzo takes a long breath. "Also, about Zoya…"

I can feel my gut twist at the mention of her name. "What about her?"

Ana shifts in her seat to watch me attentively.

"She showed up at your office. Fortunately, it was after everyone else had left." He sighs. "But then she went down to the foyer and the casino floor."

For fuck's sake. "What did she do?" I slam the car in park outside of the house and stomp to the passenger's side.

"She verbally attacked the floor manager demanding to see you, and started saying how everyone was in danger because Ivan was coming." Enzo laughs lightly. "I don't think she should stay here."

I rub my temples and follow Ana into the house.

Hades runs up and leans against her legs, nearly knocking her over, wiggling for her attention.

He doesn't even look at me.

"Fine. Set her up in the guest house here. I can't have her throwing a fit and exposing our organization to the public." I click the end button and toss my phone onto the counter.

"Rough day at work, big man?" Ana drops her purse next to my cell.

"Zoya and Galena will be coming here. They'll stay in the guest house." I'm used to being the one in control of every situation.

Lately, that has been tested constantly.

"Why? She looked completely fine when we saw her a little while ago." Her lips flatten and she twists her wedding ring.

I drop my palms on either side of her and run my nose up her neck. "You know how you got tired of being caged in by your mother? How the desperate need for freedom finally overcame the urge for safety? I think that's what is going on with her. She's been in hiding as well since this." I point at my mask. "So I'll do my best to be patient, for Galena's sake."

Movement out the window catches my focus.

Enzo's fleet of black SUV's cutting through on the back driveway to the guest house.

I can't imagine that his sex clubs are ever slow. He must want her moved out as badly as she does for him to act so quickly.

"So…is she always like this?" Ana's eyes narrow as she follows my gaze.

I shake my head. "I haven't had direct contact with her for years. It was only when I went to get you that I saw her again for the first time."

Ana tilts her chin and purses her lips looking up at me.

"Whatever." She ducks, slipping out from between my arms and grabs her bag, heading upstairs.

Hades, like the traitor he is, immediately follows her without even glancing at me.

My fist lands on the island top hard enough to make my phone jump.

This is *not* what I had in mind for tonight.

I have work to do, although I dread having to sit in my office knowing my wife is pissed at me.

When Ana comes back downstairs, she's changed into an oversized sweater and leggings, showing off the tight curves of her hips as she leans against my desk. "What, my husband, did you have planned for dinner tonight? Are we inviting our new neighbors?"

I groan as I lean back in my chair. "Come here." I hold out my hand and straddle her across my lap. "The only thing I want to eat tonight is you." My palms circle the globes of her ass and I grind her against my hardening cock.

"Oh, am I interrupting?" Zoya stands in the doorway with a smirk on her face. "I tried to knock, but there wasn't an answer."

Where is my useless guard dog?

Ana's spine straightens, and she doesn't even look at Zoya. "Yes, you're interrupting."

Zoya raises an eyebrow, but stays still. "That's rather rude, child."

Ana's nails dig into my shoulders and her jaw clenches.

She's cute when she's angry.

"Zoya, you need to call. This is our house, and you'll respect that." It's hard to concentrate with Ana's hot pussy pressing on my crotch.

"Well, I thought we were all family here." Zoya gives me a patronizing smile, then has the audacity to sit on a nearby chair. "Speaking of, why are you still wearing that ridiculous mask? We've all seen you without it."

Ana's eyes widen. "We have?"

Zoya laughs. "What, you haven't seen how handsome he

is? Why is he keeping that from you?" She pushes herself up and turns. "Mikhail, dear. Galena has no toys to play with. And I need a different bed than the one that is in that tiny house. It's horribly soft. You know I like it hard." She winks at me, then disappears.

As soon as she's gone, Ana's face darkens and she shoves her hands against my chest, leaping off my lap. "What the fuck, Miki? She's seen you without your stupid mask, but I haven't?" Tears well in her eyes. "You said you weren't ready, and I've tried to respect that. But to have her hold something so important that you keep out of reach?" Her chin wavers and her arms wrap around her waist. "Fuck you!"

Turning on her heel, she runs out the door.

God damn it. This is *really* not what I had planned.

CHAPTER 31

ANASTASIA

MY FACE BURIES into the pillow as I sob out my frustrations.

What was I even thinking? Pushing him to marry me must have been a mistake.

Maybe he's had a ton of girlfriends before I came along.

I didn't know him when I committed myself to him. Am I stupid for thinking this could work?

The bed dips when he sits next to me.

"Ana, I'm sorry." His warm palm rests on my lower back.

I hate that it feels so good when he touches me. I want to be mad at him.

"I don't know why you don't trust me? Instead, you let that...*woman* show me up? Do you have any idea how embarrassing that is? I'm supposed to be your *wife!*" New tears flood out of my eyes and I fall nose first into the damp silk again.

His fingers wrap around my shoulders, and he pulls me up to look at him.

"She's never seen my face after the—"

A searing, stabbing pain shoots through my chest, a physical manifestation of the anguish I see in his eyes. I gently placed my palm against his warm cheek, feeling the faint pulse beneath my fingertips.

"So I have to live the rest of my life with a man who will never show me his complete self? You love me. You don't want to lose me. Don't you think I deserve something more? If you really cared, don't you want me to be happy?" I sob the last words out.

Because with him, I am the happiest I have ever been. And I think it's the same for him too. We were forced together in this cruel world for a reason.

"You aren't happy? I don't make you smile?" The sadness in his voice makes my throat close up.

"You do, and that's what hurts. I'm in love with a man who believes he's a monster with no heart. And I don't think there's anything I can do to make you see that there is something beautiful beating in that enormous chest of yours. That you do, in fact, have the capability to love extremely hard, you just won't admit it. But I can't live my life with someone that won't bare their soul to me and show me the scars that run so deep they shut themselves off from happiness. I want the man under that mask to love me fiercely. To show me his darkness and let me bring him into the light. I know what I want, Mikhail. You. But not just the parts you aren't afraid to show me. All of it. Every horrible part so I can love them, too."

I turn away from him, not even wanting to read his reaction. Every word I said is the truth. I am in love with him way beyond his appearance. My heart beats for this man, my body comes alive for him and my soul is entwined with his.

"It's because I love you that I don't want to show you the parts I hate. The parts that nearly broke me. That make me weak. I love you too damn much to taint you with my flaws. I want to shield you from the dark, not drag you in with me."

As my gaze meets his, fresh tears roll down my cheeks. He loves me too? I shake my head and run my hands through his soft hair.

"That isn't how it works, Miki. Give me your demons. Let me dance in the rain with them. Why are you really hiding from me?" I whisper.

He sucks in a ragged breath, and the sight makes my own chest ache. His pain is mine.

"I don't want to lose you. Maybe I'm fucking petrified you'll see what's under here and leave." His words are almost a whisper.

I shake my head and stroke the fabric of his mask. Leaning in, I press a soft kiss next to his nose.

"You think that little of me? That there is seriously something under that mask that I'll be repulsed by? That I'll hate. Because there isn't. Nothing. Mikhail."

His eyes close and he sighs.

"If I can't even look at it, why the hell would I expect you to?"

His voice is so raw. Broken almost. His fingers dig into my thigh and I place my other hand over his and squeeze for reassurance.

"Mikhail. Stop. I am never leaving your side. I'm your wife. You are my goddamn husband. Let me ask you a question…"

Silence fills the room and a knot of nerves forms in my stomach.

"Go on."

To be closer to him, I sit on his lap and he lets out a groan, making me break into a smile.

"Now isn't the time to tease me, iskorka," he mutters, squeezing my hips.

"No, probably not. Just don't focus on my butt for a few minutes." I wink at him as he strokes a stray strand of hair away from my face.

"Your ass, Anastasia, is constantly on my mind."

"Good. Now. Listen." I give him a stern look. I take a breath through my nose before I continue.

"If something happened to me tomorrow, let's say I get hit by a car, and my face is all smashed up, hardly recognizable even. I'm laying in a hospital bed, you're probably holding my hand and plotting revenge. But would you want me any less because I didn't look perfect anymore?"

He doesn't hesitate in his response.

"The fuck. No. What I feel for you is way beyond that."

My heart races. I'm on the right track.

"Will you love me in forty years when I have wrinkles?" I continue.

He runs his fingers through my hair and twirls the curls around his finger.

"Yes."

I look down at him, fiddling with the lock.

"Would you love me if I shaved my hair off?"

"Yes."

"Why?" I press.

"Because it's you. I love every single thing about you. Your fire, your sass, the way your smile lights up a room, the way you gravitate towards me, the way your eyes burn into mine, the softness of your touch. The way you brought me back to life. You are my iskorka in every sense of the word."

Blinking back the hot, stinging tears, I feel the gentle pressure of his palm against my cheek. I lean into his warm touch.

"I'm not giving up on you, Miki. I wouldn't even know how. But you gotta let me in, show me the real you and let me love him too. It's just us here, us against everyone. You took me. You stole my heart and there's no return on that. Don't make me fight for this alone. I believe the man hiding under that mask is worthy of my love, and I'll prove it to you. Take it off, Mikhail. Nothing changes. Not a single thing. Only that you give me the final key to unlock your heart."

He nods slowly, but doesn't move his hand from my face.

"Let me help?" I whisper softly.

He averts his gaze away and closes his eyes briefly.

"Look at me, Mikhail. Not just at me, look past it, go deeper. It's me. It's only us here. I've given you every piece of me. I trust you, I cherish you, and most of all, I want to love all of you. Now show me who you really are."

He curls his thumb beneath the edge of his balaclava, then rips it over his head.

I'm so used to looking in his chocolate colored eyes, it takes me a moment to comprehend what he's done.

Reaching up, I feather a soft touch over the puckered skin on his cheek, and trace the tight pull at the corner of his full lips.

"Oh, Miki…" I trail off. "You're hot as hell." I can see the scarring that goes up his sharp jaw, but it's nothing like what I envisioned.

His mouth drops into a frown. "It used to be much worse. After it had healed, it was still bright red…almost angry looking." He shakes his head. "Even my own niece was terrified to look at me. It was just easier to cover it up. Then it became who I was." He shrugs, then cups my hand with his against his cheek.

"You make me want to be a better man, pretty girl."

I shake my head, and he frowns in response.

"I don't want you to be better, Miki. I just want you to be mine, exactly the way you are now." I keep my touch light on his scars. He doesn't flinch. He seems to be at one with me seeing him.

"It feels good," he rumbles. "I can't remember the last time anyone touched me there."

That makes me giggle. "Miki, I've had my hand every-where on you *but* there."

I curl my knees under me, and frame his face with my palms. "No more secrets, okay?" I reach forward and touch my lips to his scars.

"Or what?" For the first time, I get to see him smile. And what an incredible sight that is.

I trail my thumb down his chin. "Or it'll be my turn to spank you."

With a growl, he rolls over me, pinning me to the mattress. "I promise, no more secrets. But I can't say there won't ever be spankings."

I look up at him through my lashes and smile, wriggling in his hold as he pushes open my legs with his thigh.

"So, mask stays off when we're alone?" I ask.

"Yes. Only you get to see the real me. He's all yours."

He crashes his lips over mine for a searing kiss, one that sets me on fire. It's perfect. And he is all mine.

CHAPTER 32

MIKHAIL

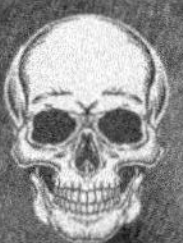

"Tell me more about what you hope to gain from this party." I'm not in the mood to be social.

But Enzo seems to have half of New York City flying in for his little get together.

"We need to flush out the mole. I've invited Drago, Ben and Sven. and told them all to invite anyone they'd like. Alexei is going to reach out to Tatiana through his network, and offer her the opportunity to get the rest of what's on the drive that Mila took." Enzo runs his fingers through his hair.

If I didn't know him better, I'd almost say he looks nervous.

But he's the most calm and collected of any of us, so that can't be it.

"Do you think Ivan will show?" I wouldn't think that he'd have the balls.

Enzo weaves his fingers together and leans over his desk, ignoring the wall of monitors behind him. "I suppose it depends on the leak. If he knows that Zoya and Anastasia are both here. he might. It's a hell of a big bait."

My chest aches at the thought of putting Ana in danger.

"Maybe she shouldn't go?"

Enzo blinks at me, then pulls back with a frown. "I need to know how Tatiana fits into all of this. You know how close Zoya is to…to…" His voice trails off as his jaw clenches. Sitting back, he draws in a long breath, steadying himself. "My hope is to find out more. There's a path with Tatiana, that USB drive she had Mila recover had a lot on there I have questions about."

"I know, and I hope you find answers someday. But I don't know if Zoya is the right path to follow." I am getting increasingly frustrated with her.

That's a battle for another time.

"Anyways. Frankie, Zara, and his entourage will be here tomorrow. He's promising extra manpower for a potential showdown with Ivan." He leans back to tap on his keyboard. "Sounds like he might be bringing Keller, Grayson and Luca."

"I imagine Jax is excited to see his old crew again. When was the last time they were out here? For his wedding?"

Enzo nods. "It'll be fun to have everyone together again. I get tired of the commute sometimes when my clubs here are keeping me so tied up."

I glance over the flickering screens behind him, each showing a view from a different room. "I guess it's a good thing?"

He grins. "Oh yes. I'm planning an after party here over the weekend, if you'd care to book a suite with your wife. Want company?" He raises an eyebrow.

I have no idea if he's suggesting another woman or himself.

"She's already more than I can handle. But that does sound fun." The thought of having Ana tied up and at my complete mercy makes my cock grow.

"I'll make sure you're set. Let Romeo know if you need anything." He types quickly, then pulls out his phone.

He flips the screen around to show me who's calling.

Zoya.

She's going to drive us all crazy.

"On one hand," Enzo says as he denies the call. "It is nice having her closer to ask questions. On the other, I liked her better when she was actually in fear for her life." His lips thin while he slides his cell back into his pocket.

"We need to get Ivan taken care of. Then, she doesn't have any more reason to hide. Maybe she can come work for you?" I tease him and stand.

Enzo shakes his head, his slicked back dark hair doesn't waver with the movement. "She's too expensive for my tastes."

CHAPTER 33

ANASTASIA

Song- Like That, Sleep Token

"HI GORGEOUS, GORGEOUS BOY." I sneak a look at Mikhail who is ingrained on his phone. He's busy, which means I can give Hades some love.

Protection dog, my ass. By the time I'm finished, he's going to be the pampered prince he deserves to be.

I bend down to his face level. His brown eyes almost soften as he looks at me. We have a special bond.

"You want some treats, boy?" I whisper and Hades sits up straighter, making himself even taller and licks his lips.

I kinda see why Miki got him for security. Seeing this beast running at you would scare anyone.

"Okay. I'll sneak you some, stay." I say the last word sternly as I stand and back away. He doesn't move, like a statue.

I back step by step towards the refrigerator. I gasp when my back hits the cool metal of the door. I glance over at Mikhail who is watching me closely. Having his chocolate eyes on me makes a blush creep up my neck.

Silently, I open up the refrigerator and grab some chicken.

"Who is that for?" Mikhail's deep voice makes me jump.

"Hades, he's been a good boy." I smile sweetly at him and then glance at Hades, sitting patiently licking his lips.

Mikhail raises an eyebrow at me.

"Why? You want some food? Have you been a good boy too?" I bite back a smile.

Slowly, he rubs his hand across his jaw and swipes his thumb across his lip, before bringing his dark stare back to me.

"Did you just call me a good boy?"

"Uh, yeah. I guess. Why, do you want to be one?" I place Hades' plate down by him.

"You're my only good boy," I whisper, stroking his head.

As I stand, I turn and I'm staring at Mikhail's chest. He grips my chin and presses my back against the counter, leaning over me, his lips just inches from mine. His hot breath pours over me as he lowers his mouth next to my ear.

"Call me a good boy again, iskorka. I dare you. There isn't a good bone in my body." He almost growls and I clench my thighs.

A grin twists up on my lips, then I lick along his jawline.

"Oh, big man." I slide my hand along his abs and cup his growing cock through his jeans. "You have at least one very good bone."

With a swift motion, he picks me up and places me on the counter, tearing off my leggings and leaving me feeling exposed to him. The way he licks his lips while devouring me with his eyes leaves me feeling drenched with desire for him.

"That is true," he whispers in my ear, sliding his fingers inside me. "But, you'll have to wait until I deem you a good girl again. You have some lessons to learn, baby."

I pull back and look at him with confusion as he fucks me

with his hand. I'm soaking him. His lips curl into a smirk, and I can't help but gasp as a wave of pleasure starts to build inside me.

"Feels good doesn't it? You already want to come for me, don't you?"

I nod eagerly, my body moving in rhythm with his hand as he tightens his grip around my throat.

I tip my head back, relishing in the pleasure overtaking me until I'm on the cusp of exploding. And then, before I can come, he removes his fingers and steps back.

"No," I whine.

Fuck.

My chest heaves, a ragged breath catching in my throat. His grip on my wrist is like a vise, his hard stare pinning me in place.

"Lesson one. You only get to come when I allow it. Your punishment today will be denying you of that pleasure. I will relieve you when I believe your punishment is served."

He pulls my panties back over my aching pussy. As he bends down to place a kiss on it, his eyes remain locked with mine.

"Delicious." He stands and slams his lips against mine, only riling me up further.

"Please, Miki. I'll be good for you. I promise."

He chuckles, a low rumble in his chest, shaking his head slowly.

"Not how this works. And don't even think about relieving yourself while you're out today. I will know. I know every single inch of you. You'll only drag this out longer for yourself the more you relent."

I let out a dramatic sigh, pouting at him while batting my eyelashes in a playful, flirtatious manner.

"Fine." I huff, blowing my hair away from my face. He grips my chin, making me look at him.

"Such a brat, aren't you?"

He gently presses his lips to mine, a feather-light touch that sends shivers down my spine.

He lifts me off the counter and hands me my leggings.

I'll behave, but I'm going to get him back for this.

I snatch my pants from him and he yanks me back into an embrace.

"Never forget how much I love you," he whispers against the top of my head.

"I love you too, big man. I'll love you even more when you bend me over like a pretzel later."

I leave him laughing to himself as I head upstairs with an extra sway in my step. If I'm spending the day frustrated, he can be too.

When I freshen up, I snap a quick picture of my ass in my black thong. I'll send that to him this afternoon.

CHAPTER 34

ANASTASIA

"I LIKE YOUR CASINO, Miki. It's pretty fucking cool." I hold on tight as he tugs on my hand past his office and towards Lara's door.

I'm kind of nervous about spending the day with his sister. I know how much she means to him. What if she doesn't like me? Or I accidentally upset her. My mouth runs away with me sometimes and Miki warned me she can be sensitive sometimes, especially around food and body image. The woman is drop dead gorgeous, but we all have our demons, I suppose. He did say she's been doing better recently. I'm really hoping we become friends. I could use some girlie time.

With a sharp rap on the door, Mikhail doesn't wait for a response. He throws it open, his hand on my back, ushering me inside. I come to a sudden stop, the force of the impact jarring me as he slams into me from behind. I try to retreat before he sees the scene I am looking at.

Lara is straddled over Alexei's lap, with what looks like her tights around his eyes.

Jesus. I squeeze mine shut, waiting for Mikhail's wrath.

Luckily, both of them are dressed by the looks of it. More of a heavy petting session.

Mikhail clears his throat and Lara bursts out laughing, ripping the tights from Alexei's eyes. He gives us a bright smile with his silver tooth showing and waves. Like nothing is going on out of the ordinary.

"Do you two ever fucking stop?" Mikhail grits out. "I set a specific time to avoid this kind of thing. Alexei, stop distracting Lara at work."

Alexei lets out a cackle and Lara rolls her eyes, sliding off his lap behind the desk and straightening her white blouse.

"Sorry, Ana." She looks at me apologetically with her blue eyes.

I offer her a smile and a raised hand.

"No worries. We will go wait in Miki's office, knock when you're ready for me."

Mikhail is already heading into the hall, intertwining his fingers with mine as we stroll down the corridor.

"I like your family. They're fun." I nudge his side playfully and he grunts.

By the time we get to his office, Lara is calling after me in a panic.

"I'm ready, I'm ready. I am so sorry." We turn to face a red faced Lara, who is holding up her car keys. I can't help but laugh. Tugging on the neck of his t-shirt, I drag him down to me and smack my lips on his.

"Here, my card." He slides out his black Amex.

He silences me by pressing a finger to my lips as I begin to speak.

"I don't care what you spend. There is no damn limit. Whatever makes you smile, buy it. Lara has very expensive taste. She can help. And maybe a little something for me to rip off you."

With no established life or job here, I'm left with no choice but to accept.

"Very good husband." I wink and pat him on the head.

My gesture causes his eyes to widen, almost in disbelief.

"I will see what I can do, big man. No limit, you say?"

"Try to max it out, I dare you."

I blush. The man has clearly more money than sense. I'm standing in his damn casino, and they never lose.

"So, looks like I am actually off mansion and yacht shopping? Maybe some fine art?"

He shrugs, the rough texture of his jacket brushing against my arm, as he pulls me into his embrace.

"I'm not with you for money, Mikhail. You could be broke and I'd still be by your side," I whisper in his ear.

"I know, baby. That's why I'm saying spend it. If I'm going to use it for anything, it might as well be to see you smile."

"You are too cute, Mr. Volkov."

"Don't push it, iskorka. Now, shop to your heart's content." He taps my ass as I pull away. Now it's my turn to blush.

I drop my heavy bags onto the floor with a thud, and sink gratefully into the worn, plush chair of the coffee shop. Mikhail was not joking when he said Lara knew how to shop.

My god. It's more of a sport than anything.

"So, are you happy with everything you've bought?"

I look down at the mountain of bags.

She literally means everything, from underwear, outfits for every season, a dress for the ball. I even bought Hades a blue diamond encrusted collar. I'm cringing at what the total might be for all of this.

The server brings our coffees, the aroma of roasted beans filling the air. When I blow on the still-steaming mug, my gaze fixes on the decadent chocolate cupcake. I pause as I reach for it.

"Would you like to share?" I ask.

Her nose scrunches up.

"He told you, didn't he?"

"A little bit." I don't lie.

She sighs, stirring her coffee.

"I'll have half, but you can have the bigger half," she says with a grin.

"Deal."

I'm not going to pry. I can just be someone there for her if she needs me.

"So, how does it feel having another sister-in-law?" I ask, twirling my wedding ring.

"Amazing. It's nice for the balance of men to women to finally be even."

She smiles brightly at me as I slice the cake in half, sliding hers over on a plate.

"I'm glad. I've never really had much in the way of family. It was just me and mom. I had no clue Jax and Katerina existed."

"Well, you've found your way into a big and slightly crazy one now." She brushes her bright blonde hair over one shoulder.

I hope I don't lose this. It means more to me than I realized.

She takes a small sip, then looks up with her mug poised near her lips. "I have never seen Miki like this. It's different, in the best way."

"Really?"

She nods solemnly.

"Since the accident, he became an icy shell of himself. You seem to have dragged that spark for life back out of him. Even his eyes are brighter."

Wow. I knew Miki was closed, but it's sure nice to hear not only is he bringing me happiness, I am to him too.

There's a pause as Lara takes a bite of her cake.

"Have you, umm, seen under his mask?" She almost whispers it, like it's a banned topic.

"Yes." I nod. "I have."

Her mouth drops open and tears well in her eyes.

Shit. Have I said the wrong thing?

"I can't believe it," she mutters to herself.

That makes me sit up straight. "What do you mean?"

"Sorry." She wipes her tears. "I just never thought Miki would find the strength to reveal himself. None of us have seen his injuries. We know what happened and we are all okay with the mask. We understand. But it's a huge step for him. I'm just proud of him."

She sniffles, so I hold my hand out across the table, taking hers and giving it a reassuring squeeze.

"One day, he might have the confidence to leave the mask behind. But, I promise, he is perfect under that mask. The scars are there, but they don't change who he is."

She nods. I hope one day Miki feels like he can stop hiding. But I will support him however he decides.

"Thank you, Ana. Thank you for bringing my brother back to life."

"He's done the same for me. I love him very much."

"I know. I can see it in the way you two look at each other."

That makes me smile, my heart bursting with happiness.

"Now I just need to get rid of that woman in our house," I grumble.

"Zoya?"

"Yea. She's obsessed with him, Lara. Uses him like he's some sort of personal slave. And so fucking rude."

Lara rolls her blue eyes. "Ignore her. You have what she wants. I'm sure Miki will find a solution soon. Trust him. His heart lies with you, we can all see that. Until Dad is gone, he wants to keep everyone safe. It's for Galena more than her. It will work out, I promise."

I chew on the inside of my mouth. Something isn't quite sitting right with me about Zoya. I'll find out what.

CHAPTER 35

MIKHAIL

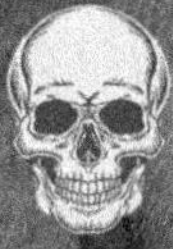

Fᴜᴄᴋ ɪᴛ's ʜᴏᴛ. Sitting in the sun with half of my face covered under a black mask isn't ideal.

Ana and Lara decided on a pool day, so Alexei and I get to relax with beer while they swim and sunbathe.

"I feel like a bartender," Alexei grumbles as he returns from delivering the cocktails he made for the girls.

"While you're up, we need two more beers."

"I really am a fucking donkey today." He throws his hand up and stomps back to the kitchen. Leaning back with my fingers woven behind my head and my feet on the table, I find some relief from the sun thanks to a passing cloud.

Ana looks stunning in her deep red bikini. I can't tear my eyes from her. I inwardly groan as she rolls over onto her front on the sun lounger. Now that fine ass of hers is on display.

My hands almost twitch to spank it for teasing me.

Sliding my phone out of my shorts, I pull up our messages.

Me: That ass would look perfect if it was red to match.

When her phone dings, she grabs it from under her sunlounger and flicks up her oversized sunglasses.

I can see her grin from here as she types back.

ISKORKA

If we go for a dip in the pool you can grab it?

I can't help but chuckle. If I do that, I won't stop.

ME

I wish. Why did we invite guests over?

She responds in seconds.

ISKORKA

Because family is important and I'm not going anywhere. Make my ass as red as you want when we're alone.

Alexei drops heavily into the seat facing me, banging our beers onto the glass table.

"Done. You can get the next ones. I can't make any more cocktails, I will become a raspberry if I touch anymore."

I arch a brow. He's so dramatic.

"You tell Lara that."

I look back down at my phone.

ME

I'll hold your ass to that later. Now, pool?

She sits up on the chair, turns to face me, and beckons me closer with a finger. Grabbing my beer, I lift my mask discretely and take a gulp before making my way over, shading her when I stand over her.

"Damn. You look good in swim trunks." Her gaze roams my body, and she bites her lip. "I want to lick your abs."

I step forward, grabbing her messy bun and tip her head back so I can look into her eyes.

"All yours, baby."

Ana sneaks a look behind. Lara is fast asleep on her beach chair. With a mischievous grin, my wife leans forward, running her tongue all the way up my six-pack as she stands.

"Yum."

Holding her face in my hands, I lean in to kiss her, sneaking my mask down to my chin.

"Yum, indeed, pretty girl. Let's get in the water." I brush my lips against her ear. "We gotta cool down my dick."

She giggles when I smack her ass as she pads over to the stairs and gets in the pool.

I perch on the ledge, dangling my legs in the cool water, before dropping in and keeping my head above the surface.

With a push, I swim to Ana, forcing her against the wall and containing her.

She wraps her legs around my waist.

"That is not helping the situation."

She clings to my neck, and I walk around the pool with her. With each step, her ass knocks against my dick.

"Hey, Miki. Ana. Look up and smile." We both look at Alexei standing at the edge of the pool with his phone in front of his face.

"Say, potatoes."

Ana looks at me, confused.

"He means cheese." I roll my eyes.

She looks back at him and smiles. My vision, however, remains with her.

I love her smile.

I love her.

Once that is over with, she leans back and floats on her back.

God, this is making it worse with her legs tightening around me.

My hands grip onto her ass and I squeeze, watching her breast floating on the surface of the water.

"It's my turn to lick you," I tell her.

My hands skate up her sides.

I need to get out. Or drag her upstairs.

She maneuvers herself back up and wraps her arms around my neck.

"Why don't you and Alexei put the BBQ on? That might distract you."

"Good idea. Because I'm ten seconds away from pulling your panties to the side and fucking you here."

She leans in and bites my shoulder.

"Nope." She bursts out laughing and untangles herself from me, swimming away back to the stairs.

Smacking her ass like I'm beating a drum as she climbs out of the pool, I follow her, grabbing my towel from the chair as she wraps herself up in her red one.

"Good swim?" Lara yawns as she speaks.

"Refreshing," Ana chirps back and wiggles her brows at me.

Wiping off the excess water from my arms, Ana's face morphs into fury as she looks behind me.

I turn my head to find Zoya walking towards us down the path from her house.

She gives me a little wave. I ignore her and turn back to Ana.

I'm already dreading the show Zoya will put on.

If it wasn't for Galena, I would have booted her on her ass by now. I've never taken notice of her advances over the years.

Now, they infuriate me because I know it's upsetting Ana.

I have no interest in Zoya. Never have, never will.

I'll just make it clear that I belong to Ana. It seems to work.

Before she approaches the group, I step behind Ana and wrap my arms around her waist, pulling her back against my chest.

"Miki, Lara, Alexei," she greets us all with a smile before her gaze lands on Ana.

Her eyes darken.

"Anastasia," she says her name like spitting venom.

I hold Ana tighter, reassuring her.

"Zoya. Why don't you come and help me grab the beers?" Lara says, jumping up from her seat.

"Hmm." Zoya's eyes flick between me and Ana before taking a slow step towards my sister.

Lara ushers her off, giving Ana an apologetic smile.

Ana spins in my arms.

"Nice of her to leave her dignity at home," she grumbles.

I didn't take notice. I try to avoid that entirely.

"I mean, her swimsuit is so far up her crack it's gonna disappear in a minute."

I let out a chuckle. My girl has a way with words.

"Trust me, I was not looking at her ass."

Ana scowls at me. "You wouldn't fucking dare, Mikhail."

I seize her by the throat and lower my head.

"Trust me. There is only one ass I want and will ever want, and that belongs to you. Now, stop the jealousy before I spank it out of you. Okay?"

I need to remind her she is mine and, of course, I am hers.

Zoya is nothing to me. No matter what she wears or how much she flirts. My eyes are always fixed on my wife.

"I do trust you. It's just irritating. She tries to make me feel like I am the other woman? I'm your wife for the love of

God. Her lack of respect makes me stabby, Miki. Like, it's a problem. I see her face and I want to smash it against the concrete."

Godammit. I get feral when she gets all aggressive.

Like a cute little package of love, spirituality and pure violence.

"I kinda enjoy watching you get riled up."

"Good, because it might become a reality one day."

"Noted. I've got you."

Zoya clears her throat behind us.

"I've got your beer, Miki baby."

Oh fuck.

"Zoya," I warn her, taking the beer from her and being careful to avoid even brushing her hand.

Alexei hasn't said a word, just watching this whole interaction with interest.

"Bitch," Ana mutters under her breath.

"I'll get rid of her," I whisper in Ana's ear as she pulls away.

Lara hands Ana a fresh bright pink cocktail and Alexei his beer.

"You good?" Lara mouths to Ana, who gives her a brief nod.

She's gritting her teeth. She is not happy.

Zoya bends over and picks up the sunscreen, turning to me. "Could you rub all over my back, please, Mik?"

I close my eyes and suck in a breath. She's on her fucking own with this one. Ana steps in front of me, and I let her.

Zoya needs ripping into. Maybe she'll learn.

"Are you fucking kidding me? Get some self respect, Zoya. You are in *our* place. Flaunting yourself around like some prized whore will not win over my damn husband. Now get the fuck back to your house and stay there before I really lose my patience with you."

Zoya's face flashes with anger. She looks to me to provide back up and I shake my head.

Not happening.

Fuck, listening to Ana get all possessive over me is way too hot to stop.

"You won't be here long enough for it to make any difference," Zoya snaps back, putting her hand on her hip.

"I'm not going anywhere, Zoya."

A vicious grin spreads on Zoya's lips.

"Well, neither am I. I'll always be in your life. I am part of the family. So you'll have to suck it up and you'll always have me on the outside, waiting for you to slip up and lose him."

Not a chance.

I have to hold myself back as Lara steps to my side.

"How far do we let this go?" Lara whispers.

"Ana can handle herself. Don't worry."

"Well, you'll be waiting for the rest of your life. Mikhail is not yours, Zoya. Get it through that thick skull of yours. You fucked his father. What man in their right mind wants their dad's sloppy seconds? Revolting. You're disgusting, letting that old creep fuck you."

"The Volkov men are a good fuck though. Aren't they, Mikhail?"

I start to step forward when I see Ana's hand swing back, but I'm too late. She's already smashed her palm into the side of Zoya's face.

Zoya stumbles back with a shocked look towards me. "Miki. Control your whore."

My fists clench. Lara and Alexei hold me back as rage flashes through me. I'd kill her with one hit.

"Let Ana deal with her." Lara smacks my arm.

And she does.

Zoya goes flying across the ground like a rag doll, Ana stomping closely behind before she yanks Zoya up by her hair.

"Never call me that," Ana spits out and shoves her in the pool.

Ana jumps in after her and I debate stopping her.

But watching her go all out like this is something special. My woman is crazy in the best way.

"Miki. She's going to fucking kill her. Galena needs her mom." Lara's eyes are wide as she looks towards the water then back to me.

I sigh.

Alexei is by the edge of the pool cheering Ana on as she holds Zoya by the back of the head under the water, occasionally dragging her up for air.

Lara sets her drink down. "I'll get Ana. I don't want you accidentally killing Zoya either."

She has a point. I'm pretty fired up. It wouldn't be an accident though.

Lara dives in and grabs hold of a furious Ana. As soon as she realizes it's Lara, she lets go and backs away.

I don't know what Lara whispers to Ana, but it calms her down.

Zoya is screaming to me about Ana being a maniac. I zone her out, rushing over to help Ana out of the water.

"You good, baby?" I ask, with my hands on her shoulder.

"Yeah. I feel much better now. I got that out of my system."

"Lara," I call out. "Make sure she's out of my sight before the time I return."

I hear Zoya shouting my name as I guide Ana back into the house.

"Feisty one, aren't you?" I kiss the back of her head.

"Yep. Remember that. Don't piss me off, I will fight you."

"Got it, baby. I'd let you win."

She turns to face me, pulling the strings of her bra.

"I've been really naughty, haven't I?" She pouts.

"So fucking bad, pretty girl. So bad that I am going to have to punish you for this kind of behavior."

I tower over her, rubbing my fingers along her throat.

She sticks her bottom lip out, a smile teasing up the corner of her mouth. "Please, sir. Teach me a lesson."

Ripping the bra from her, I cup her breasts and pinch her nipples, making her yelp.

"Bedroom. Run."

CHAPTER 36

ANASTASIA

Song- WOOF, FKA Rayne

I DON'T NEED to turn around to know he's standing in the doorway, watching me. With a little grin, I carefully fold my new clothes from my latest shopping trip and place them in the drawer, leaving the small red bag on the dressing table.

"Anything you want to show me?" His deep voice sends electricity through me and my cheeks blush.

"Maybe? Maybe not. Depends."

His muscular arms wrap around my waist and I lean back into his chest.

"I missed you." He breathes, his warm exhale ghosting across my ear.

As I spin in his arms, I can feel the muscles in his chest beneath my hands, and I gaze up at him.

"Are you trying to sweet talk me into something, big man?"

He shakes his head, a sly smirk twisting his mouth as a low chuckle.

"I missed my wife. I missed her on my tongue, coming on my cock, I missed her making me laugh."

For fuck's sake. Now I'm horny.

"Well, if you must know, I bought a little something you just might enjoy."

His hands firmly grab my ass and he pulls me tightly against his body.

"Put it on for me, pretty girl." He leans in and runs his tongue along my jaw, I tip my head back and he carries on along the column of my throat.

"Mmm, keep doing that," I whisper.

"Are you going to be a good girl and do as I say?" He works his way between my breasts and back up to my neck and starts biting and sucking on my skin.

"Do I have to, right now? I don't want you to stop."

Running my hands down his tight black top, I can feel each defined ab as I make my way to his belt.

"You only get to play once I see it on you. Those are the rules."

Running my tongue along my teeth, I lean back and grab his face in my hands, tilting it upward to meet mine.

"New rules. You gotta earn the right to see me in my new pretty set." I bat my lashes at him for full effect.

His eyes scan over my face and a low grumble comes from him. Kinda like Hades does when anyone comes to the door.

The corners of my mouth twitch. I fight to contain my laughter at the sight of his completely straight face.

"Did you… just growl at me? Like a dog?" I ask, biting the inside of my mouth to stop myself from laughing.

It was hot, I have to admit.

"Go on," I urge, giving him a seductive smile. "Make that noise again, it was sexy."

"Anastasia," he warns, his eyes narrow.

God, his voice is dreamy.

"Hmm?" I reply sweetly, twirling my hair around my finger.

"Don't start."

Oh, I'm going to start. Pushing this man's buttons is my new favorite pastime. And the rewards, or punishments rather, are totally worth it.

"I like the growly, Mikhail. You could bark for me if you want to. Maybe that will inspire me to get all dressed up for you, so you can rip them back off me."

I step away, shrugging off my cardigan, the soft wool falling to the floor as I'm left in my sports bra and leggings.

"Go on. Bark for me, big man, and I'll give you everything you want."

A shadow falls over his eyes as our gazes meet. The change is subtle yet palpable.

Fuck. I'm playing with fire.

The way he runs his hand along the strong, defined line of his jaw, sends a jolt through me, and my heart starts to race.

And the way his tongue swipes across his bottom lip has me imagining all the places I want him to lick. Damn.

Just when I think he's about to grab me by my throat, he steps back.

"Strip and get on all fours. Crawl to me, iskorka. Let's see if that's enough to get me to play your games, shall we?"

He smirks, and I want to grab his handsome face and kiss the life out of him. But I really want him to bark for me. How far I can push this dynamic before he bends me over and spanks my ass raw?

Slowly, I begin to ease my bra off, feeling the cool air on my exposed skin, but I come to a halt.

"If I strip for you, Miki, you'll drop to your knees and beg for me. And that's before I even start crawling. I know you want me as bad as I want you. So be very careful what you wish for."

He walks towards me, each step echoing in the silence, then his fingers grip my chin.

"You're right. So fucking right," he whispers against my lips. As I go to press my mouth against his, he stands upright.

Maintaining eye contact, I remove the bra and casually toss it at him, a mischievous smile playing on my lips as I do. With ease, he catches it and clenches it tightly in his hand, his intense gaze locked on my chest.

"All good, big man?"

Instead of tugging down my leggings, I let my hands slip below the hem and into the soft fabric of my panties.

"Fuck," he mutters under his breath, his voice barely audible.

"Wow, the thought of you barking. It really has me wet," I tease.

As I slip one finger inside, he releases another low, guttural growl from his throat.

"Yep. That's doing it. Keep going, Miki."

He adjusts his pants making me smirk at him. I probably have sixty seconds left of teasing before he takes over.

I snatch the bag from beside me and pull out the black and gold lace bodysuit, holding it up in front of me.

"Crotchless," I tell him, raising an eyebrow. I want him to eat me out while I wear this for him.

"Put it on for me. Now."

The urgency in his tone sends a shiver down my spine and ignites a fire within me.

"Turn around, I'll tell you when you can see it." I pin him with a glare.

With a curt nod, he unbuckles his belt, the smooth leather sliding through his fingers as he removes it from his pants, and wraps it around his fist.

Oh, I'm in trouble.

CHAPTER 37

MIKHAIL

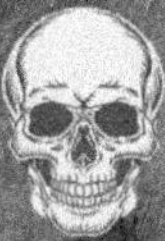

Song- Toxic, Omido, Rick Jansen

My cock is aching, straining against the zipper.

She knows how to dig her claws into my heart to get what she wants from me. And I let her. Mainly because I love teaching her a lesson, but also partly because I crave her sassy, bratty side.

It makes my cock throb.

I like it when she fights back and I fucking love it when she teases me, thinking it's a game she could ever win.

"You've got ten seconds, Anastasia."

I squeeze the leather of the belt wrapped around my hand for some sort of relief.

I want her on my mouth, on my cock, consuming me in every way she can. I want to be hers as much as she is mine.

"Three. Two."

"Ready!" I can hear how flustered she is.

I slowly turn around to face her, and I nearly pass out. My chest constricts, out of love and pure desire for my wife.

Her wedding ring shines under the bedroom lights and my

fingers itch to choke her. God, so hard for her little performance.

I scan the length of her body, the gold chains on the black lace, I think my dick might explode. The way her dark curls cascade over her shoulders, almost outlining her tiny frame.

Those hips. I want to grab them, dig my fingers in while I slam my cock deep inside her, holding her in place as she screams.

"Oh fuck." The words fall out of my mouth.

Killer. Black. Leather. Stilettos.

She wins. The word crotchless spins around my brain and I drop to my knees. Her dripping pussy is all I can think about, and I'm determined to do whatever it takes to have her on my face.

And I'm not even angry about it. Her in that outfit is enough to send any man on this planet wild and yet I am the one lucky enough to call her my wife.

Mine.

I, Mikhail Volkov. Head of the family. Ruthless killer. Am down on my knees, salivating over my wife to the point I am willing to bark for her so I can have her sweet pussy on my face.

"You are so beautiful, iskorka. So fucking beautiful."

My chest tightens, I'm squeezing the leather around my fist so tight while she does a full spin for me.

Her ass. The lace. I take a deep breath. My wife can have whatever she wants from me.

With a short sharp breath out, I let out a deep-throated growl, and then I fucking bark like a dog for her.

She clenches her thighs together and runs her finger along her lip. I've given her what she wanted, now she will be sufficiently punished. Just after I have my fill.

"Here. Now." I motion her with my finger.

As she takes a step forward I flip my palm at her.

"You want me to act like a mammal, so will you. On your knees and crawl to me."

Her eyebrows raise and she shakes her head slowly.

"If you don't get on all fours and crawl to me, I won't let you come for a week. I'll make your life a sexually frustrated hell, pretty girl."

I'm not joking either.

She drops to her knees and places her palms on the floor in front of her, giving me the perfect view of her full cleavage.

"Stunning, baby. Come here."

She tips her head down and I groan in frustration.

"Eyes. On. Me."

They have the power to seduce any man and bring him to his knees.

Her blue eyes lock with mine as she slowly crawls towards me, swaying her hips. By the time she is close enough to me, I'm wild for her.

I reach out and grab her, rolling her onto her back and pinning her down with her hands above her head.

"How wet did me barking get you, hmm?"

Sliding my fingers between the fabric of her crotchless bodysuit, I thrust two fingers in easily.

"Fucking soaked."

"Hmm," she moans in my ear.

The sound of her slickness fills the room. She wants to play games, now it's my turn. I withdraw my fingers and swipe them across her glossy lips.

"Open." I command and she does as I say.

Inserting one finger, she closes her mouth around it.

"Lick it clean."

Her tongue runs along my skin. I then bring the second up to my own lips and repeat the process, tasting her sweetness.

I stand, leaving her spread out on the floor. I hear a little frustrated groan come from her and smirk.

Freeing my aching cock from my boxers, I stroke it as she waits for her next instruction.

"On your knees, your sassy mouth needs to be punished."

And then her ass will be too.

She maneuvers gracefully to her knees as I tower over her. Her sparkling necklace shining under the dim lights.

She blinks up at me through her thick lashes. Damn, she's beautiful.

"Can you fuck my mouth now, please, sir?"

She licks her lips and I hold in my groan.

"You may. And remember what I want when I'm finished?" I tilt my head to get a better view of her.

"I remember, sir. I'll let you see."

I stroke her cheek and grip her chin.

"Good girl."

I let out a moan as her lips wrap around my cock, gripping onto the back of her head, I dive down her throat.

Fuck, the way she gags around me, yet opens up almost has me coming on the first stroke.

Taking a deep breath, I fix my eyes on her and find her looking up at me as I fuck her mouth.

Damn, the eye contact shoots electricity through me.

Even when the tears spill down her cheeks as I thrust my hips harder, holding her firmly in place.

Every time I hit the back of her mouth, she gags and my muscles tighten. Her nails dig into the flesh on my thighs, a welcome pain to distract me.

As my climax starts to burn through me, I relax for a

moment, letting her suck and lick the tip. It sends shivers right through me of pleasure.

"Your mouth is sinful, baby. So fucking good," I praise.

She moans around my cock, shit, I'm close.

With a few final thrusts, I yank her back by the hair and she sits down on her legs, opens her mouth wide and tips her head back.

"So fucking good for me, aren't you?"

Running my fingers through her hair, my other hand strokes my dick, I press the tip against her tongue and spill into her mouth, watching as the ribbons of white coat her.

Wiping the remains from the tip, she tilts her head down slightly, keeping her pretty lips open, offering me to look at the mess I've made.

"You can swallow now, baby. Every last drop for me."

She closes her mouth and I watch her neck bob as she swallows. Fuck, it has me hard again. Leaning down, I grip her by the throat and pull her to her feet and slam my lips over hers.

"I-I need to come, sir. It hurts. Please."

The desperation in her voice has my cock standing to full attention again.

"Did you think getting me to bark for you would go unpunished? Really?"

"Please, Miki." She pouts.

I bite back a grin. Absolutely no way is she getting away with that sass. But, I might let her think so for a minute.

I drop to my knees and place her foot on my shoulder, and she rests her hand on my other one to steady herself.

This is for my own pleasure.

I gently lick along her dripping pussy, her moans echoing through the room.

"So sweet," I mutter, swirling her clit with my tongue.

I keep going long enough for her leg to shake next to my head and before her climax can build any further, I remove her leg and stand, picking her up by the waist.

Taking a seat on the edge of the bed, I lay her over my lap facing down and run my palm over her perky ass.

She grips onto the bedsheets and tenses as my hand cracks down on her ass.

"Fuck!" she screams.

I rub my hand over the forming red welt as my cock throbs against her stomach.

"Such a perfect ass, Anastasia. I can't wait to claim that too."

"Please do."

My fingers dig into her hip.

"Fuck. You have no idea what you do to me, iskorka."

I'm always hard around her and my heart is constantly fluttering too.

Before she can reply, I slap her again, this time harder.

Her cries fill the room.

"Sir, please. Fuck me." She pants out.

I tut, slapping her lightly this time.

"Spanking isn't the end of your punishment, baby. You think I wouldn't notice you're dripping down your thighs?" I run my fingertips along her wetness. "This isn't even the warm up, pretty girl."

She wriggles in my hold and I tighten my grip around her waist. Leaning in, I run my tongue over her bodysuit, all the way up to her shoulders. Clasping my hand around the back of her neck, I spank her again. Her back arches as I press into her throat, hitting those pressure points.

"Miki, please, I need you so bad," she almost sobs.

And I *almost* give in.

As the door crashes open, I pull Ana into my arms.

"For fuck sake, Hades." I grit out as my panting dog sits in front of me.

"Out!" I bellow, pointing at the door.

His dark eyes fix on Ana in my arms and the fucker growls at me.

"I wouldn't dare." I keep my tone firm.

"Maybe, bark?" Ana whispers cheekily in my ear.

I stand and drop her down on the middle of the mattress as she descends into a fit of giggles.

"Hades, bed. Now!"

I usher him out of the room and close the door.

"What are you doing to that dog?" I mutter, shaking my head. He's becoming more of a princess with each day that passes.

"He's there to protect us, Ana. Remember that before you pamper him."

She sits up on her elbows and flicks her dark hair over her shoulder. Seductively, she spreads her legs, revealing her glistening pussy.

"You are naughty. And, you're seriously pushing it."

With all of the self restraint I can muster, because my god, I want to fuck the sass out of her so hard right now.

But, I am teaching her a valuable lesson.

So I grab her knees and close her legs, causing her to pout at me.

"I'll relieve you when your punishment is up, baby." I wink at her and head to the bathroom to grab some lotion for her ass.

When I return, she's already laying on her front with her hips in the air for me.

"Good girl," I whisper, sitting next to her on the bed and start to massage the lotion in.

I don't know who I am punishing more, me or her.

CHAPTER 38

ANASTASIA

MIKI HAS BEEN GONE for hours.

He texted me telling me not to wait up and he'd snuggle me in bed when he's home. But I napped earlier so I'm not tired.

I flick through the TV, but nothing really grabs my attention. I need to buy some books or something.

Pushing myself up from the couch, I head to the kitchen and brew a fresh batch of coffee. It will probably stay warm enough for Miki. Maybe I could run myself a bath? It's getting late. I should just listen to Miki and go to bed.

"Hades!" I call out.

He's been snuggled up next to me on the couch, but didn't follow me when I got up. Opening up the refrigerator, I grab his chicken and the creamer for my coffee.

His paws click against the floor and he plonks his butt down in front of me.

"Aww. Good boy."

I tear off some of the meat and hold it out.

"Wait." I point my finger.

"Okay. Go on."

He jumps forward and gently takes the food from between my fingers and munches it.

"Paw." I hold out my palm and his heavy front foot thumps into my hand.

"Good boy, Hades."

He takes the treats and I stroke the top of his head, scooting around him to finish making my drink.

Hades' deep bark makes me jump. I look over and he's pointing at the back door. Stepping behind him, I try to see what he's barking at.

There's a quiet knock.

Fuck.

I tiptoe over, ushering Hades with me. He makes me feel safe and protected when Miki isn't around.

Peering through the latch, I don't see anything. So I open it with the chain still on.

"Ana. It's me," a little voice says.

Galena.

I quickly help her inside.

"Are you okay, sweetie?" I crouch down to her level.

She curls her arms across her belly.

"Mommy is asleep and I kept hearing weird noises, so I got scared. I thought Mikhail might be home to help me," she sniffles.

I hold out my hands.

"Would you like a hug?"

She nods and shuffles into my embrace.

"Shall we play some games?"

Hades nudges his head against my side, nearly knocking me over.

That makes Galena giggle.

"He's being naughty, isn't he?"

"He's huge."

"He's a big softie. Aren't you Hades?"

I nuzzle my face against his and he licks my jaw.

"Ew!" I laugh, wiping the slobber away.

"He needs a collar. You know, in case he runs away." She tentatively reaches out to pat his shoulder.

"Oh. Do you want to see something cool?" I stand holding my hand out to her. Her tiny hand slides into mine and I lead her to my room with Hades following closely on our tail. I rummage through the wardrobe and find the little white bag, pulling out the sparkly blue collar I bought for Hades. I was waiting to surprise Miki.

Or, wind him up. He keeps reminding me how Hades is not a family dog but a security dog.

I'm not having it. I'm on a mission.

By the time I'm done he will be sleeping at the end of our bed.

"Do you think he will like it?" I show Galena the collar.

"Yes!" she squeals and claps.

"It's so pretty."

"Hades, here."

He trots over and sits in front of me.

I put the leather around his neck and secure the buckle.

"Beautiful boy."

I can't wait to see Miki's face.

"Okay. So TV and candy or a game of hide and seek?"

It's the first thing I can think of. Miki's house isn't exactly overflowing with games for kids.

"Hide and seek!" She jumps up and down with excitement.

"You go hide first. I'll count. I'll give you one minute."

Turning to face the wall, I cover my eyes with my hands.

"One, two, three…"

I hear her run off, still giggling to herself. I turn around and Hades is sitting where I left him.

I keep counting in my head until I get to thirty and call it out and then continue to sixty.

"Ready or not, here I come."

I make my way out of the room, Hades close behind. Opening up the spare bedroom, I stay silent waiting to hear her.

Nope.

I look through all the bedrooms. Hmm.

Maybe downstairs.

With a light jog, I head to the kitchen, opening up the bigger cupboards she might fit in.

I jump backwards as the front door opens.

"Jesus."

I look up and Miki stalks towards me.

He closes the distance quickly. As he's just about to take his mask off, Galena comes bounding out from behind the couch.

"Miki!" She crashes into his leg.

"Hey, little sis." He picks her up into his arms, then leans over pressing a kiss on my cheek through his mask.

"Hey, beautiful," he whispers in my ear and I blush.

"What are you doing here?" he asks galena.

"Mommy is sleeping and I was scared."

Miki frowns looking at me.

"Scared of?"

"Don't know. Just a few bangs."

"I'll check it out, then we can get you back to sleep. Sound like a plan?"

She nods and he places her down onto his feet.

"Hades!" Miki calls out and he trots to his master's feet.

"Ana. Would you care to explain to me why my guard dog is sparkling?"

Hades tilts his head and I cover my mouth to stop laughing.

"He looks cute. Leave him alone."

"Cute? He isn't meant to be cute! I can't go out with a dog with a sparkly collar on him."

I roll my eyes and he glares at me.

"galena, say goodnight to Ana."

She gives me a bright smile. "Night, night."

"Sweet dreams." I blow her a kiss as Mikhail leads her out of the back door.

Hades pads over and sits on my feet, leaning his head against my legs.

"We are in trouble," I whisper, softly stroking his head.

I don't take the collar off, it's far too amusing watching Miki tick.

Pouring him a cup of coffee, I set it on the kitchen island and take a sip of my own. As soon as he returns, he tears off his mask, tossing it down on the counter.

"Now I'll deal with you, pretty girl."

I place my mug down and stand up straight as he approaches me, my heart picking up a beat with each of his steps.

"Oh yeah? Want me to help with that?"

I bend over the counter and wiggle my ass at him. I yet out a yelp as his palm cracks down on my behind, the force sending me forward.

"Spanking doesn't work on you, that was just for me." His hand smacks again on the other side.

I push my hair away from my face as he rubs his palms over my ass.

Hades erupts into a fit of aggressive sounding barks. Mikhail moves back.

"Stop." Mikhail's voice is deep and stern.

I turn around as Hades growls at Mikhail and I frown, watching their standoff. No, this isn't like my big softie. So, I step in front of Mikhail.

"Hades, sit." I point my finger at him.

Immediately he does as I say.

"Good boy." I praise him, spinning to face a very confused looking Miki.

"How in the fuck? What have you done to my dog?"

I shrug, kind of pleased with myself.

"I guess he prefers me now."

Mikhail looks past me, glaring at Hades. "Traitor."

I hit his chest. "Be nice. He's just protecting me."

He snakes his arms around my waist and holds me tight.

"Fine. I can't be mad at him for protecting what is most important to me."

"Aww." I reach up and stroke the rough skin of his jaw.

"You are both my big softies." I grab his cheeks and pull him down to kiss me.

It feels good knowing that I'm not alone in this world, I have not one, but two fierce protectors. And I'd do anything for both of my boys too.

"We best get some sleep, the big ball tomorrow. I have to look refreshed." I tap his chest and snatch his hand.

"Refreshed or freshly fucked?" Miki asks, following behind me.

"You tell me."

His deep menacing chuckle makes my pussy pulse.

"You are very much still being punished, pretty girl. But, I suppose we can put that sassy mouth of yours to use."

CHAPTER 39

MIKHAIL

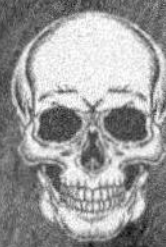

I use my shoulder to push open Vox's door and step into complete chaos. I might have to blow this place up for the trouble it keeps causing me.

A simple collection for protection, yet countless times has ended in bar fights.

The Reapers, since Brody and his father's death, have been a tiny operation, they never rebuilt. They aren't a threat.

But fuck me, the ones that remain like to make a scene. And it's about time I taught them a lesson.

I watch from the sidelines as Jax beats a man's head on the bar and Alexei strangles another with his thighs on the ground.

Blood flies from Niki's mouth onto the floor as he approaches and claps me on the shoulder.

"Why this time?" I ask.

Nikolai shrugs. "I'm not entirely sure. I thought the Reaper shit was done with."

I scratch my mask.

"Not unless they're still in contact with Father."

I scan the room. They look pretty useless. Not any help to Ivan.

Jax tosses the guy on the floor, and I call him over.

"What happened?"

He rubs his hand across his forehead.

"Fuck knows. Bill came out with a wad of cash. As I went to grab it, that asshole I just beat down tried to snatch it. Then more of them appeared."

So they knew it was collection day. It was calculated.

"Take Bill and shove him in Niki's car. Let's see what he knows. We have to take care of any leads to Ivan."

They both nod and head over to the bar.

"Alexei, with me."

He looks at me with a wicked grin and rolls himself off his victim then jumps to his feet.

"Can I drive?" Alexei asks as we walk out to my Corvette.

"Not a chance in hell." I swing the keys around my finger as we approach my matte black beauty.

"No fun." He pouts and I slap him on the back of the head.

"You have enough money. Go buy your own."

"Nah. The bike keeps me entertained. Don't need another death trap."

Alexei is unusually quiet as I drive to the warehouse, his leg bouncing up and down.

"You think Ivan is going to come back?"

"Here? No. I think we are going to have to take the fight to him. He knows it's too risky to step foot on my territory."

He nods, deep in thought. "When?"

"When, what, Alexei?" I grip the steering wheel tighter.

"When can we take him out? I know Lara is worried he's

going to come back for her. I just want to kill him so she can stop worrying."

I sigh. I've just gotten back from Russia. We aren't ready. Especially now that I have Galena and Ana to protect.

"Enzo is still investigating the information on that drive. It might have answers we need. Or the leverage to get us backing in Russia. We have to do this right. I've got the scars to prove what happens when it goes wrong going up against him."

Ivan will keep doing shit like this to show he can get to us. It's nothing we can't deal with while we wait.

"For now, we protect what's ours, understand, Alexei? And when the time comes, we end that fucker, okay?"

I know how he feels. I won't live my life constantly worried about my father coming after her.

This has to stop.

"Can we throw a party once he's dead? You know, like when royalty dies?"

I chuckle.

"No clowns this time."

As we pull up to the warehouse, Niki and Jax are dragging Bill into the building. I slide out the single-edge razor blade from my inside jacket and hold it between my thumb and finger.

"Don't bother taking him inside. I don't have time to drag this out." I tell them, grabbing the older man by the throat and pinning him against the wall.

"Simple yes or no. Are you working with Ivan Volkov?"

The fear in his eyes amuses me. I'm sure he's just realized I am more of a threat to him than Ivan ever was.

I'm not one that comes out to play often. I let my men deal with it for me, except when I do decide to appear, I seem to put the fear of god in everyone.

"N-no." His voice shakes.

Taking a page out of Ana's book, I stare into his eyes. He rapidly blinks, his green eyes becoming less clear as his pupils dilate.

"You're lying. Let me rephrase that question. Are those Reapers working with Ivan?"

He tries to swallow against my palm. I squeeze tighter, making his eyes bulge.

"Maybe," he croaks out.

I sigh, shaking my head.

"Okay, how about a deal? You tell me the truth. If you are working with Ivan but admit your treachery, I might think about keeping you alive. You lie to me one more time, however, I will find your wife, slit her throat—" I hold up the razor in front of his face. "—and make you watch."

I release my grip, and he sags against the brick wall.

His hands are shaking by his side as his skin pales an awful gray.

"Fine. Yes. Ivan orchestrated the robbery."

I run my hands through my curls.

"Anything else to tell me? Directly with you or with the Reapers?"

He avoids eye contact.

"With me. I got the Reapers in to help me. He threatened my family, Mikhail."

I let out a menacing laugh.

"And you think I won't follow through with my threats?" I hold the blade against his throat and press under his chin.

"It's funny. People often think Ivan is worse than me, but they don't know me. You see, there is a reason I stay hidden. I lock this evil away from the world. The monster Ivan himself created. I am your worst nightmare, Bill. Not Ivan."

"P-please don't hurt my wife." His bottom lip trembles when I lean in.

"See, that is where me and my piece of shit father are different. I respect women. He does not."

A quick slice across his neck, and warm blood gushes over my hand.

I release him and throw him to the ground as he suffocates to death on his own fluids.

"Niki, you got a towel or something in the trunk?"

He shakes his head and laughs.

"Umm, I got something in there." He scratches the back of his neck as I head towards his black Hellcat.

"Careful!" Nikolai shouts as I open up the back. I leap back as a bloodied Reaper in a leather vest hurls himself at me.

Throwing my hand up, I launch my fist straight at his nose, hearing the crack against my knuckles, and he falls to the floor.

"What in the fuck, Nikolai?" I hiss at him, shaking out my fist. "If I'd have known, I'd have my brass knuckles on."

"Good punch though, Miki. You'll be in the ring in no time," Jax chuckles as he grabs Bill by the feet and starts to drag him inside the warehouse.

"Towel's on the back seat, Mik," Nikolai grunts, bending down and picking up the unconscious Reaper from my feet.

"Have fun. I'm going home," I tell them, wiping off my bloodied hands.

CHAPTER 40

ANASTASIA

CATCHING eyes with Mikhail in the mirror as he enters the room I smile.

His gaze drags up from my heels and he smirks, licking his lips.

"Absolutely fucking gorgeous, Ana," he mutters as he steps behind me.

"Do you think my dress is too short?" I tug at the hem, feeling self conscious. I fell in love with this red sparkly outfit at the store. It hugs my figure perfectly, covered in delicate sequins. I even got lipstick and heels to match. But, now that I have it all on, it kinda feels cheap. Like it might draw too much attention to me. I want to make my husband wild for me. I know how much he loves my ass. But, it's only for him to see.

"If I had it my way, we wouldn't be going, and I'd fuck you in that dress. It's beautiful."

He runs his hands over my ass cheeks and squeezes, pressing me against him. I blush feeling how hard he is.

"See what you do to me?" His voice is deep and filled with hunger.

I'm biting my lip, eager for him to just take me to bed.

"Yeah. I just don't want that happening to other guys."

The amount of creeps that think it's okay to stare or try to touch me when I'd go out with my friends, it's enough to make me want to wear a dress that goes down to my ankles.

"That kind of thing worries you?" He quizzes.

I look up at him. The slight purse of his lips spoke volumes.

"Yeah. I'm a woman. I think every single one of us has had to deal with unwanted attention from a guy. It's just part of life."

"Trust me, no one in that room who values their life will even think about looking at your ass, let alone touching it."

He nuzzles my cheek, the soft touch sending shivers down my spine and causing my eyes to flutter closed.

"I don't want you getting in trouble because of my butt, Miki."

"That ass is mine. I'll protect it at all costs, pretty girl. You wear the dress. You look gorgeous in it and it makes you smile. I'll stand right beside you, ready to kill any mother-fucker that makes you feel uncomfortable. Deal?"

I laugh, but his face is stern.

"You haven't got to kill anyone, Miki."

With a dramatic roll of his eyes and a frustrated grunt, he let his annoyance show.

"Fine. Severely disfigure is the best I can negotiate on this one."

I run my palms up his chest, wishing I could rip his shirt open and lick his tattooed abs.

"I'll get changed."

Last thing I need is a bloodbath.

As I go to pull away, his arms tighten around me.

"If it makes you more comfortable, change. But listen to

me, I think you look incredible. Your ass is completely covered. You fell in love with that dress and it makes you smile. Fuck the rest of the world. I'll deal with them. Just do whatever makes you happy."

Running the back of my hands along the raised, puckered scars on his cheeks, I feel the roughness of his skin as he leans into my touch. I hardly notice them anymore. His strikingly handsome face, with his chiseled jaw and charming smile, is so captivating it renders his flaws insignificant. They are part of him and I love all of him.

"That is the cutest thing anyone has ever said to me. I'm lucky I have you, big man. You are one of the good ones."

He chuckles, grabbing my hand and placing a kiss on the front.

"Cute for you and only you, sweetheart."

My fingers tighten on the cool, crisp lapels of his black suit jacket as I shove him backward. He must have been surprised as he stumbles back, his back hitting the wall. Pulling on his tie, I yank his lips down to mine and snake my arms around his neck, crashing my mouth onto his.

"Mine, Mikhail. Always mine."

That niggling doubt that Zoya keeps clawing at inside me turns me into a monster sometimes. I love this man and I will do anything to keep him by my side. I know I am his woman. His wife. But, sometimes it is just nice to be claimed.

"Oh, iskorka, you will forever be mine and I am yours until I die, baby."

CHAPTER 41

MIKHAIL

Song- Dangerous, Royal Deluxe

I PULL out onto the freeway, the engine roaring as I slam my foot on the accelerator. Her in that dress has me so sexually frustrated I can't concentrate on anything other than bending her over in it.

It's been two days since I started her punishment. Spooning her in bed has been torture. I'm constantly hard.

The next best thing is slamming the corvette around to release some adrenaline. I at least get some blood flow to my brain before the gala rather than it all being in my dick.

"Hey, Miki."

As I take a left, my hand rests on her thigh, gently stroking.

"Yes, pretty girl?"

"Have you ever had a blowjob while you've been driving?"

I choke on a cough, my dick throbbing against my suit pants.

"Fuck. No, I haven't, actually."

I want her pussy, not her mouth right now.

I look at the sat nav on the screen. Ten minutes ETA.

"How bad do you need to be fucked, baby? Do you think you've been good enough to end your punishment?"

I swear she moans under her breath. My fingers dig deeper into her thighs.

"So bad, Miki. I can't think straight, I just want you. I've got it bad for you, sir. And I've been really good, haven't I?"

A rumble erupts from my chest. She hasn't really behaved. She's teased me to no end. Pushing my buttons, but I wouldn't have her any other way.

"I'm not wearing panties," she whispers and I nearly swerve the car.

I come to a halt at the stoplights, push back my seat to give me room, but enough to still hit the pedals, then unbuckle my belt, pulling my cock out.

I sneak a look at her flushed face and her eyes light up.

As she goes to lean over, I stop her.

"No. A blow job isn't going to fix this. You're going to be a good girl for me. Straddle my lap and ride me while I drive."

As the lights turn green, I slowly pull away, much to the displeasure of my beast of a car, it's pushing me to go quicker.

"You've got eight minutes to get me off, baby. I want you walking in there with my cum dripping down your thighs under that tight little dress."

"Jesus, Miki."

"Fuck your voice, Ana, it makes me hard just listening to you. On my lap and ride my dick."

It's not going to take me long, I'm desperate for her.

With one hand on the wheel, I help her get into position.

With my hand on the back of her head, I nestle her face against my neck so I can still see the road.

"You're going to have to guide me in," I whisper. My words hardly come out, I'm so turned on.

I feel her soft, glossy lips press against my throat as her dainty hand guides the tip of my dick against her hot pussy.

"Sit on me. All the way down."

Her teeth sink into my throat as she lets herself drop, little moans escape her as she does.

"Fuck, Miki," she hisses.

I might have to pull over. Or explode in her. Pressing the accelerator, I grip the wheel so hard my knuckles turn white.

When she rolls her hips against me, sucking and biting on my neck, I grab her ass and up the tempo.

"More, baby. I need more. Be a good girl and fuck me properly. Make me fill you up like you deserve to be."

I slap her ass as she grinds against me, taking all of me inside her.

Keeping my eyes on the road is a challenge, but I do. I'm letting her have her fun with me.

"Such a good fucking girl, aren't you?" I slap her hip again.

"For you, always," she pants.

Her walls strangle my dick and my thighs tense.

"I'm so close, iskorka. So fucking close. God, you're perfect."

Her moans grow louder in my ear and it nearly tips me over the edge.

Fuck it.

Instead of taking the left to the venue, I swing right, holding her in place by her waist.

It seems quiet enough. It's dark and my windows are blacked.

I keep the engine running as I pull to the side of the road.

I barely flip it to park before I grab her face and crash my lips over hers.

Gripping on to her hips, I hold her in place and thrust mine up, relentlessly pounding into her. I muffle her moans with my mouth.

"Come for me, pretty girl. Come all over my dick like a good girl."

Her cries erupt through the car, and I roar out her name until my lungs burn, filling her to the brim with my come.

I pull her flushed face back to look at her and I smile. Fuck, she's perfect.

"Punishment is officially over. I can fuck you whenever now." I pull her bottom lip back with my thumb.

"Good. You have a lot of making up to do." She grins.

"That isn't how this works." I pin her with a stare.

"Miki, we aren't meant to follow anyone's rules. We make our own. We are exploring, right? What makes us both happiest?"

I rest my forehead against hers.

"You. Iskorka. Anything you do makes me happy."

And I mean it. Whether she's being bratty and sassy, pushing every damn button of mine she can find, or when she submits and lets me ruin her.

Anything she does is everything I need in life.

CHAPTER 42

ANASTASIA

Song- Me and the Devil, Soap&Skin

"Wow." My mouth falls open as we enter the grand hallway. It's like something you'd read about in a fairytale.

Huge chandeliers, with servers in bow ties holding champagne on a tray. Fresh red roses perfectly arranged in vases, and even a string quartet. Of course.

"Enzo knows how to throw a very elaborate event."

Miki tugs at his bow tie, clearly uncomfortable.

"You look sexy." I elbow him in the side and he looks down, arching his brow with a smirk.

"Don't tempt me. I'll lock us in the nearest room and have my wicked way with you."

Goosebumps erupt over my arms. I want that.

"I bet there is a huge library in here, there has to be."

This place has that old world sense about it. I bet it has one of them rolling ladders and some dusty books.

"We can go hunt it down if you want?" He nods towards the staircase.

"We can at least show our face in there first."

Miki told me he has lots of friends coming to Vegas for this. I want to see this part of his life and he made it clear he wants to show me off as his wife.

He swipes us up two flutes of champagne and leads us to the ballroom.

I recognize his family huddled in a corner laughing with each other. Alexei's cackle carries over the crowd. I half expect him to be swinging from a chandelier by the end of the night.

Instead of heading to them, Mikhail beelines for another group of men. As soon as we approach them they stop talking.

Jesus. They're scary.

The tall one at the back is covered in tattoos like Miki. He's a beast. The blond one next to him is pretty similar, but with a short cut like maybe he's military.

The guy in the front, with the navy suit and dark hair grins and extends his hand to Mikhail, who firmly shakes it.

"Mr. Falcone. Good to see you again." Miki greets him.

"Same goes to you, Mr. Volkov." He looks at me and extends his hand. "You must be Anastasia." His deep Italian accent is kinda nice to listen to.

"I am." I accept his firm handshake.

"These are my guys. The muscle, Mr. Keller Russo. This one here, Grayson Ward. And my right hand man, Mr. Luca Russo."

I nod my head. They all seem nice. Not as rowdy as Mikhail's group. But I bet just as deadly.

"Lovely to meet you all."

Mikhail wraps his arm around my shoulder.

"We can catch up later over a few vodkas." He looks to Luca. "Or Brandy? Is that still your poison of choice?"

"Can't beat it." Luca holds up his glass.

Jax appears from beside us and clasps Keller on the shoulder.

"You ready for a fight?"

I frown. What is he talking about?

Frankie clearly notices the confusion on my face and chuckles.

"Keller is the world heavyweight champion. Him and Grayson here trained up Jax."

"Oh, cool." I can't imagine what they'd all look like in the ring.

"So Keller is fighting Jax?" Mikhail asks, looking at Jax who excitedly nods.

"Yep. Charity match at the start of next year, we're donating to a Men's Mental Health Charity. I'll take it off as vacation, don't worry boss."

The men erupt into laughter.

"I expect our invite." Mikhail tells him.

"You can get in the ring if you want, Miki vs Grayson?" Jax sniggers.

Grayson grins. "I'll give you a run for your money, Mikhail."

Miki huffs beside me. "Yeah, I'd like to see it."

Jax claps his hands together. "This could work you know. Luca you can fight Alexei."

Luca quickly shakes his head and laughs. "Only if you take any weapons away from him. He fights dirty."

"Who is taking on Nikolai?"

The men all turn to Frankie.

"I'll fight anyone. I'm sure I can give the big guy a run for his money."

As if on cue, Nikolai slaps Mikhail on the shoulder.

"I heard my name and 'fight' in a sentence. Who's head am I ripping off?"

Frankie's eyes go wide.

"Jax and Keller's charity boxing match next year. I signed us all up."

Nikolai gives him a sly grin.

"Nice." He cracks his knuckles for full effect.

Nikolai and Jax keep the guys chatting and Miki leans down, stroking my hair away from my shoulder.

"Shall we go to the bar? Then maybe search for that library you want to see?" he whispers in my ear and my body heats up.

"Sounds good."

He presses a kiss to the side of my head.

"We will be back, tell Enzo I'll find him later."

He leads us away. I'm looking forward to getting Miki to read to me. I wonder if they have any spicy books up there?

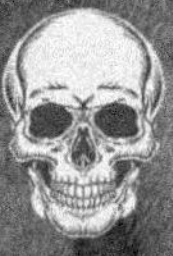

Song- Glass Houses, Bring Me The Horizon

"Who is that guy over there?" Ana nudges my side. I follow her line of vision and squint.

And then it hits me when I see his neck tat. The fucking clover just behind his ear.

Declan Quinn.

The man who, much like myself, hides in the shadows.

But in a room, he certainly holds a persona. Covered in tattoos, a long tailored black jacket to show the bulging muscles and a fist full of rings, finished off with a flat cap. He looks every bit the unhinged Irish Mafia boss.

He's also a very good contact to have in your pocket.

The best part, he also runs a damn chocolate factory. One very much to Enzo's tastes so I have heard, Enzo was very busy helping Declan turn Decadence into not only arguably the best money laundering scheme around, but the most erotic sex club I've ever heard of.

He's basically a kinky 21st century Willy Wonka, but instead of eating chocolate all day, the man indulges pussy.

The shit that goes down in that place even makes my eyebrow raise.

I squeeze Ana's hand. As amazing as his attributes are, he isn't someone I want near my wife.

Frankie stops me in my tracks before I get to the bar. Ana spins around and smiles sweetly at us both. God she's beautiful.

"I'm just going to grab our drinks, Lara is at the bar, I'll stay with her until you're done," she whispers in my ear.

"Sorry, Frankie, give me a second."

He nods to me, pulling Zara tightly against his side. I did wonder where she was, Frankie never leaves her.

I glance up at Lara and Alexei laughing at the bar and smile under my mask. I know they'll protect my girl. She's safe here as far as I can tell, Enzo has the place covered.

Not that I'll take my damn eyes off her. Not after her confession about feeling uncomfortable around men earlier.

"Okay, baby. I'll only be here. I'll be over in a few minutes."

She presses her lips to my cheek, I wish my mask was off so I could feel her lips properly.

As she saunters off to the bar, I grind my teeth and watch the crowd's eyes follow my wife's ass around the room.

"You good, Mikhail?" Frankie's deep Italian voice drags me out of my burning inferno.

"Fine," I huff, clenching my fists by my side.

"So what do you think of the plans for the docks I sent you?"

"I'll send Niki and Jax down to you to scope it out. I can't turn down more weapons can I?"

I don't take my eyes off Ana as she approaches the bar. Lara wraps her arms around her and they're chatting while Alexei orders up the drinks dramatically.

"You really like that girl, don't you?" Frankie says.

"Love." I correct him.

He chuckles. "When I heard you were married I assumed it was for a deal, not love."

I rub my jaw. "It's complicated."

"True love always seems to be," Zara chimes in. I'm still not sure how I feel about her being the NYC commissioner now. But, she's Frankie's wife, it works for business too.

Alexei whispers something to Lara and she turns to face him while Ana rests her elbow on the bar as her drink is slid across to her.

A tall guy with blond curly hair nudges closer to her.

"He one of yours?" I nod in the direction of the guy.

"No. Nothing to do with us," Frankie replies.

The unknown man leans back and looks down at Ana's ass.

I can feel the rage boil within me.

I step forward just as his hand snakes around her back, right above her ass.

She jumps away from his touch and bashes into Lara. Before Alexei can intervene, I grab my blade from my inside pocket and flip it open.

I grab him by the back of the neck and slam his head into the bar. Turning him to face me, my fingers grip his throat. His green eyes fill with fear, but that only fuels me further.

"Did my wife give you consent to touch her?" I spit out.

He shakes his head, beads of sweat pooling on his forehead.

Alexei cackles behind me. Nikolai will no doubt be there when I turn around.

"Well? Asshole?"

"N-no. I didn't realize she was your wife."

I nod slowly, pulling him upright. He's a few inches shorter than me and nowhere near my build.

"Oh, so if you knew she was my wife, you wouldn't have touched her?"

"Never. I'm sorry."

Pathetic.

"But, if she wasn't my wife, you wouldn't give a fuck if she consented to you grabbing her like that? Like a piece of fucking meat?"

"Uh," he stammers.

"Did your mother not teach you manners? Like when it's acceptable to touch a woman?"

Blood trickles from his nose and he shakes his head.

I turn to Ana who seems to be fascinated by this, a little grin on her lips.

"You good, iskorka?"

She nods. "I'm better now, big man."

I turn my attention back to this piece of shit.

"Apologize." I tighten my grip around his neck just before I let go and his back crashes into the bar.

"I'm really sorry," He says, looking at me.

I roll my eyes. "Not to me. To Anastasia."

The color drains from his face as he turns to her. She doesn't look amused.

"I'm very sorry. It won't happen again."

She scoffs. "Yeah right. Men like you can't help yourselves. Fucking pigs. Probably why you're so desperate. No girl in their right mind wants a guy like you."

I nod and smile at her, she'll know I approve, she reads my eyes when the mask is on.

"Can I go now?" he asks, rubbing at the red marks on his neck.

"No." I pause, wiping the blade over my palm.

"Now I teach you a lesson on touching and consent." I snatch his right hand, the one that touched my wife, and press it on the bar.

"See now, you will have a reminder. A scar. That will haunt you for the rest of your life and remind you not to touch without asking."

I know the pain of the memory of a scar. This might make him think twice.

Before he can reply I stab him through the middle of the hand, hard enough the tip of the blade goes through to the wood of the bar.

He screams out in pain.

I lean in as the tears stream down his face.

"You're lucky I didn't cut both your fucking hands off."

I turn my attention to Ana, and she slides her fingers through mine. I pull her tight against me and rest my head on the top of hers, inhaling her sweet scent.

"I told you, I shouldn't have worn the dress." She hiccups against my chest.

I squeeze her tighter. I'll make sure there isn't a room in this world where my wife can't walk in and feel safe.

I'll scorch this earth of men like that asshole, not just for her but for all women.

"At least I didn't kill him. I wanted to."

She pushes back and looks up at me.

"I'm proud of you. I think you got the message across."

My chest swells and I guide the back of my hand gently over her cheek.

"I love you, pretty girl. No one touches my wife."

She rises onto her tiptoes and presses her lips on mine through the fabric.

"Do I get to stab anyone that touches you too?" she asks playfully.

Zara giggles behind us. I assume she's probably a woman who has done something like that for Frankie.

"Yes, baby. I'll even hand you the damn knife."

"Can I start with Zoya the next time she puts her disgusting hands on your shoulder?"

I can't help but laugh at her comment.

My feisty girl.

I need to be careful she doesn't. Zoya is really pushing it with us both. She barely survived the drowning episode.

"I'll take care of it, I promise." I tell her.

"Good. Because I'm sick to death of her."

I lean in and rub my hands down her back and rest them on her ass.

"Can you still feel my come dripping out of you?" I whisper against her ear, feeling the heat of her blushing radiating off her.

"Yes. I wish I wore panties."

I groan, remembering the fact her perfect pussy is exposed.

"You are my wife. The woman with my DNA dripping out of her in a room full of hundreds of my associates. You own my heart, pretty girl. You always will. You have nothing to ever worry about."

She nods with a small smile.

I know there are niggling doubts, mainly from Zoya's spiteful words.

Looks like I'll just have to keep proving myself to her, I'll do that for the rest of my life.

She is it for me.

I DIDN'T EXPECT that seeing Mikhail pound that man's face against the bar would turn me on so much.

It makes me want to feel him inside me again. He's been holding back for so long, torturing me, that I just want to catch up.

"Hey, big man?" I let my fingers work under the seam of his shirt. "Weren't you going to show me where the library is?" Batting my eyelashes, I hope he gets the hint.

His jaw clenches beneath his mask making the little muscle at his temple pop as he scans the room.

"What's the matter?" I try to see what he's looking at, but his gaze keeps shifting.

"We're here to try and draw someone out, but no one has made a move yet. It's starting to make me nervous." His thumb rubs a small circle in the small of my back.

I tilt my head and stare up at him. "Wait, you're all twitchy because nothing's happening? The people playing those instruments up on stage will be very disappointed to hear that." I gesture at the cello nearest us. "Maybe we really should go for a walk?" I rise onto my tiptoes so I'm closer. "I think maybe you still have something left in the tank making you antsy."

When his eyes finally land on me, I know I'm getting through to him.

He snugs me tighter so I can feel the bulge in his pants. "You're right, let's go take a look around."

"Enzo, I'm taking Ana to the library." Mikhail announces as we walk past.

Enzo looks up from his laptop that's hiding behind the bar. "Sounds good, just stay away from my office. It's armed to catch anyone if they're feeling particularly nosey." He gives Mikhail a wink before dropping his gaze back down to his screen.

"Mikhail?" I whisper as we push through the crowd.

"Yes, my love?" His chest vibrates.

"What did Enzo mean by that?" We finally get away from the crowd and step into the cool hall.

He points to a door on the left a good distance from the library.

It has a sign that says *Employees Only* in big red letters.

His voice drops. "It's a dummy office. This whole event is designed to try and pull Tatiana and Ivan out. If anyone is stupid enough to want to go in there, all hell will break loose."

My mouth drops into an "O".

His thumb grips my chin. "You make it too easy to want to shove my cock in there when you make that face."

"How about we find a couple of nice…thick—" I let my fingers trace down his muscular stomach to his belt. "—books to use for me to kneel on?"

He practically carries me through the ornate double doors, whisking me through the aisles of the dusty tomes until we reach a wall of stout encyclopedias along the back wall.

Pulling one of the heavy leather-bound editions down, he lets it drop with a thud.

"Is that tall enough?" He asks, unzipping his pants and freeing his cock for measurement.

"Maybe one more." I want to get a good angle, like when I'm kneeling on the bed.

He grabs another, lining it up to fall on the first.

But when it lands, the boom seems to echo through the entire library, and the ground waves beneath our feet.

"Mikhail!" I scream, falling against him.

Billows of smoke and dust roll between the stacks to choke us. He might have a mask, but the air makes my nose burn.

Burying my face against his jacket, he pushes his silk handkerchief against my cheek.

"Hold this, stay low." He grabs my wrist and weaves past the rows of books, hugging the wall when we start to hear voices yelling in the hall.

"Mikhail? Anastasia? Are you okay?" Enzo yells through the haze.

"Yes! What happened?" Mikhail calls out. He pulls me with him to the exit.

Rubble litters the corridor, chunks of wood and concrete scatter over the fine marble.

When Enzo appears out of the cloud, a broad grin covers his face. "I caught one of the fuckers."

CHAPTER 45

MIKHAIL

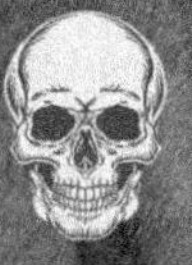

A MASS of rapid footfalls grow closer from the far end.

Frankie leads his men, but they all fall to a halt a few feet away.

"Is everything okay?" He asks, looking worriedly between Enzo and I.

Enzo nods, his smile not breaking from his cheeks. "Yep, my trap worked."

The color returns to Frankie's cheeks. "I fucking hate explosions."

"Same. Are your guys good?" Keller asks from behind him.

"I think so. we were the only ones on this end when it went off." I keep Ana pinned to my side and glance around.

Jax, Nikolai, and Alexei all look mildly amused, but unharmed.

"We're going to call it a night." Frankie holds out his arm for Zara to join him, and runs his palm over his face. "I've had my fill of bombs." He gives a lopsided grin, but I can tell he's uncomfortable.

I've heard the rumors of his past, I can't say as I blame him.

"We're fine, thanks for coming." I give him a quick wave, then turn to Enzo. "So, who's in there? Is it one of Tatiana's men, or Ivan's?" My hands itch to get a hold of them.

Both factions have caused us a hell of a lot of grief.

Enzo shrugs. "There's an access through the back. My camera was blown when the explosives went off. I guess Romeo got a little excited with the charges." He raises his eyebrows and shakes his head at his assistant.

"Sorry. I wanted to make sure the door sealed." Romeo holds up his hands with a smirk on his face. His dark hair is peppered with white flecks of concrete and plaster.

We all look like we've been in a snowstorm.

"Jax, will you take Ana back to the ballroom? We're going to have a little talk with whoever was in there." I hold Ana by the shoulders and press my mask to her forehead. "Are you okay to go?"

Her big blue eyes widen over the handkerchief, but she nods and moves to her brother.

"Nikolai, Alexei, come with me." I motion them, then turn to follow Enzo.

Enzo hits a panel in the wall nearby and an invisible entrance appears.

We push through the narrow tunnel that spills into the back of the dummy office.

More papers and debris litters the floor, but not nearly as much rubble.

I don't recognize the man who's digging into the pile where the door used to be.

He turns quickly, throwing his palms into the air. "I didn't mean to, I was looking for the bathroom."

"I find that hard to believe, unless you really can't read."

Enzo moves lithely to the side, letting the three of us bigger guys pass him. "There was a clear picture of a toilet on the two doors down the hall, yet you chose to come in here."

Alexei and Nikolai each grab an arm of the thin man.

"Who are you?" I grunt, standing in front of the intruder.

"I'm no one. Please, I'd like to leave now." His dark eyes dart between Nikolai and Alexei. "I didn't do anything, honest."

"What is your name?" I ask again, more forcefully. "Cooperate, and I'll probably let you go."

"Wait, what do you mean by 'probably'?" he asks, nervously licking his lips.

"I'm 'probably' going to rip you limb from limb for not answering my fucking question," I growl. Reaching forward, I grip his throat and stare into his eyes.

The fear fades until he locks mine with a hard glare.

"That's what I thought. You'll be lucky to survive this. Who sent you?" I jut my chin to Nikolai, the signal to begin.

Niki and Alexei each bend the arms at the elbows and pull, stretching the lean man until I hear the pop of a dislocating shoulder.

He grunts, but doesn't scream.

Impressive.

"Tell me before I cut your arm off." My favorite blade always sits at the small of my back, but now it appears in my hand, taunting him at his sleeve. "Was it Tatiana or Ivan?"

His jaw clenches, but his eyes narrow. "You really don't know who you're playing with, do you?"

"Why don't you tell me?"

"There's bigger players than them, and you're a fool if you think I'm lying," he sneers. "One day you'll learn the name Kovalyov."

I look towards Enzo. "Who is he talking about?"

Enzo's mouth twists. "I'm not sure, but I have heard the name. It's only come up in a few documents, and all backdoor shit." He shrugs. "I don't know."

I turn back to the man who's almost dangling between Nikolai and Alexei. "What were you hoping to find here?"

His pinched eyes survey the room. "Information that was taken from us that you had no right to see."

"Well, that's vague as shit." I glance at my Rolex. I'd rather be out with my wife than in here.

"Enzo, do you have any other questions for our new friend?" I let the tip of my knife tap on the unknown man's chest.

Enzo shakes his head. "I need to do more research now. But I don't think this asshole is going to tell me anything new."

I nod in agreement. "Niki, pull harder."

He groans. "Aww, Miki, I got a nice tux on and am taking Mila to Enzo's club right after this. Can you make this *not* messy for once?"

Alexei shrugs. "Yea, Lara would kill me if I tried to kiss on her all bloody again."

I take a deep breath and let it out. "Fine. You're both pussy whipped."

Enzo chuckles behind me. "Says the man who married someone the first day."

"I can't win with any of you." I sheath my knife and step forward, wrapping my hands around the head of the man between Niki and Alexei.

With a hard jerk, I twist his head around, snapping his neck.

He slumps, lifeless.

Enzo waves his hand. "Leave him, I'll send in the crew." He moves to the hidden tunnel.

Before I reach it, I hear the thud of the body hitting the floor.

"Quick, don't step in the piss puddle," Alexei laughs at Nikolai.

"Some days, I swear I'd rather be a gardener," groans Nikolai behind me.

CHAPTER 46

MIKHAIL

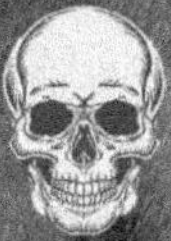

"There's a few of us gathering at the club. Our Irish friends seem to want to carouse while they're here, and Declan wants me to give him a tour. Feel like swinging by and bringing some of your guys in case things get...out of hand?" Enzo leans against the bar next to me.

None of Tatiana's men haven't shown, but for that matter, neither have Ivan's.

Now that the spy has been taken care of, Enzo will have a lot of research to do in the coming days.

But tonight it's just a party, and it's nice to have a moment of normalcy.

Except Declan's men getting rowdy near the band.

"Think it's time?" I grin at Enzo. I wouldn't mind getting Ana to his club. I know he saved me a room.

Enzo purses his lips with a slight lift of the corner of his mouth and nods. "We got some recon, might as well have some fun."

"Do you actually cut loose and use any of those rooms?" I push the straw of my drink beneath my mask and finish it off.

Enzo shakes his head making a lock of his dark hair come

loose and fall over his eyes. "No, there isn't a woman left alive who can satisfy me." He pauses, looking seriously into his own glass.

He lifts it, tilting towards me in a toast. "Here's to finding your soulmate." With a single swallow, he tosses the remainder down and sets it on the counter.

"I've never been to a club like that," Ana whispers as Enzo walks away.

I pat the swell of her ass, smiling beneath my mask. "Don't worry, iskorka, I promise you'll enjoy it."

Leading her towards the exit, I stop near my brother.

"Nikolai, round up Jax and Alexei. We're heading to Enzo's club as a little extra muscle in case Declan's crew gets too rowdy." I raise my eyebrows, hoping he gets what I'm suggesting.

"Ah, I'm there. Does he have rooms booked for us?" Nikolai grabs Mila and pulls her close, his hand straying suggestively down her snug dress.

"Yep. It'll be nice to have a night off for once." Leading Ana towards the limos, my cock hardens in my pants just thinking about what I'm going to do to her.

"Wow." She marvels as we push into Ashes. "There's so many people here." She hugs herself a little tighter to me.

"Don't worry, baby. We won't hear anyone once we get inside." I take a firm grip of her hand and guide her through the waiting crowd.

I'm glad to see Enzo so successful. Maybe one day he'll find someone to make him truly happy in all of this.

But I'm not dwelling on him tonight.

My eyes are only focused on my beautiful wife.

As we enter the hallway, Enzo leading us through, I glance over and Ana's eyes are darting all over the place. My cock twitches just thinking about the fun we can have in the private room.

Although after the events of the ball, I hope to fucking god no one stares at her ass.

We are here to stop a scene, not cause one. Not that I give a shit.

As we step inside, I lead her straight to the bar.

The Irish seem to be behaving, loud as hell, but not causing issues. Declan would be stupid to cause issues in my territory. Seeing as they're here via invite for Enzo and club expansions.

After the explosion, we can't be too safe. My father will go to any lengths to ruin us.

I nod to Declan as he rests his elbow up on the gold bar opposite. His striking pale blue eyes don't so much as glance at Ana.

He knows as well as any other man in here not to. I give him a curt nod before ordering up a champagne for Ana and a shot of vodka for myself.

"Wait, can I have a vodka? I want something stronger."

I pull her in front of me and cage her in against the bar.

"Make that two, please," I shout to the bartender.

He slides them across the smooth wood and I toss down a few bucks.

Picking up both of the shot glasses, I hand one to Ana.

"Na zdorov'ye, *to health.*" I clink my drink against hers.

"Na zdorov'ye, *to health,*" she replies quietly. Damn, her soft Russian accent makes me want to throw her across the bar and ravish her.

Lifting up the bottom of my balaclava, I quickly toss the liquid in my mouth and let it burn down my throat, slamming the glass down.

Ana takes a small sip and coughs.

"Either swallow it all or spit it in my mouth. We don't waste good vodka."

She turns her nose up and hands me the shot.

"The smell of it is making me feel sick. I can't."

I tilt my head, this isn't the first time in the last few days she's complained about not feeling well. I'm glad the grin is hidden under my mask.

I toss back her shot. If I'm right, she doesn't need alcohol anyways.

"Do you come here often?" she asks, batting her lashes.

I run my hands up her sides.

"Do you use that pick up line often, baby?" I whisper in her ear.

She shakes her head, running her palms up my chest. Fuck, just that touch alone sets me on fire.

"But to answer your question, I don't. Only for work or to see Enzo. Not interested otherwise, only now if I'm bringing my hot as sin wife here to play with." I wink and she blushes.

"Good boy." She licks her lips and I pin her with a stare.

"Did I not teach you a good enough lesson about calling me that, hmm?"

She pouts at me and strokes her fingers through my curls.

"Maybe not, I guess. Maybe this student requires some extra lessons?"

"Fuck, Ana," I groan.

Leaning in, I rest my chin on her shoulder, inhaling her floral perfume.

"I need to bury myself inside you now."

She turns her head, pressing a kiss to my cheek.

"Lead the way, sir."

CHAPTER 47

ANASTASIA

Song- Who Do You Want? Ex Habit
https://lost.exhabitmusic.com/whodoyouwant

Mikhail's hand rests protectively on my back as we navigate the dimly lit, smoky club, the bass vibrating through the floor. It's fascinating. The bar area just seems like an extravagant resting place for rich guys. I guess the naughty side goes on behind these doors.

"Does our room lock?" I ask as we continue down the hall.

"Yes, baby."

There's a gold door coming up to my left. When we approach, I stop and turn to face Miki.

"What's in there?" I ask, placing my hand on the gold metal handle.

Miki flicks his eyes up to the sign and I follow his line of sight.

Public viewing.

Interesting.

I'm intrigued. I've never even thought about coming to a place like this.

"Can we?" I arch my brow.

He shrugs, his shoulders bunching, but his grip on my hand remains firm.

"Sure. I'd rather go to our private room, though."

Miki swipes his card on the reader and I push open the door. I hesitate as the moans and grunts fill my ears. Straightening my spine, I step in and squeeze Miki's hand. There's lots of couples. As I scan the room, most of them are getting off on couches in front of the gallery area.

My gaze lands on the viewing area, like a staged dungeon. Bed in the middle, an X cross. Chains everywhere. A woman's screams rip through the room and I step back to be closer to Miki.

I'm not sure this is my thing. I'm a one man kinda girl.

It almost feels wrong watching someone else.

As I look at the couple, wait, there's two guys and I can see the ass of a woman. Kind of. She's being fucked from behind by the lanky guy and then I think sucking the dark haired one's dick.

He tugs her head dark back and the lanky one pulls out. She sits naked on the edge of the bed and looks over in my direction.

Well, not mine. She has her eyes on my husband.

It's fucking Zoya.

She holds up a finger to him and motions for him to join.

He stiffens behind me and holds me closer, wrapping his arms tight around my waist. I don't know whether to laugh or be furious. Both. I hate this woman with every bone in my body.

"What the fuck is she doing here?" he hisses.

I need to leave.

I turn to face Miki. He's looking at me, not her, thank fuck. I might have lost it.

"You wanna go join her, hubby?" I say sarcastically, sliding my hands up his black shirt.

He shakes his head, the vein popping on his temple. Oh, he's pissed.

"You better not be jealous of her being Eiffel Towered over there," I whisper aggressively.

"No. I'm pissed off because who the hell has galena? I didn't save her for her mom to fuck around in my associate's club."

Oh, he's mad at Zoya.

"Maybe she needed a good two dick fucking to get over the devastation that she can't have you."

He slides his hand back in mine and drags me through the door, straight back to the bar.

Enzo is at a table nearby and Miki comes to a halt.

"Why did you let Zoya in?"

Enzo shrugs.

"She said Lara was babysitting. She needed a good fuck. I know her from a past life. Didn't think it would be an issue." He looks between me and Miki.

"Don't let her in again. I sacrificed a lot to keep her and Galena safe."

"No problem. Go loosen up." Enzo knocks back his whiskey.

We silently head to our room, it's all a blur as my jealousy bubbles over. As we enter, Miki slams the door shut behind me, the sound echoing in the sudden quiet.

I give him a quizzical look. Is he mad really because of her safety or is there more?

"Strip for me, baby," he commands, removing his mask and tossing it on the red carpet.

I chew on the inside of my mouth. He remembers our rules. I love seeing his handsome face.

"Fine. But I have a question," I say, sliding the strap of my dress down my arm.

"This isn't a place for talking." He smirks.

"Tough. Listen."

His brow furrows. "Two minutes."

I roll my eyes. Fine. I'm desperate to see what he has in store for me, anyway.

"Truthful answer only. Were you jealous watching Zoya with those guys?"

"Fuck no. She can do what she wants when she's back home, and there isn't a threat to Galena."

I nod. I understand. But, something inside me can't help but keep pressing. I have to be sure.

I unzip the side of my dress and let it pool to the floor. His mouth drops open when his eyes rake over my body.

I bought my white sparkly bra when I was out with Lara. I have a few sets to surprise him with.

"Fuck, pretty girl." He rubs the growing bulge in his pants.

"You reckon those guys in that room would like this?" I run my hands over the glittery fabric and sway my hips seductively.

His jaw ticks and his eyes darken as he steps forward.

"What the fuck did you just say?" he seethes, making me stumble a step back.

"I mean, she's doing well. Those guys looked like they knew how to give her a good time. You sure you don't want to join them like she asked?" I tip my chin up.

I don't know if my anger is directed at her or him.

"I mean, why else would she want you to join if she thought you'd reject her? Have you slept with her before?"

"No. Never. And never fucking will. Do you want to fuck those guys?"

His hand shoots out and he grabs my throat, shoving me into the padded wall.

The anger on his face has me snapping my mouth shut.

Did I push him too far?

I swallow as his fingers squeeze, making me struggle for air.

"N-no," I cough.

He releases me and my body sags against the wall.

"I don't want to fuck them. I'm just saying, maybe that's something you used to be into? A bit of sharing? Watch me get fucked by another dude. I mean, or you and another guy? Zoya looked like she was having a great time there."

He rubs his hands over his face. "Stop. Fucking. Talking. Anastasia."

"So two dicks is a no go for me?" I mutter to myself.

I let out a squeal as he grabs me by the waist and throws me over the leather spanking bench in the middle of the room.

"Is that what you fucking want?" he roars.

I scream out when something hard smacks down on my ass.

I almost see stars as the pain sears through me, tears rolling down my cheeks, but I'm also turned on. What the hell?

"I just want you!" I shout at him. "Why would I want another guy's dick in me when I have you? I'm fucking worried you're going to leave me for Zoya!"

I start to sob, hot tears streaming down my face, blurring my vision. I don't know where this jealousy is coming from. It also doesn't help that ass really fucking stings.

I shove myself up from the cold, hard bench, and throw myself at his chest, feeling the force of the collision.

"I just want you." I grab a fist full of his shirt and with all my strength I push him back on the plush, silky bed. Landing on top of him, I straddle him.

With one hand grabbing around his throat, I squeeze and kiss him.

"Now how about you fuck me and prove I only ever need your cock?" I bite his lip and a growl erupts from his chest. His eyes are black as he rolls me onto my back and forcefully opens my thighs.

His face, I don't recognize it. There's no love in his eyes. Just fury.

My heart beats frantically. I push on his chest and he snaps his eyes to mine.

His stern facade momentarily melts, replaced by a softer look that lasts only a second.

"Red," he whispers.

He runs his hand through his hair and lets out a ragged breath.

"Fuck. Red. I'm sorry, I don't trust myself." He climbs off the bed and storms towards the door. Without thinking, I rush after him, my heart pounding, and throw myself in front of him, blocking the doorway.

"No. Miki," I say sternly.

His head tilts as his jaw clenches. "Move. I don't want to hurt you. I couldn't live with myself. And the shit I just envisioned doing to you was wrong."

I frown, taking in his words, but I stay frozen on the spot. "No. Talk to me. Please."

He lowers his head, and I run my hands up his huge biceps through his shirt.

"Come on, big man. It's me. Tell me what's going on. You

haven't been right since the last room. If it wasn't Zoya, what was it?"

He huffs, and I stroke his cheek to offer reassurance without smothering him.

"I didn't like watching you looking at them. I can't stand the thought of you wanting more. Like Zoya was doing, two guys. There's a whole sexual world out there. I unlocked that for you. I fear maybe you'll want to explore outside of what I can offer. And I'll never share you, Ana. Never. You are mine. It would kill me if you wanted something I can't give you, or the thought of another man touching you."

He takes a shaky breath, his knuckles white against his clenched fists.

"I can't do it. I'd kill them. But there's that little doubt in my head."

His face turns red, his eyes almost murderous. I take a step forward and rest my hand over his heart.

He looks away, his nostrils flaring.

"Stop it. That's never going to happen. Do you hear me?"

I push his beautiful face back to me, making him look me in the eyes.

"You are enough, Mikhail Volkov. I only want you and will only ever want you. There isn't another guy on this planet that compares to you and what you give me. You, big man. You are all I will ever need. I promise."

He runs his hands up my sides and leans in for a kiss.

I press my finger to his lip to pause him. "Are we good now? We can play? Your head is back with me?"

He playfully licks my finger and smirks before gently taking it into his mouth and swirling his tongue around it.

"Oh, I'll make it up to you. I'm sorry, pretty girl. I'd never forgive myself if I hurt you. I had to stop."

Pulling my finger back, I replace it with my lips, wrapping my arms around his neck and jumping into his arms.

I'll climb him like a damn tree.

"I'm never letting you go," he grunts out, running his tongue along the side of my neck.

"Good. Never want you to. You're stuck with me. Now, about making it up to me. I think me on that bench. Show me how sorry you are with your tongue, then use whatever you used before on me."

His hand digs into my ass. I tighten my legs around him as he walks us over to the bench.

Laying me down on the cool leather, my hot skin sticks to it. Draping a leg on either side, he lifts my ass up.

"Forgiveness in the form of orgasms. God, I love you, baby." His warm breath beats against my pussy and I shiver.

"P-please, Miki. Sir." I wiggle my hips, desperate for his mouth.

CHAPTER 48

MIKHAIL

Song- Heavenly Bodies, Arankai

With a feather light touch, I run my fingers along her ass and all the way down her back.

"I have something for you first."

Retrieving the diamond chain from my pocket, I hold it up to the light, standing in front of her.

"That's stunning." Her eyes twinkle, much like the gems.

I had it encrusted with some blue diamonds to match the collar she bought for Hades. Except this one is one hundred times the cost.

"Your own collar. Mine," I say with a grin.

"Oh, kinky." She winks, pulling her hair up from her neck, allowing me to secure it.

"To some it could be. I just thought you'd look sexy as hell wearing it. I think it's safe to say our dom and sub dynamic isn't quite the usual."

She giggles.

"No from what I googled, I am far too sassy and mouthy

for that. And actually, I wouldn't mind tying you up one day and having my way with you."

That makes me inwardly groan. I'd do anything for this woman and let her explore me how she likes.

"We have our own rules, baby. I'm still in control, even if I do allow you to tie me up one day." I softly stroke the blonde strand away from her face.

"I'm your little naughty submissive." She pouts and I pull her lip back with my thumb.

"That you are. Now, I better get back to earning your forgiveness? And then I'm chaining you up and spanking you for that sassy mouth."

"Deal." She gives me a wide grin.

God, I fucking love her.

Retrieving the paddle, I take my place behind her, I drop down to my knees to worship her pussy. Spreading her ass apart, I dive in and feast on her.

Just how she likes it. I bring her close enough to the edge, using the paddle to lightly tap her ass to ease her into this.

As her moans grow louder, I stand.

"Who does this ass belong to?" I rub my hands down her back.

"Y-you," she stammers.

"Good girl."

Smack.

"Do you think you've behaved well enough to come yet?"

Gripping the red welts on her backside, I push two fingers into her soaking pussy.

"Oh my god," she cries out.

I smack her again, this time even harder.

"I wouldn't bother calling out to God, baby. You're better off trying your luck in hell first."

Leaning down, I plant a gentle kiss on the fresh welt forming on her flawless ass.

"You're doing such a good job, pretty girl. I'm proud of you."

I explore the curves of her spine with my tongue, tangling my fingers in her long locks before sinking my teeth into her throat.

"I really need to come, sir," she pants out as I tug her head back.

Her beautiful blue eyes lock with mine.

That passion. Hunger. Love. It drives me crazy.

"Seeing as you've been so good, I'll let you decide." I keep thrusting my fingers inside her as I speak. "My tongue, my fingers or my cock?"

With my fingers curled inside her, her back arches, and I break into a grin. She's struggling to hold it together.

"I need your cock inside me, Miki."

"Excellent choice, baby."

I pull my fingers away, lift her trembling body, and help her stand.

"I've wanted to tie you up so badly for weeks."

Bringing her to the X cross mounted on the wall, I pull down on the chains connected to handcuffs.

"Stay facing the cross and bend over."

A mischievous grin dances on her lips as she looks at me.

"Aren't I supposed to get on my knees in front of it and pray?"

My fingers trace the curve of her chin as I lean down, my lips ghosting over hers.

"By all means, if you want to get down on your knees for my cock, go ahead. But you'll be begging for it, not praying."

With a forceful smack, our lips collided, the impact sending a jolt through me.

"Maybe I'll pray that I don't choke to death." She winks. With a firm grip on her waist, I push her down until she is bent over.

Securing her wrists in the cuffs connected to the chains, I pause for a minute, letting her anticipation mount while I go grab the leather flogger.

I run the tails delicately down her back, admiring how she's spread her legs for me, letting me see her glistening pussy. It's ready for me to fuck.

The flogger cracks sharply as I flick my wrist and strike her with it. A raw, desperate cry rips from her throat, calling my name, and I can't take it anymore.

I need to be inside her.

I release my cock from my pants and firmly grip her hips as I push as deep into her as I can.

"Fuck, iskorka. So good."

With one hand firmly on her ass to hold her in place, I grip her shoulder with the other, meaning I can hit that bit harder.

I pound into her with force, not holding back and adding in the occasional smack on her ass.

I go so hard my ears ring as my climax nears.

"Miki!" Her screams tear through the room.

"Now!" I don't have any other words in me.

I grunt out her name as I spill into her. It rips through me violently.

I let her ride out her orgasm, gently thrusting inside her, feeling her walls tighten on my cock.

"Such a good girl, aren't you?" I praise her, stroking her back. "There is no escaping me, iskorka. Mine forever." I tell her as I withdraw.

With a click of the cuffs, I carefully lay her spent body on the bed. Her dark curls, damp with sweat, sprawl across the cool cotton sheets. The silence is heavy, broken only by the faint thump of my own heart.

Like a fucking angel sent to the devil himself.

"Did you enjoy that?"

Judging by her post-orgasm smile, I know the answer.

"Hmmm, was so nice. Might need a nap before we go again."

"Lemme get you cleaned up and put some ointment on your ass, then we can relax for a bit before we go again."

She rolls onto her front and wiggles her butt in the air. I wince looking at the marks.

"You're going to be sore, baby. But the red looks great on you." I wink at her.

It really does.

Anastasia covered in my marks is a sight to behold.

I PULL the blanket away from my neck as I wake up from my nap with a yawn. A smile beams on my face. Aww, he must have tucked me in. I vaguely remember him pressing a kiss on my forehead as I was drifting off. I'm so damn tired all the time at the moment. I thought perhaps jet lag, but there is no way this would go on for so long.

It's probably the fact Miki keeps me up all hours of the night, bending me around like a pretzel. Kicking off the blanket, I stand with a stretch and look at myself in the floor-standing mirror opposite the bed. Ruffling my fingers through my hair to make the curls bounce, I swipe on some clear gloss. I think about putting on some leggings, but I bet big man will like seeing me in his shirt, even if it is more like a dress.

I'm giddy as I head down the stairs, almost with a skip in my step, thinking about wrapping my arms about my husband. That still feels strange to say, but it feels right. He is mine.

That smile is wiped straight off my face when I hear her voice. My nose wrinkles and my fists clench. That high-pitched noise she makes when she laughs is as annoying as a tire screeching. My blood boils. Why is she here? Again?

Doesn't she see she's a fucking third wheel here and is not welcome? I don't think I could have made it more obvious. Plastering on a fake smile, I can't let her see I'm annoyed. I'll kill the bitch with kindness... for now. I've pictured strangling her to death when she smirks at me. Drowning her in a pool wasn't enough. It's a shame Lara pulled me off.

As I round the corner to the kitchen, Mikhail is resting against the counter with his enormous arms crossed over his chest. As I cast my gaze to the kitchen island, my blood fucking boils.

She's sitting there, drinking out of *my* coffee mug, licking her lips and fake laughing at *my* husband. Her eyes meet mine across the room briefly and she doesn't acknowledge me. Her attention is straight back on Mikhail as she stands. Of course she has her tits on the verge of falling out of her tight white top.

Cringe.

I tug on the hem of Miki's shirt and clear my throat, just as that piercing cackle comes out of that vile woman's mouth. Mikhail's dark eyes burn into mine and a blush spreads over my cheeks. A single look from him and I melt on the spot.

His eyes crease under the mask. He's smiling at me and my heart races.

"Iskorka." He motions me over to him with his hand, never breaking eye contact.

I can feel her gaze burning into the side of my head and I can't help but smirk. Not that I bother to even look at her.

I step in front of Miki and wrap my arms around his waist. He instantly returns the embrace. I bite down on my lip as he brushes my hair away from my ear and leans down. The fabric of his mask brushing against my skin.

"Fuck, pretty girl, you're in my shirt. I need you to stay exactly where you are to hide how turned on I am by you," he whispers in my ear.

I turn my face into him as he tugs me closer, his hard cock pressing against my stomach, and I'm desperate for him. I want him so badly, it's infuriating he can't fuck me on the counter. Because *she* is here. I've had enough. I want to fuck my husband when and where I want, not be confined to our damn bedroom.

"Tell me what you'd do." I rub my body against his.

"I'd throw you over that island, push up that shirt, pull your panties to the side and fuck you with my tongue first."

I squeeze my thighs together as his fingers dig into my waist. My body is tingling as I picture him on his knees for me. Fuck. I bite back a groan.

"Well, maybe, if we didn't have a guest in our house so much, I'd be able to get down on my knees right now and sort that big problem for you out." I can't hide how pissed off and horny I am in my voice.

"She's going in a minute," he says, this time louder. Oh, perfect.

"Am I?" Zoya replies full of sass.

"Fucking bitch," I mutter under my breath. I go to turn in Mikhail's arms but he holds me in place.

"Yes. Zoya. Our conversation is finished. I would like to spend time with my wife." The sternness in his voice is only turning me on. And the way he says "my wife" has me ready to fold for him.

"You can spend time with her while Galena and I watch films in your cinema room. You know she loves it in there."

That isn't how this goes. The rule is they live in the

outhouse. We live in Mikhail's house. She's lucky she's even on this estate, let alone standing in our fucking kitchen.

"Not today." He cuts her off.

"Miki, you can always join us, if you'd prefer. Maybe let Anastasia have another nap while the adults talk."

I shake my head and push away from his chest. I want to kill her. Before I can turn around, I catch a glimpse of Mikhail's dark eyes. They tell me everything. They are the key to his soul. That is how I read him. His eyes give both warnings and silent declarations of love.

I wonder how hard I would have to smash her head against that marble counter to shut her the fuck up?

His eyes flick up to the stairs and back to me with a nod. My nostrils flare as I try to get a hold of my rage. He raises his eyebrows at me, the look that says, "if you don't do as you're told, you're about to get a spanking".

I can't resist. I'm going to listen to his silent warning, but first, I step forward and go up on my tiptoes, grabbing hold of his collar and yanking him down to me. I smack my lips against his. Well, I can feel them through the fabric of the mask. I tug him down further and brush my mouth over his ear.

"Fix this and then come and fuck the rage out of me before I really do kill her."

A low growl erupts from his chest. I'm going to get in trouble for teasing him like this. But, I'm dead serious. I am done with her and her shit stirring.

"You're *my* husband. It's my pussy who keeps your cock warm every night. Remember that, big man."

I stroke the side of his face over where his scars are, and he closes his eyes with a sigh. I'm not sure if it's out of annoyance for the situation, the fact he's turned on by my outburst or he genuinely is softening into my touch. I'm not mad at him, it's her. And I'll let him deal with it.

Without even looking at Zoya, I turn and head up the stairs with my head held high, entering to our bedroom. Closing the door behind me, I head to the bathroom.

CHAPTER 50

MIKHAIL

Song- Ex Habit, over my dead body.
https://ffm.to/overmyd3adbody

"Do not *ever* speak to my wife like that again," I grit out every word through my teeth.

Fuck. Ana has me turned on, but that quickly morphed into rage when Zoya spoke down to my wife.

My respect for her is gone, even though I will protect my little sister with my life.

But, I have to put the woman I love first.

I saw the anger burning in her eyes, the murderous look flashed across them. It turned me the fuck on. But I can't have her going down that path. I protect her. My hands will be dirty for her.

And she's right, this is our home. I want to enjoy my wife at every possible opportunity. I want to have her walking round this house in my shirts with my cum dripping down her thighs. Fuck.

"I didn't say anything bad. It's not as if I called her a

spoiled bitch with an attitude problem that clearly loves a man too good for her."

I clench my fists, keeping myself rooted on the spot.

"Get out, Zoya. Last warning, my kindness to you only goes so far."

She rolls her eyes and stands, resting her palms on the counter, and pushing her breasts forward. These games of hers have to stop.

"She's only your wife on paper, not in your heart. You can't love Mikhail."

"Out. Now." I raise my voice so loud she jumps back with a gasp.

She shuffles towards the patio doors and slides it open.

"You can do better, Mikhail. I know you."

She doesn't. Nobody knows me the way Ana does. And how wrong that statement is. Ana is too good for me.

"There is no one better in this world than my wife. Nobody. This needs to stop."

Zoya's eyes glass over, quickly replaced with fury. Great. I don't have time for her, I gotta deal with my little crazy princess upstairs. Perhaps letting Ana kill her in the pool would have solved these issues.

Zoya opens her mouth and I shake my head. With a sigh, she closes the door and I watch as she walks down the path. I head over and twist the lock, then double step up the stairs and shove open our bedroom door. I stop in my tracks, raking over Anna's gorgeous figure as she pulls the hem of the top up, revealing her perky ass in those red lace panties.

"Keep the shirt on," I command.

She stops immediately, and I grin.

"Good girl."

I step into the room and kick it closed with my boot. She spins to face me with a sexy smirk.

Those lips.

I need them around my cock.

Closing the distance between us, as soon as I reach her, my hand shoots out and grabs her by the throat, slamming her back into the mirror. I feel her swallow against my palm and release my grip a little.

I'll let her say what she her piece and then I'll fuck the rage out of her and then punish her for talking back.

"Go on, pretty girl. Let it out."

"Mask off. You know the rules. Talking and fucking. No mask."

As her hand touches my cheek, I snatch her wrist and spin her, pressing her face against the mirror and holding both wrists behind her back with one hand, letting her ass press against my cock.

Releasing her throat, I use that free hand to untie the back of the bandana and toss it on the floor. I don't want to look at my reflection, so I carefully peel the black shirt over her ass and run my palm against her soft skin, digging my fingers in to grab it. I'll keep my focus on that.

"Now you're in position, tell me what's going on in your head."

"I don't want that woman in our house."

I don't hesitate. "Done."

I push forward, pressing my dick against her ass harder.

She frowns.

"Words," I tell her, hopefully it's not too many of them because my cock is about to explode.

"Why was that so easy?"

I spank her, and she lets out a little shriek.

"You come first. You're my wife. I have made that clear. No one speaks to you that way. Not her. Not anyone. This is your home. I love you."

I dig my fingers into the freshly red skin and grind my hips against her.

"And, we can't have my innocent, untainted wife going to jail for murder, can we?"

I run my hand under her shirt and up her spine. I'd never let that happen regardless.

"She speaks to me like that again. I'll shoot her."

"Hmm, is that right, iskorka?"

Good thing she didn't hear the rest of what Zoya had to say. The woman would have a bullet lodged between her eyes. I don't want to break galena's heart like that. I have to keep her safe and happy.

Taking out my pistol from its holster, quietly I slide back the chamber and remove the bullets, shoving them in my pocket.

She shivers as I run the gun along her back and then drag it along her throat, tipping her chin up.

"Do you even know how to aim a gun?" I question, watching her eyes in the mirror.

My pretty girl is turned on and scared at the same time, and it's making me hard as hell.

"Ever held one?"

She shakes her head, and I pull her panties to the side and slide my finger inside.

"Dripping. Interesting." I give her a wicked smirk in the mirror, trailing the gun over her chin and press it against her lips.

"Lick the barrel, iskorka. Be a good girl and do as you're told."

Her tongue sweeps out and licks along the side. Jesus Christ.

"You going to stay very still for me?" I stroke her cheek

with the weapon and work my fingers deeper inside of her pussy.

"I-I will." Her voice shakes.

"Color?"

She pauses before she replies. "Yellow. But I trust you."

I get down to my knees behind her, pulling her panties down over her hips. I tap the inside of her thigh with the gun and she spreads them wider for me. Enough for me to eat her out properly.

She presses her ass against my face as I feast, licking her and fucking her with my tongue, all the while stroking up and down the inside of her leg with my pistol.

And she is soaking for me.

Edging the muzzle of the gun up higher, I stop at the entrance to her pussy. I know it's not loaded, but she doesn't necessarily know that.

"Trust me?" I ask, licking her again.

"Y-yes."

I push it in far enough for her to yelp, which is soon followed by a moan when I circle her clit with my finger. I slide it in, just until the first ridge, and pull it back out, replacing it with my tongue.

"You might not know how to shoot a gun, but you sure know how to fuck one, pretty girl."

I slap her ass as I get to my feet, spinning her round to face me. Her big eyes sparkling and a naughty smirk on her lips.

"Now, how about my cock? Fill you up properly, like the greedy girl you are, hmm?"

I'd love to see my girl pregnant.

She nods frantically as my hand wraps around her throat. I grab her waist, hoist her up, and slam her back against the mirror.

"Take the gun out of my hand," I tell her and she tilts her head, studying me.

"You can hold it. I trust you."

She takes it from my palm and holds it between us as I work to get my cock free from my pants and thrust inside her. She wraps her arms around my neck, pulling me closer, the gun resting on my back as I pound into her, tightening my grip on her throat.

Her mouth falls open, those little breathy moans just setting me on fire with each thrust.

"Is that better, pretty girl? You prefer stretching around my cock, don't you?"

She nods, her eyes fluttering closed.

"I want to feel you come inside me, big man. I need it."

A primal growl erupts from my chest and I crash my lips over hers, possessing her. Her nails scratch up my neck as I dive deeper inside of her.

"You want me to fuck a baby into you, pretty girl?" I grunt out.

"Fuck, Miki," she cries out.

"I want everything with you," she says as her fingers dig into my throat.

"Good girl. Mine to breed. Fuck, you're perfect."

Holding her firmly in place, I can feel she's close. So with a few last thrusts, as hard as I can, pressing the points on her throat to send her wild, she loses it and comes apart on my cock. I join her in release, filling her up with every drop of me.

Mine.

I bite down on her bottom lip and suck, loosening my fingers on her neck.

"You good, baby?" I whisper against her lips.

"I'm very good. Very full." She teases with a sexy smirk. "Just how you should be."

331

CHAPTER 51

ANASTASIA

Song- Hymn To Virgil, Hozier

FRUSTRATION BOILS over as I pace the room, my finger slamming down on the dial button again and again, each press a stinging reminder of my mounting anxiety. When it connects to Mikhail's voicemail, I let out a scream that echoes in my ears. My heart pounds in my chest as I stop, staring at the pregnancy test lying on the bed. The positive one.

Mila brought it for me yesterday, but I've been too scared to take it. I know something is off. I don't have periods because of my pill, but I had a break after the kidnapping ordeal in Russia.

These hormones, tender breasts, nausea. I took a sex ed class in school. It's enough to make me want to take a test to be sure.

And fuck me, I was right. Now I'm furious.

When I couldn't find him in the house, I thought I'd check where Zoya was. Surprise, surprise, she also wasn't there.

He told me he would get rid of her. All her shit is still there. Clearly she's manipulating him yet again.

It clicks over to voicemail. Fuck. Him.

"Mikhail. You have five minutes to call me back, or I am packing a bag and leaving. I mean it. I need you."

I swallow past the lump in my throat. I'm petrified. I don't want to leave him. I love him. Hell, we are starting a family together. Why won't he answer my calls? Where the hell is he?

The phone vibrates in my hand, a familiar buzz that makes my heart race. I answer on the first ring, and my anger starts to melt away as I hear his deep Russian accent through the speaker.

"Ana, baby. Are you okay?"

The sound of a woman's laughter, giggling in the background, acts as a trigger, and my rage erupts, returning with a vengeance.

"Where are you, Miki?" I say through gritted teeth.

"I just had to take Zoya to get some shopping for G. I won't be long."

My vision blurs.

Her.

Whatever Zoya needs, she gets. I don't trust her. And I don't fucking like her one bit. I see the way she looks at my man. The way she tries to get her claws in and hit his weakness of caring for his little sister.

What if she is the one he really wanted all this time? I was never meant to happen. They've known each other long before I've been around. Maybe this is just some fucked up game that they're playing?

"Ana? Are you okay? Talk to me."

Tears roll down my face. Am I destined to live as the other woman? Even in what would be our family home?

Wondering if it really is me he wants. Always having that bitch making orders.

I suck in a breath.

No. I want more out of life and love. I deserve more.

"Just come home. We need to talk."

I cut the call before he can reply and sit on the edge of the bed, placing the little white stick on my lap.

"Well, maybe it will just be me and you, baby," I whisper to my flat stomach.

How the hell is this even possible?

I let the tears fall. I love this man. Truly and deeply. But I can't live without knowing if I own his whole heart. Even if the tiniest part belongs to Zoya, that isn't enough.

No woman should feel like they are in competition with another for a man's heart. I won't allow that to happen to me. Even if it will kill me to walk away. I will put myself first and figure out the rest later.

I blow on the steam off my coffee, the heat warming my face, as the front door slams shut with a resounding thud.

"Iskorka." His voice carries through the mansion.

"In here," I reply quietly.

I turn and rest my ass on the counter, holding the mug in front of my face with two hands.

He stops opposite me, studying me. I raise my brows at him. I am Anastasia. I am a bad bitch. And I will either get what I want or I'll hold my head up and walk away.

"You've been crying?" His brows furrow as he steps closer.

I hold up my hand to stop him from coming any closer and he tilts his head to the side.

"Where is *she?*" I ask, flicking my eyes towards the front door.

"Who? Zoya? I told her to go straight to her house."

Of course. Maybe it's so she can hide the freshly fucked look he gave her?

"What's this about, baby?"

Baby. The word hits me right in the chest. I'm growing his. A new life in all this crazy.

I carefully place my coffee down on the counter and straighten my spine, looking up at him. I'm not scared of him, nor to challenge him.

"Do you love her, Miki?"

He squints at me, a look of skepticism on his face, and shakes his head, the movement a subtle but definite rejection. Yet, it isn't enough.

"Hmm." I'm not sure if I believe him.

"The fuck?" he mutters and takes a step towards me.

"Stay where you are and answer my goddamn question with words. Do you have feelings in any kind of romantic way towards that bitch?"

The rage starts to build in my chest, a tight, suffocating feeling that threatens to consume me. Her snide comments, the looks. She radiates such jealousy. The little ways she fawns over Miki to try to make me feel small. The constant interruptions. Reminders of his care for her.

"I'm going to need you to explain what the hell is going on here, Ana."

I let out a laugh and push myself off the counter, closing the distance between us. His gaze pierces down, the darkness in his eyes almost consuming him, but I catch a glimpse of the amber specks that lie within. Those little bits of light in there.

My fingers trace the contours of his chest, and I offer him a smile that looks sweet and warm, the contrary to what I really feel. They say you have to scare a man sometimes to get them to reveal the truth. Mikhail is no different. Under this hard exterior, there is a man who loves deeply in there. A man who would be an amazing father, a protector. A perfect husband for me.

"I will ask you one more fucking time, Mikhail. I want to know, is my husband in love with another woman? Do you feel even a minuscule bit of what she feels for you?"

He strokes the back of his hand along the side of my face, and I pull it away.

"What she feels for me? Ana, where is this coming from? I'm yours, baby."

I clench my fists against his chest, my nails digging into my flesh.

Not good enough.

"She's in love with you. Do you love her back? It is a simple question. Because if you do, I can't be here. I'm not competing with her for my own husband's attention. I know my worth. You are either all in with me or I'm out. Was I just someone to keep you entertained until you could have her? If you've played me... I swear to God I will break you, Miki."

I see the creases appear around his eyes. He's fucking smirking under his mask.

I push against his chest and he grabs both of my wrists, a small growl escaping from him.

"Break me? Please, enlighten me how. And then I will give you a lesson in *breaking* for this little outburst."

The son of a bitch. My heart races, a deafening roar filling my ears as his grip tightens, preventing any chance of escape.

Fine. I let a small, sadistic smile creep up on my lips. I want to slap the grin from his. I look straight into his dark, unblinking eyes, my words measured and cold.

"You want to know how I'll break you? I'll find a guy, I'll let him fuck me, hard, on your bed, in your precious corvette, on your bike. Every fucking surface in your home. Even your desk at work. And then you know what I'll do… I'll hunt her down, drag her by her hair back here and slit her throat. To be honest, I will probably leave her on your cum stained bed for good measure. And then you will have neither of us. Because I will be gone, out of your life just a distant memory and you can wallow forever about how you let the one women who would love you unconditionally, who would give you everything she had despite your demons, how you let her slip away because you couldn't answer a single. Fucking. Question."

I'm almost out of breath by the time I finish. God, it felt good. It's probably all true, I am crazy about this man. I've told him before I would fight for him, for us, and I am. And now even more so for our baby.

He lets go of my wrists and a sinking feeling washes over me. What if he isn't answering because I'm right? He doesn't want to upset me. What do I do?

"Sounds like you've really thought this through, beautiful." He drawls out, reaching behind his head. He fumbles with the balaclava, his hands shaking as he pulls it free and throws it to the ground, the fabric crinkling as it lands.

I keep my eyes fixed on him. I've seen his scars. I love them because they are part of him. But I know not to stare. It's his biggest insecurity and it will take time.

"Don't sweet talk me. But yes. I have. I don't get played by men, Mikhail. Even you. So tell me the truth… do you love her?"

I can feel every aggressive beat of my heart against my ribs.

"God, it's a good fucking job I love you crazy," he mutters, rushing forward, his arm wraps around my waist and his mouth just a breath from mine.

"No. Fucking. Way. Ana. I love you and only you. I feel nothing for her, she is just an inconvenience I am trying to get rid of as we speak. I'm protecting my sister that is as far as it goes. But love… Ana, my heart is all yours. I promise."

I stare into his eyes, but he doesn't blink, he knows what my witchy ass is doing.

I believe him.

"You might want to sit down, Miki."

His brows furrow, panic appearing on his face.

"Nothing bad, big man. Just, umm, a shock?"

He runs his hands along my cheeks and presses his lips against mine.

"I'm sorry if you've ever felt anything less than the most important person in my life, baby. I will never let that happen again."

I shake my head, almost feeling a bit silly for my reactive outburst.

He has never himself made me feel that way. He always shows how much he cares and loves me.

It's her. Grating on me, picking at my insecurities with her digs, flirting around him.

And my little surprise doesn't help. I am all over the place.

"Yeah, well, when I tell you the news, you might understand my outburst. Although, I appreciate your apology, Miki. I love you too." I chew on the inside of my lip.

"Come with me." I hold out my hand for him to take.

CHAPTER 52

MIKHAIL

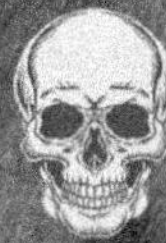

Song- Alkaline, Sleep Token

I DO as she says and sit on the edge of the bed.

She's cute when she's nervous.

"What is it, baby?" I ask, placing my hands on my lap as she fidgets on her feet in front of me.

Then she fiddles with her wedding ring.

"So you know how you keep saying you want to put a baby in me?"

"Yes…"

I try to stop the smile erupting on my face.

My heart hammers in my chest out of excitement. I just need her to say the words out loud.

"Well, you have been successful in your efforts, big man."

She pads over to the drawer and pulls out a white stick and places it in my hands.

I stare down at the two red lines.

Our baby. Our future. This changes everything, for the better.

"And here I thought I couldn't love you any more than I

already do. Come here." I open up my arms and she throws herself into them.

She nuzzles her face into my neck and I pull her slender legs over my lap.

"Thank you, iskorka," I whisper into the top of her head.

Her warm tears roll down my neck and I pull her face up to mine.

"This is the start of our new life, baby." I settle my hand on her stomach and she smiles.

"You think I'll be a good mom?" Her bottom lip quivers and I press my lips against hers.

"Not just good. The fucking best, baby. That heart of yours, that strength you have, the way you spark up a room when you enter it. You will be incredible and I cannot wait to watch you."

She truly is something special. I knew it from the second I laid eyes on her.

"I'm so fucking happy, pretty girl. Happiest man on the planet right now." I wipe away her tears and her white teeth appear as she smiles.

"I'm really happy, Miki. Just a bit scared."

"I will be by your side every step of the way."

I press my lips to hers, a silent declaration of my love. This is my chance to do some good for once. Ana has proven to me that I do, in fact, have a heart.

And it's now dedicated to her and our child.

I will burn down the world to keep them safe.

My thoughts are jumbled and chaotic as Mikhail guides me toward the car, the sounds of the city swirling around me.

"Ana?"

I blink a few times, the blurry vision clearing to reveal we have stopped, and he was already opening the passenger door with a soft click.

"Sorry, world of my own." I shake my head and swerve past him.

His hand wraps around my waist, pulling me close against his side. I tilt my head back, getting lost in the dark depths of his eyes.

"You've given me the best possible gift. You've given me a future, us a family. Thank you."

I'm excited. I can't wait.

It's just all coming sooner than I imagined and it's almost hard to breathe.

How am I already over four months pregnant?

Will I end up like Zoya? Trapped away to be safe?

So many questions. Yet when I look at Mikhail, his face

softens, a subtle easing of the lines around his eyes, and the worry etched there melts away, calming me.

He's got us.

Me and our little baby boy.

"I love you, big man." I rub my stomach and his gaze follows my hands. "And I love you, little guy," I whisper.

"I love you both so much."

He lifts his mask, the scent of woodsmoke and something else, something definably him, fills my senses before his lips claim mine.

"I'm hungry." I give him a little grin.

"For what, pretty girl?" He strokes my face.

"Your cock, obviously. Starved, Mikhail. I might faint in fact." I dramatically put the back of my hand to my forehead.

His deep chuckle makes me giggle uncontrollably, calming the chaos in my brain.

"Get in the car, Anastasia," he says as a low grumble and I squeeze my thighs.

Just like our wedding day.

"Don't make me run. I'm too pregnant now to be chased."

He gives my backside a playful tap. "I'll give you whatever you want, baby. We will make it work."

I press the tip of his nose with my finger.

"You big softie. This kid is gonna be so spoiled."

He nods, his face falling into a mask of shadows, his eyes darkening with unspoken anger.

"Our son will have a loving childhood, Ana. I promise. I'd never let my kid go through the torture of what I had to deal with. If I ever start to resemble my father, lodge a bullet between my eyes."

Rising onto my tiptoes, I gently brush my lips against his soft cheek.

"We've got this, big man. You are nothing like your father

and you never will be." I flatten my hand over his hard chest. "Your heart is far too big."

I slip out of his grip and slide into the seat. He closes the door and gets behind the wheel.

As always, his broad hand grips my thigh and I rest mine on top, stroking his skin.

I still can't get over how pregnant I am. It doesn't make sense.

"Miki…"

"Yes, iskorka?"

"How the hell am I four months? I don't get it. Isn't the pill 99% effective? I've never missed a day? I'm so confused."

I look down at our entwined fingers and he doesn't reply.

"In a good way. I'm happy, Miki. God, I can't wait to have a family with you. Honestly. But, I'm just a little confused. I guess it could have been back in Russia before you got my prescription?"

I stare at his side profile. His jaw tightens and I frown.

"Hello? Earth to big man? Are you even listening?"

He clears his throat.

"You're being weird. Spit it out." I grab his hand and shove it back in his own lap.

"I, err."

Is he… nervous?

"Mikhail Volkov. Stop this. You're stressing my confused little brain out."

He lets out a sharp breath, pinching the bridge of his nose.

"I switched your pill out. You've not been taking anything real."

My mouth drops open as I register his words. And then I burst into a fit of laughter, complete with slapping my hands on my thighs, and tears rolling down my cheeks.

"Yeah, right? Stop trying to make me feel better. That's ridiculous. Who does that?" I shake my head, trying to get my breath back.

"Me. A man desperate to get you pregnant. A man who loves filling you up to breed you. One who never wants you to leave him."

That shuts me up completely.

I fought back the bile rising in my throat, a bitter taste coating my tongue.

"You fucking what?" I hiss.

"I don't regret it." He keeps his eyes on the road as I clench my fists.

"Stop the damn car." I slam them on the dash.

"No," he replies calmly.

"If you don't stop the car, I'll fucking jump out," I seethe.

"The fuck you will," he growls.

I huff as he strokes my stomach softly. The baby.

"Fine. You win. But I'm not talking to you."

I turn and cross my arms over my chest as I face the window, the cold glass chilling my skin.

"I'm not apologizing," he mutters.

I snap my face to him, my cheeks burning. From a mix of anger and desire.

It's fucked up, yes. But it's cute.

"Next time, ask me first."

His handsome face breaks into a warm smile, diffusing the anger that had been simmering within me.

"Next time?"

A grin stretches my face as I nod.

"I want a big family. You started the ball rolling so you gotta give me more babies."

"Deal."

We finish the drive home in silence, his hand protectively

stroking my tiny bump. It's that small I thought it was just bloating.

He helps me out of the car once we pull into the driveway, linking my fingers through his to lead me home.

As soon as the door shuts behind us, he pins me against the wall and his lips are on mine.

It's hot and sinful.

Lifting me into his arms, I wrap my legs securely around him and my arms tight around his neck.

With kisses peppering his cheek, he guides us down the long hallway, the quiet echoing with each step.

"Fuck, I can't wait to be inside you." He mutters between kisses.

"Fill me up, big man."

As he gets to the stairs, I pat his back to stop him.

"Wait. Can we go put the ultrasound pictures on the refrigerator, next to the cute picture I put there of Hades?"

He chuckles softly and kisses my cheek. "Yes, pretty girl."

Mmm, I smell coffee. I roll over and, as predicted, find Mikhail's empty spot next to me. I climb out of bed and stretch with a yawn and do my usual morning routine, then grab one of Miki's tops and put it on.

"Morning, handsome," I call out as I jog down the stairs.

"In here, baby," he yells back from the kitchen.

With a big grin on my face, I rush to him and slam my body against his for a cuddle.

Nestling against his chest, he strokes my hair and presses a kiss to the top of my head.

"I prefer waking up next to you, or with you inside me," I murmur against him, feeling his cock grow through his jeans.

"Me too. But we have a umm, guest," he whispers in my ear and I groan.

I know precisely who he means, and a fiery anger boils within me, making my heart pound.

"Get. Rid. Of. It." I say and put my best fake smile on as I push away from him.

Turning to her, sitting on the fucking bar stool like she belongs here in her yet again tight black dress and a tit explosion.

Does she not realize Miki is an ass man? She's barking up the wrong tree entirely.

And he's mine.

"Morning," I say to her and she scowls.

Kill her with kindness.

Or a blade through the throat would be my preferred option.

I don't trust her. I don't like her. And her grubby hands need to stay away from my baby daddy.

Miki opens up the refrigerator and her eyes go wide.

Ha. I bite back a laugh.

"What's that?" She points to the door as he closes it.

"Don't tell me Alexei and Lara are going to be littering the earth with his crazy genes."

Is she fucking serious?

"There's nothing wrong with Alexei or Lara. In fact, I hope one day they do have kids. They'd be cute as hell." I step in front of Miki with a hand on my hip.

"Mikhail?"

"Fucking hell," he mutters under his breath in annoyance.

"That's our baby, Zoya." Miki announces and places a

protective hand on my waist, tugging me snug against his side.

I'm struggling to hold back my laughter as her mouth drops open.

She's taking it as well as I imagined. I can hear her black heart breaking.

Shame.

"How? What?" She's lost for words. Her hands shake as she takes a sip of coffee.

"Do you want me to give you some biology lessons? Or, maybe you can ask those two guys at the club?" I say. Miki chuckles under his breath.

"But, you've known her for five minutes, Miki. This is ridiculous. You realize you're stuck with her for life now? How could you be so reckless?"

A growl erupts from his chest. He steps forward and slams his palm down on the counter.

"Anastasia is my wife. I want her next to me until I take my last breath. I want lots of kids with her, starting with our baby boy. You'll do well to keep your intrusive thoughts in your head before I remove my help. My family comes first, Zoya. Remember that."

She slinks off the barstool and the fake tears slip down her cheek.

I roll my eyes.

"But I am part of your family." Her voice breaks.

"No, Zoya. Galena is part of my family. You lost that right. Now get out of my house." Mikhail seethes, turning his back on her.

She's a master manipulator. She found that little soft spot in Miki's heart for Galena and she's exploiting it.

Not for much longer. Even poor Galena fears her mom. I can sense it. I've watched her tense when her mom touches her. She barely says a word around her. Poor kid. I can see why Miki is trying, I don't blame him.

It makes me love him more.

He's going to be an incredible dad.

Mikhail watches with a stern face as Zoya rushes out the back door.

"That got rid of her," I say as the door slams behind her.

"She's testing my patience. Enzo needs to hurry up with alternative living arrangements." Miki takes off his mask and rubs his face.

"Has she always been like this?"

He shakes his head.

"Not this bad. I barely spoke to her or saw her over the years. Since I told her not to come in the house, she's now using Galena as an excuse every time. Today it was that Galena is sick and needs some medicine. I don't believe her."

"What about speaking to Enzo? Get her moved away from us. It's healthier for us all. We have to think about the baby. I don't trust her, Miki. Do you really know her? Can you say she won't try to hurt me? I get a bad vibe from her."

He places his hand on either side of my waist and rubs my stomach under my top.

"She wouldn't fucking dare come after you. But yes. I'll push him to speed this up. I don't care if she has to leave kicking and screaming. I've had enough. You need to be as relaxed as possible. Leave it to me, I can get something figured out within a few days."

Relief washes over me.

"I'll drag her out myself if you want."

He smirks at me and runs the tip of his finger down my nose.

"God I love it when you get feisty, iskorka."

CHAPTER 54

MIKHAIL

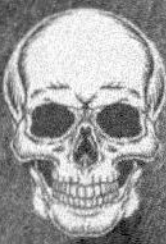

"C OME HERE." I pat my thigh for Ana to sit on.

She pushes a dark curl behind her ear, picks up her hot cup of tea, and slides her tight ass onto my leg.

Hades lies on the floor beneath the table, lightly snoring in the warm sliver of sun that spills there from the window.

"Did you want to go to the office with me today? We can catch a concert afterwards." My hand falls to her growing belly as I sip my coffee.

There's a part of me that doesn't want to let her out of my sight now that I know she's pregnant. I want to bubble wrap her and strap her to my back to carry her everywhere.

"Who's babysitting Zoya then? Doesn't she demand *all* of your time?" Ana's nose wrinkles and she wiggles on my lap.

I shrug and pull her tighter. "Niki or Lara can take care of her, too. Lara would be the best choice, Zoya apparently can't stand Alexei."

Ana laughs. "I believe that. He doesn't even acknowledge she's in the room." Her small hands cup my cheeks, running her thumb over my scars. "You're too nice. My big softy, trying to be the good guy."

I growl, pulling her palm to my lips. "I am not."

She gives me a wide smile. "Liar." She drops down hard onto my lap, nearly crushing my left nut.

"My little iskorka, I'm going to show you just how horrible I can be." I flip her over so she's lying across my knee.

Damn her for giggling. She's making me grin along with her.

"Mikhail!" Zoya's cry shatters our moment before she bursts into the room.

"Of fucking course." Ana pushes herself up and smooths her hair back with a glower darkening her features.

I take a deep breath, and tug up my balaclava. If nothing else, it will hide just how absolutely furious I am that Zoya keeps barging in.

"What the hell do you want? And how did you find out the code for the doors?" I bellow loudly enough that Ana winces.

Zoya rushes in, panic flaring her eyes. "She's gone! He took her!"

"Who? Galena? Are you sure she didn't sneak away from you?" It wouldn't be the first time. My little sister seems to hate staying with Zoya.

I can't say I blame her.

"He took her. She isn't hiding, I looked everywhere. I just know he did. Get Enzo to check the cameras!" Zoya clutches her dress at the neck, and collapses into the chair next to the table.

"How does he keep finding you all of the sudden?" Ana asks, then turns towards me and wrinkles her nose.

"I don't know. He wants me, wants Galena. What am I going to do?" Zoya sobs, covering her face.

I pull out my phone and call Enzo.

"Pull up the feed on Zoya's house," I grunt before he says a word.

"What the hell did she do now? he sighs.

But I can hear his keyboard clicking in the background.

"She's saying Galena has been taken. I need to know who did it." I stare hard at Zoya.

"Of course she's been taken! I can't believe you're sitting there, not offering any comfort." She bites her lower lip and looks at me through her lashes.

Her pranks for attention have been escalating. There are some days I hate that I made a promise to protect her.

"Shit." Enzo stops making background noise. "Yea, she's telling the truth. It's one of the same fucking goons that took Anastasia. It has to be Ivan."

"Fuck." I drop my forehead to Ana's shoulder. "See if you can catch them at an intersection."

"Not gonna happen." He pauses. "This is from, um, six hours ago."

My jaw ticks watching Zoya.

She purses her mouth and blows me a kiss before Ana can see her.

What the hell has she been doing for six hours?

"We have to get her back." Zoya stands and moves next to me. "Please? Take me to Russia, I'll talk to Ivan. Galena isn't safe with him."

"She isn't safe with you either." Ana pouts, then leans on my chest to put her body between Zoya and I. "You should go yourself and get her back," she snaps at Zoya.

"You know, Ivan had me first. He only took you because he couldn't find me." Zoya flips her wrist, shooing Ana as if she's a nuisance.

"Gross." Ana makes a gagging face.

It's like when she's choking on my cock. It makes blood rush to my crotch seeing her do it.

"You can have that dirty old man. He's a creep." Ana pushes off my lap

"You're just mad because you'll always be a second choice. I could have had your man too, if I had wanted him." Zoya sets her hand on my shoulder, but before I can protest, she pivots on her heel and moves towards the door. "Please, Mikhail. I do need your help. I want my baby back," she says before she leaves.

Ana cups her own belly, and rubs her hands over the budding life growing there. "I feel for her, I really do. But why does it have to be you?"

I rise to pull her close. "I hate this, too. Let me find out what Enzo says, and I'll see if I can set up a team. There's a chance I'll need to go, though. Galena is my responsibility, as the leader of this organization, it will always be mine." Tugging down my mask, I kiss the top of her head.

"Go get ready. You can still come with me to the office, I just don't think I can promise the concert until this gets figured out."

CHAPTER 55

ANASTASIA

I FUCKING HATE HER.

She's taking him away, and there isn't a damn thing I can do about it.

"You need to stay. For the sake of you, and our baby. I don't want either of you in danger." Mikhail throws another shirt into his bag.

"This is bullshit! Get one of your other guys to do this! Someone! Anyone!" I grab the folded up tee and toss it back at him. "You don't have to go. You're in charge, make one of your minions go with her. It's her own fucking fault." I let myself flop onto the bed, my belly poking up towards the ceiling.

"Galena is still my sister. I swore I'd keep her safe," he growls, putting the same item into his bag again. "I take my responsibilities very seriously, in case you can't tell." He bends, pressing his lips to my lower abdomen, then shifts my legs away from the night stand to pull out his pistol.

"I don't want you to go." Maybe if I add some tears it will stop him?

"Pouting will only earn you a spanking. I'll be back

before you know I'm gone." He holds out his palm. "Come on, I want to show you something before I go."

I roll my eyes, but let him pull me up.

I don't want to admit I probably was going to need his help anyways. With this growing baby bump, I'm like a turtle on my back.

He leads me downstairs, then calls Hades to come to him.

The nails clicking on the hard floors precedes the giant dog in his lazy saunter.

Mikhail reaches into a closet and pulls down a large stuffed animal, tossing it onto the floor.

Hades turns his nose, but remains focused on Mikhail, wandering closer to me and lowers his head.

I give him a scratch behind one of his clipped ears.

What is my husband doing?

"This is an important lesson. Hades is trained to attack on a single command. I've been anticipating Ivan, but now I want to know that you're protected." He takes my arms, and puts me behind him.

"Watch me closely." His hand raises and he points towards the stuffed toy. "Hades, mayday, mayday, mayday!"

Hades leaps forward, growling, and pounces on the fuzzy animal.

Within seconds, nothing remains but tufts of stuffing and fabric.

"Abort!" Mikhail grunts as he claps, then turns to me. "Did you see what I did?"

Hades drops on his butt, panting, with chunks of white fuzz still clinging to his dark muzzle.

That poor little hippo didn't stand a chance.

"Remember, it's three times before he'll attack whatever you're pointing to. He'll die to protect you, just as I would.

But he won't stop until the target looks like that." He gestures at the spreading mess. "So use him wisely."

"Maybe I'll make him do that to your luggage so you stay?" I grumble, letting myself lean against Mikhail's broad chest.

His chuckle vibrates against my ear. "I'll be back soon. I'll feel better knowing you're here, with him." He kisses the top of my head.

"Meanwhile, you're going to be thousands of miles away, with *her*." The thought makes me want to scream.

"Stop. I can only handle one crazy woman in my life. Once we get back with Galena, I'm sending them to New York. Frankie already agreed he'd keep an eye on her for me." Mikhail flicks his wrist to look at his Rolex.

"I'm sorry, iskorka. I have to go." His warm hands cup my cheeks and he crashes his lips against mine. "I love you both," he whispers before picking up his bag and walking out the door.

Hades tilts his massive head, and meanders to his water bowl.

He's pure terror in action, wrapped in a loveable goofy grin when he lolls his tongue.

I'm glad he's on my side.

CHAPTER 56

MIKHAIL

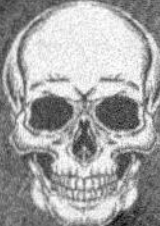

"I DON'T KNOW if we can trust Drago. Something was off last time. My father knew I was here." I signal the waiter to bring me another shot.

"There aren't a lot of choices available who have been vetted." Enzo sighs. "Otherwise, your best bet is to get in and out like you did last time. I just don't think Ivan will make things easy on you a second time."

I watch Zoya leaning over the bar to chat with the bartender. Her lips are so close to his ear, I can't see what she's saying.

"She's pushing us to go to the safe house one last time. I guess there's a few things she wants to pick up that might help Galena once she's back. We'll be at the new one within a few hours." I glance at the door again.

Drago should be here soon.

This is one of the biggest night clubs in the area. Hopefully, it's public enough that there shouldn't be any troubles.

He's impossible to miss when he walks in. He's nearly as big as I am, maybe bigger, stalking across the room as if he owns the place.

"Welcome back, Mikhail. I've heard much has changed since the last time I saw you." He holds out his hand to shake before he sits. "Congrats on the new wife, and kid on the way. A regular family man now?" He winks, crossing his ankle over his knee to reveal his tattoos extend all the way to his feet.

"You're well informed, friend." It makes me nervous how he knows. "Perhaps your eye for detail can help. I need to get back into Ivan's compound to rescue my sister."

Drago's blue eyes widen. "Lara? She seems very capable. I haven't heard from Alexei—"

"No, my littlest, Galena." I nod towards Zoya who approaches us.

Drago's leg falls, flattening his shoe against the floor with a thump. "Tatiana! I didn't—" His head tilts. "My apologies, I mistook you for someone else."

Interesting.

Drago's easy smile covers his mistake as he takes her palm and brings the back of her fingers to his mouth. "A pleasure."

"Thank you. Are you here to help me get my daughter back?" Zoya sits close enough to me that her knee brushes my thigh.

Drago squints at me before smiling. "I'll do my best. Ivan is a formidable foe, but I assure you, I'll do everything I can to help."

Every time my father's name is mentioned, the hidden scar on my face itches.

"I'll owe you for this one." I know he can't see it, but my jaw clenches.

Going into debt, in our line of work, is never something I like to do.

Drago grins and leans closer. "I like the sound of that."

"This calls for a drink." I raise my arm to the waiter. "Bring us a round." I circle the table with my finger in the air.

When the glasses appear, I hold mine up to Drago. "Here's to new friends." I swallow the burning liquor.

Standing, I notice Zoya's drink sits untouched. "Not thirsty?" I herd her towards the exit.

"Not really in the mood for alcohol." She dabs her eyes. "I miss my daughter so much."

"Don't worry, we'll get her back." The drive to the safe-house is short.

Which is good, because the effect of the bourbon is hitting me stronger than I expected.

I guess married life is making me a bit of a lightweight.

"Wait here." Zoya points towards the couch. "I just have a few things to get from Galena's room, and then we can go."

Fuck, this seat is comfortable. I sink into the thick cushions.

My eyes are so heavy, I'll just close them for a moment.

CHAPTER 57

ANASTASIA

THE HOUSE is empty and quiet, except for Hades snoring on the floor nearby. His presence is comforting, especially now that I know he could take care of any threat that might come near me.

I'm lost without Miki and I am petrified. Something doesn't sit right with me. My gut is screaming that something is wrong.

Zoya tried so many ways to get between me and Miki. Did the pregnancy tip her over the edge?

I can see in her eyes, she isn't stable.

The more my thoughts spiral, the more I debate phoning Lara. She might understand.

It startles me from my tea when my phone rings.

"Ana, this is Enzo. There's something odd about the feed from Zoya's house. Do you feel up to a field trip? I won't be able to make it that way for a few hours."

"Um, sure. I can go look. Where am I going?" I pat my leg to make Hades follow me.

Mikhail might have pissed me off when he left, but I'm not going anywhere without the dog now.

"There's a camera in the hall and another in an office area. Neither registered any movements when Galena was taken, but I can't see why." His voice sounds distant over the ticking of his keys.

I grab the spare set of keys from the wall and use them to open the smaller house.

I don't know what she was complaining about, this place is still ten times bigger than the tiny apartment I lived in with my mother for years.

"Okay, where am I going?" I wander through the living room to find the only hall near the kitchen.

"Yea, I got you on the feed. Take that right, and look up towards the end. You should see the camera up on the wall."

Following his directions, I step around the corner and can see something up near the ceiling.

"Wait!" he yells. "Where did you go?"

"I'm in the hall, like you told me to be. There's something stuck up there. Like, a piece of paper." I can see it taped over the lens.

"Fuck." His exhale whispers over the speaker. "You disappeared as soon as you would have come into this view. Okay, check the office too, please."

"Come on Hades." I step through a closed door, but don't see anything really amiss. "What am I supposed to be looking at?" I ask Enzo.

"There's another camera above the desk. It's hidden though in the smoke alarm. Can you send me a picture of it?"

I can't really see anything wrong with it, but I send the photo.

"Damn it," he groans. "They swapped it."

"Who?" I have a hard time believing Zoya did this.

"There was this one angle when Galena was being taken. It looked like she was smiling up at the guy. I didn't think anything of it at first. See if you can find anything else?" He clicks off the line.

What is going on?

Rifling through the papers on the desk, I find a small stack of letters bundled in the back.

They're all addressed to Zoya, and show crease marks like they've been folded tightly.

When I open the first one, I almost drop it.

All I can focus on is the signature.

Ivan.

Scrambling, I redial Enzo.

"What did you find?" he asks calmly.

"She's working with him!" I shriek.

Fumbling through the pile, I find one of the older ones from before she left Russia.

—I'm so glad my housekeeper moved next door and found you. Getting to reunite with my daughter has been everything I had hoped.

I've found Sergy's daughter. I know by taking her, we'll be able to draw Mikhail back to Russia.

Once he's gone, I'll be able to give you anything you desire—

My hands shake, I'm so angry.

"Tell me what you found." His voice cuts through my spinning thoughts.

"He found her, in Russia. They've been talking for months." My words come out in a jumble.

They kidnapped me just to get Mikhail? Is that why Zoya made him bring her over, to get closer?

What the hell is happening?

Housekeeper. I bet it was that bitchy old lady who was fitting my dress.

I knew I hated her.

"We have to save him." I blurt. "He's never going to come back if we don't." Pain in my heart nearly drops me.

I can't lose him. He's my entire world now.

"I'll get the guys together. Go back to the house, I'll send Jax over to hang out just in case." Enzo sounds like he's furiously typing.

"No, fuck that. I'm going. He's my man. I'm not going to let that bitch hurt him." I stomp to the main house, Hades on my heels. "I'd rather Jax go with me. I know he'd keep me safe, and can help knock that crazy woman down if needed."

I've come to absolutely love my brother since I've gotten to know him, and his wife.

These are my family. I'm not going to let Zoya mess this all up.

Enzo sighs. "Okay. I'll get the jet ready and rally the troops."

"Good. I'll be ready within twenty minutes." I go directly upstairs and start packing.

I might be pregnant, but I'm not broken.

I'll gladly fight to save my husband. And as much as I hate Zoya, it will be a pleasure to see her fall.

CHAPTER 58

MIKHAIL

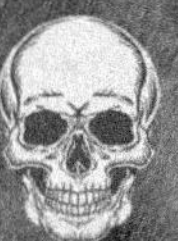

Song- Dead To Me, Ashes to New.

Fᴜᴄᴋ, my head hurts.

But when I try to rub it, my arm doesn't move.

What the hell?

Groggily, I open my eyes to find myself tied to the metal rails behind the couch.

My guts roll.

Son of a bitch.

"Oh!" Zoya appears from the back room. "You're awake. Hello, handsome." She lets my balaclava hang from one finger. "I've missed seeing your face. It isn't fair that you've held it away from me to show only that ungrateful brat you call a wife."

"She *is* my wife," I growl. "Let me go, and I promise I won't kill you." I tug at the cuffs, but they dig into my wrists.

"Hmm, no, I don't think I will. Not until you've come around. You see, if I let you go, that means Ivan gets his turn." She smiles as she straddles my knee. "And I'm just not quite ready to see you die. Yet."

Slowly, she lowers herself until she's sitting on my lap. Her palms flatten against my chest and she leans into me. "I could keep you here for a very long time, if you'd like?" Those red lips move closer, pursed to meet mine.

I jerk my head and meet her nose with my forehead, making a resounding crack.

"Ah!" she screams and leaps back, blood gushing from her nostrils down her chin. "You monster!"

"Did you forget who my father is?" I sneer. "That rotten apple didn't fall far from the tree. Let me go, and I swear that will be the worst that happens."

I add tension to the restraints, silently flexing to test the weaknesses.

I think I can get out, I just need to buy some more time.

"Don't tell me you really thought this would work? That I would crumple to my knees and beg you? I'm a fucking Volkov, whether I want to be or not. And Ana carries my *child*, heir to my empire." I spit at the floor by her feet. "You're nothing to me, Zoya. And you've repeatedly proven how little you're worth."

Her normally beautiful features mottle in anger and she runs from the room, her hands covering her bleeding face.

This is going to suck. I have no doubts that Zoya is going to hurt me.

But I can't let her think she can control me. I've known her for too long, and have learned more about her in the last few months than I ever wanted.

I'm only here for Galena.

What I didn't expect was for her to reappear with two wads of tissue shoved into her nostrils, and wearing nothing but a bra and panties.

"You have got to be kidding." My jaw clenches in disgust.

"If it's all about the baby, I should have the heir. I deserve it. After all, what's good for the father, is good for the son." She moves closer and reaches for my pants.

I might violently vomit on her.

Instead, I swipe my leg hard enough to catch behind her calves, sending her sprawling across the floor.

"This isn't happening." Straining, I can almost feel my right arm gaining ground on the bindings.

"Now you're going to pay for that." Zoya pulls herself up and whips a long silk robe around her body. "Ivan isn't going to be as nice."

"Ivan is who did this to me, Zoya! Don't you remember that night? Why would you work with him? He was horrible to you!" I want to yell in rage.

I lost so many people that night because of her. To have her run back into the arms of my father after everything I did...

Crushing.

"I was young and foolish. I see now how he truly cared for me. He treated me like the princess that *I am*." She pulls her phone from the table and types furiously into it. "He'll be here soon, and he's going to make you pay."

"How? The only thing I have left is my life! He's destroyed everything he's touched. Think about it!" I'd rather die than let him hurt Ana.

She's my world. Her and our baby are all that is important.

If this is all about me, maybe it's my time.

I'll gladly take my last breath if it keeps my family safe.

At least I can die now knowing what love feels like. Even if it was brief, she gave me a reason to stop just surviving and start living.

So if this really is the end, I can crash out of this world picturing my pretty girl's smile.

I'm just glad she's back in Vegas and safe.

"And locking me and my daughter away for half a decade was the answer? I've been miserable! At least Ivan took me out, showed me off. He may be a little rough, but I could see the world, and have all the best that it has to offer." She lashes out and kicks my shin. "You kept me in a hovel, barely surviving. That is no way to live."

"Jesus, Zoya. I know how you were raised. Your father taught you the value of hard work. You're no princess. Stop acting like you're entitled to more." I'm beginning to regret every penny I sent towards her.

"You keep Daddy's name out of this. When he gets out of prison, he's going to come after you for how you treated me." Her finger jabs inches from my face.

"Zoya, he died in the gulag." I squint and watch her. I haven't mentioned it before, but surely she had to have known?

Her fingers wrap into a fist. "You're lying," she hisses.

I'll go to my deathbed before I tell her it was Alexei. "I know for a fact. He's gone."

The rage leaks from her expression, but then her lips purse. "No, you're just saying that to hurt me. I hope Ivan tortures you for weeks for that." She flips her dark hair over her shoulder and stands.

A knock at the door startles us both.

"He's early!" She turns on her heel, and hurries to open it.

"Zoya, so pleasant to see you again. This is my associate." Drago's deep voice carries into the living room.

"Drago! In here!" I call out.

"No, you really need to—" Zoya protests as he pushes past her.

"Mikhail, what kind of kinky shit are you two up to?" He grins, then winks.

A blond woman with thick sunglasses follows him in. Her heels click on the tile floor before stopping and giving me a long look up and down. "You're Mikhail? I expected you to be bigger." She lowers her shades just enough to let me see the smile in her brown eyes.

Then she turns to Drago. "You're right, she does look familiar."

"I told you." Drago gives me a smug look, raising a brow when he spies the handcuffs. "Do you want out of those?"

"Yesterday would be fast enough." I tug on them hard enough to make them rattle.

"Leave him be. Who are you?" Zoya crosses her arms and frowns at the blond woman.

I'm curious too.

"Forgive my associate," the mystery woman croons. "My name is Tatiana."

THE LONG FLIGHT doesn't help my nausea. I thought most of that was past after the first trimester.

Apparently bumpy landings into Russia kicks it back in.

"Are you sure you want to do this?" Nikolai stops me from getting up.

"Yes. I have no doubts. I want to see that bitch burn." I set my jaw and push myself out of the seat.

Jax and Alexei follow, with Hades padding next to me off the plane.

I feel like I can conquer the world with them around me. Now I just need Mikhail back.

"Enzo gave me the coordinates to the safe house. He spotted them go in, but all of the internal cameras have been decommissioned." Nikolai pauses. "Ana, I want you to know, there's a chance Mikhail might not be okay."

I nod. "It goes with the job, right? I get it." I've never deluded myself that being part of organized crime was a safe position to be in.

The best place to be in that line of work is to be the one in control.

Nikolai pats my shoulder as Alexei holds our bags.

Jax hops behind the wheel of the big SUV, clicking his tongue bar against his teeth. "Where to, Niki?" He glances into the rearview mirror and meets my eyes.

I know him well enough to see the nerves tightening the lines around his mouth.

None of us may come back from this.

"Let me check. Enzo sent us the coordinates, I'll plug it into the GPS." Nikolai leans to the dash and punches the numbers in.

"You should let me drive, I know this area better," Alexei whines beside me.

"No." Nikolai clips, not even looking up.

"I did fine last time I was here." Alexei crosses his arms, leaning against the window.

Jax laughs from the driver's seat. "Dude, last time you were here, you spent months in the gulag. I really don't think that's a huge vote of confidence."

"I was set up! Tatiana is a shrewd bitch. I wonder if we'll ever see her again?" Alexei turns to me. "She tricked me. Don't ever make a deal with her, she's like that Rumper-guy. Always up to no good."

"Rumpelstiltskin?" I know the children's story. I can't imagine meeting someone like that in real life.

"Yea." He grins wide enough that I see his silver tooth. "She'll own your *soul*."

"Is she really that bad?" I can't imagine anyone is worse than Ivan.

All three men nod solemnly.

Great.

"Let's put it this way. My father had my wife and I captive. Tatiana just walked her happy ass in and got us out because she felt like it." Nikolai stares out the window. "That was hell."

The mention of Ivan and his atrocities makes a shiver go down my spine.

What are we walking into?

"We're here." Jax puts the truck in park near a nondescript house in the suburbs.

It looks like every other neighborhood.

"Which one?" Alexei peers between the seats at the row of carbon copy buildings.

"That darker brick in the middle." Nikolai points.

I jump out first.

"Hey, wait. You can't just walk right in there." Jax jogs to catch up to me.

Hades side-eyes him, but moves to let him closer.

"Why not? What are we going to do? If she's in there hurting him, I need to go in." It makes perfect sense to me.

"I told you I liked her. She thinks like me." Alexei laughs as he strides next to Hades.

"You're all going to get killed," Nikolai grumbles from behind.

But I hear him work the slide on his pistol. He's ready too.

"Should I kick it in?" Alexei bounces on his toes next to me.

"I can shoot the lock." Nikolai moves to aim.

"Whoa. Why don't I try it first?" I step in front and the handle easily turns.

Alexei pushes it open, then all I can hear is him yelling. "What the fuck?"

CHAPTER 60

MIKHAIL

"TATIANA? I didn't expect you to be so…short." I try to smile, but all I want to do is rip Zoya in half.

"Oh, funny guy." She turns to Drago. "You didn't tell me he's a comedian," she says sarcastically.

She tugs on her blond hair, pulling the wig from her head revealing her black locks and folds her glasses.

"I'd like to know how you plan on getting out of your little—" She waves her hand vaguely towards my cuffed arms. "—predicament."

"I'll be fine." I know her tactics too well. If I ask for her help, who knows how I'll end up owing her?

Zoya steps closer, her face pale.

"Natalia?" she whispers, reaching for Tatiana.

"Who?" Tatiana scoffs, stepping away from her.

The door flies open, making everyone turn towards it.

Alexei?

What the fuck?

Hades pads in behind him, and my stomach sinks.

No, not Ana too.

"You were supposed to stay home." I watch her eyes flick

from me to the barely clad Zoya, and anger darkens her features.

"This bitch made it hard to do. I found proof she's working with Ivan this whole time." Ana rests her palm on Hades' shoulder.

Nikolai and Jax crowd the entrance.

"Niki, Ivan is on his way," I grunt, gesturing with my chin for him to go out.

Nikolai nods, then grabs Jax's elbow and drags him outside.

"I'll go with them." Drago steps past, following my brother.

"Tatiana, always a pleasure." Alexei steps away from her to move closer to me. "Do you want out?" He doesn't wait for my answer, leaning forward he pulls out a handcuff key from his pocket and starts to unlock my wrist.

"You always carry one of those?" I blink up at him as a slow grin forms on his face. "You know, I don't really want to know why."

"Your sister is feisty." He chuckles as he moves to the other side.

"I'm so done with this family!" Zoya screams, and dives towards a drawer in the table.

Before any of us move, she's brandishing a short pistol.

But then she points it at Ana.

We all freeze, watching her.

"Mikhail, we could have overtaken Ivan and ruled together. Maybe if this fucking brat wasn't in the way." She waves the barrel over Ana's bulging belly.

"Zoya, no!" I cry out, still locked by one arm. "I'll kill you myself!"

"You're just a jealous bitch." Ana raises her jaw defiantly.

It makes me love her even more. She's brave beyond measure in the face of danger.

"I was *first.*" Zoya spits. "Always remember that."

"Put the gun down." Tatiana demands. The tone of her voice tells me she's used to having her commands followed.

Hades growls from next to Ana, but doesn't move.

"Why should I listen to you? You're in no position to make demands either." Zoya waves the gun towards her, then recenters it on Ana.

"You're going to shoot a pregnant girl? For what? Some unfounded search for glory?" Tatiana raises her palms. "Maybe we can make a deal?"

"No! It's my right! I deserve it!" Zoya's mouth wavers as she wildly swings her weapon around the room.

"She's crazier than I am," Alexei whispers as he fumbles toward the other cuff.

"Alexei, you need to get her out of here!" I shake my arm, holding out my hand for the key.

He drops it into my palm, but it falls into the cushion of the couch.

Fuck.

Alexei scrambles, running towards Ana.

Zoya glances at him, then squeezes the trigger.

It's like the world slips into slow motion as my eyes lock onto the look of fear and shock frozen onto my wife's face.

"No!" Tatiana jumps towards Ana.

Ana and Tatiana tumble to the floor. Alexei pins Zoya beneath him, prying the gun out of her hand and shoving it towards Drago.

"Ana!" I shout with my ears still ringing from the blast.

But I can't see her. My hand dives into the cushions to try and find the key, but it's nowhere within my reach.

"Natalia!" Zoya screams, drowning out any other sound

with a high pitched keening as she pulls herself away from Alexei.

With all the rage and strength in my body, I strain against the cuff until the bolts pull from the wall, bouncing off the floor when I jerk it loose to slip myself free.

Then a tiny voice breaks through my fury when I hear Ana saying the words I taught her.

"Mayday. Mayday. Mayday." She falls limply back to the floor as I rush to her.

Hades leaps away from the wall and grabs Zoya's shoulder in his crushing jaws, shaking his head, his teeth rip into her flesh as her new shrieks of agony fill the room.

He tackles her down, pinning her to the tile, jaw gnashing, he slings chunks of skin and muscle, spraying everyone near with blood.

I barely notice, collapsing to my knees next to my pale wife.

"Ana, please, are you okay?" My thumb brushes her cheek, then I wrap my arm behind her head, shielding her from the ravaging dog and the mess he's making of Zoya.

At least the screams have stopped.

All I can hear is his growling and tearing as he pulls her throat free from her body.

"Abort," I say softly, staring only at Ana's closed eyes.

Hades drops to his haunches, licking the gore from his lips.

"Mikhail? Tatiana got shot. What do you want me to do?" Alexei presses a corner of her shirt into her shoulder.

"Get Drago. She saved Ana. She deserves anything she wants for that." I pull Ana up onto my lap, rocking her slowly against my chest.

"Come on, iskorka, wake up." I can't see any injuries.

All I can hope is that she and the baby are okay.

Alexei scoops up Tatiana and darts out the door.

I can hear the wild revving of the engine when Drago leaves. I'm guessing he's rushing Tatiana to a doctor.

Maybe I should have carried Ana out there too?

Hades whines, sniffing her arm, and bumps it with his bloody nose.

"I know, buddy. I hope she's okay." My palm rests on her belly.

I can feel my baby moving. I just need her to wake up.

Gunfire outside makes my heart race, but I don't move.

Ana is my priority now.

My brother and the rest can take care of everything.

Until a slow clap comes from the door to the house.

"Well done, son." Ivan grins, watching me. "You've saved me the trouble of killing her myself." He pushes himself away from the frame and holds his arm towards the porch.

Galena moves closer, gripping his finger in her tiny hand.

"How did you get past everyone?" I growl, hunching myself over Ana.

"Oh, they're currently, hmm, preoccupied." He strokes his gray beard, then squats next to Zoya's body, while pulling Galena onto his knee. "Your mommy was a very bad girl," he says.

I wish I could send Hades on him as well, but I'm not sure that Galena wouldn't get hurt in the process.

Galena buries her face against his shoulder, and her back shudders with sobbing.

"Stop crying," he snaps. "She's gone."

Ah, there it is. The loving father.

I hate him.

"What do you want, Ivan?" I growl.

"The same as I've always wanted. My daughter, and my

wife. Now that you're mongrel has killed Zoya, I'll take yours instead." He stands, smirking as he looks down at Ana.

"I don't think so." The words to send Hades after him sit on the tip of my tongue.

If only he wasn't using Galena as a human shield.

There's more sporadic gunfire outside.

Fuck, I hope Niki and the boys are okay. My bastard father has already caused so much pain, I can't handle any more loss by his hands.

"Do you hear that? That's the sound of your men falling, one by one." Ivan bends and grips my chin, but I smack his arm away. "Your scars didn't heal quite as nicely as mine. That little bitch needs to pay for what she did to me." He points at his own cheek where a pucker sits above his lip.

"It's too bad she didn't aim for your heart, but the target is too small." I feel her shift on my lap.

A small moan escapes her lips before she opens her eyes.

She rubs the back of her head and looks up at me. "Mikhail?"

Relief floods through me. "Are you hurt?" I ignore my father.

Whatever he's planning is nothing compared to the ache of having her unconscious.

"No, I think I just got the wind knocked out of me." She glances around and cringes when she sees the mess of Zoya lying just a few feet away.

But she freezes when she sees Ivan.

"Galena, baby? Are you okay?" Ana calls out.

"Mommy's gone," she sobs.

Ana takes a deep breath. "Do you remember that game we played, when you hid from me?"

"Yes." Galena's voice is hesitant.

Ana stares into my eyes, and winks. "Do that one thing," she calls out to Galena.

"What are you up to?" Ivan stalks closer, just as Galena twists in his arms and runs towards her room.

"Mayday!" Ana screams, but before the next can follow, Ivan cuts away, running out of the house.

"Go, Mikhail. End this." Ana shoves at my arm, pulling herself away.

I bolt up and chase my father outside.

MY ENTIRE BODY ACHES.

What the hell happened? All I can remember is the shot, and falling, then saying the trigger words before the world went black.

It takes me another moment after Mikhail disappears before I stop feeling quite as woozy.

What do I do if Mikhail fails? I never want to go back with Ivan. I have to take care of my baby now.

No, I can't think like that. Nothing will happen.

Mikhail has to win this.

Another gunshot echoes through the house.

I might be sick. Was that him?

He'll come back for me.

I stay still, trying to catch my breath.

Fuck it. I have to get up and get Galena safe.

"Come on Hades. No, please don't touch me." I push the back of his shoulder away so he doesn't lean on me like he normally does.

The bloody bits hanging from his fur and muzzle are almost enough to make me want to puke.

Another shot makes my ears ring.

Please don't be him.

Rolling myself onto my side, I manage to get my knees under me and slowly push up.

I love my baby already, but I'm so fucking uncoordinated because of it. And I'm winded just trying to stand.

When I finally get to my feet, I can see the clear picture of the mess that Hades inflicted.

"Damn, dude. I'm *really* glad you're on my side."

I have to find Galena so we're ready to go as soon as Mikhail comes back for me.

An ache spreads through my chest thinking that he might be hurt, but I don't dare look outside.

If I don't see him, he's still okay in my head.

Creeping through the hall, I find the master suite.

More letters? What the fuck? How long did Zoya talk to him?

"Galena?" I poke my head into the second bedroom. "Sweetie, are you in here?" I pull open the closet and look inside, but she isn't there.

Shit. I bet she's under the bed.

I'm going to have a hell of a time getting up again if I kneel.

"If you're down there, you won, baby girl. You can come out now." All I can do is lift the foot of the comforter and hope she crawls out.

"Is he gone?" Her tremulous voice is muffled under the mattress.

"Yes, but we need to leave, too. We'll go hide together in the back until Mikhail comes back, okay?" I hate that I might be lying to her.

Guiltily, I need the comfort of her company as badly as I need Hades.

"Okay." She shuffles herself until I see the tips of her shoes poke out beneath the frame.

When she stands, her bottom lip trembles before I pull her tight to me for a hug.

Bending as low as I can, I brush her curly hair away from her eyes and give her my best smile. "You're so brave, Galena. I'm so lucky to have you as a friend. Should we go?" I hold out my hand, waiting for her to take it.

She bites her lip and sniffles, then nods. Slipping her tiny fingers into mine, we tiptoe out of the room and move towards the back of the house.

"I think we'll be safe here, do you want to wait with me and Hades?" I wish I had a weapon, but I haven't seen any sign of one.

She looks hesitantly at Hades, who still has blood smeared on his chest, then turns against my side, burying her face into my hip.

"It's okay, sweetie. He's protecting me."

"Mommy didn't like you," she says into my shirt. "I heard her talking to Daddy about it a lot."

"I know." As tempting as it is to say something negative about Zoya, I know Galena isn't the person to say it to.

When another shot goes off, my stomach turns.

Please, Mikhail, be safe.

CHAPTER 62

MIKHAIL

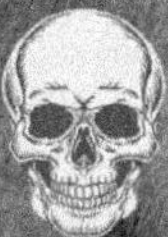

Song- Empire (Let Them Sing) Bring Me The Horizon.

As soon as I burst out of the house, I freeze.

Nikolai, Jax, and Alexei are all on their knees with two men behind them holding a gun to their heads.

Fuck.

"It seems I still have a few tricks up my sleeve. Not bad for an old man." Ivan chuckles and turns towards me, his arms spread wide.

"If I eliminate your little group, I'll own Vegas, *and* have that sweet little bitch as my own. I can raise my grandchild to be the heir you *should* have been." His face mottles as he points at me. "Instead of the traitorous disgrace you all turned out to be!" His hand sweeps over Nikolai, Alexei, and Jax. "The only thing that would be sweeter in this moment is if that ungrateful brat of a daughter of mine was here as well."

I can see Alexei's hands tighten into fists behind his head.

The man behind him lowers the barrel of his pistol next to Alexei's ear and fires into the dirt before he bends closer. "Don't even think about it, pretty boy."

397

My own clench by my thighs in frustration.

I can't do a damn thing.

"You brought this all down on yourself. If you weren't such a monster, people wouldn't want to run from you," I grit through my teeth.

This is a tough spot and I have no idea how to get out of this.

Ivan turns slowly, looking at the backs of my family and friends.

"I ran this the way it needed to be. You're weak, Mikhail. You never should have been in charge. Look at them. They chose you to protect them, to guide them, and where did it leave them? Kneeling in the dirt like dogs. They're going to die, because of *you.*"

He spins, pointing at Jax. "Shoot him first. It's his father's fault that my whore of a wife left to start with."

"No!" The word barely escapes before the shot echoes across the parking lot.

Jax falls over, slumped in a pile.

Fear grips me.

He trusted me.

The man behind him steps away, then again, weaving drunkenly on his feet.

What the hell?

He turns toward Ivan, silently opening and closing his mouth until a spill of blood covers his chin and he drops his weapon into the dirt.

Then he crumples first to his knees, then lands face first onto the ground. His eyes are wide and unblinking.

"What the fuck?" Ivan twirls, peering at the trees.

His other guard aims his gun at the woods wildly, glancing at his fallen teammate. "Ivan, we need to go."

"No!" Ivan bellows. "This ends now!"

When the next shot fires, I catch the flash of the barrel through the trees.

The second guard teeters, then collapses.

"Alexei, get Jax!" I yell, running forward to yank the gun from the falling man before he hits the ground.

Whipping around, I point it at my father.

Nikolai appears, grabbing his arms and pinning them behind his back.

Ivan sneers as Sven and Ben appear from the dense cover of the forest, both holding high powered sniper rifles on their shoulders.

"Of course it's the Butcher's men." Ivan spits.

"Got him covered?" I ask Nikolai.

He nods as I run by. I need to make sure Jax is okay.

"Alexei?" I squat next to him. "Tell me."

Alexei has his shirt pulled off and is holding it tightly against Jax's shoulder. "He should be good. Might fuck up his right hook for a while." He grins, showing his silver tooth. "Come on, Jax. I've seen you take a harder hit from Maeve."

Jax groans and rolls onto his side. "Dude, that shit hurts."

"We've all been shot, Jax." I glance back at Ivan who's defiantly staring down the twins. "Alexei, can you take him inside and make sure Ana is safe?"

"Sure thing, Miki." Alexei winks at me, then lifts Jax to stand.

As they head towards the door, I turn my full attention back to Ivan.

Alexei reappears, and I motion him to join me.

Dropping the gun, I grab one of the big Bowie knives off the side of the fallen guard.

"Get his other arm." I gesture to Alexei.

"Do you think this is the end? You fucked up letting

Tatiana leave. She's so much worse than I am." Ivan struggles between Nikolai and Alexei, but they hold him firmly.

"I've dealt with her before." I hold the tip of the blade beneath his chin. "It's your rotten soul that I'll be happy to purge from his earth."

Dropping my arm, I sink the point deep into his gut.

"You fuck." Ivan exhales heavily. "You'll never win."

With a visceral sawing motion, I work my hand up, splitting his abdomen with every thrust.

"You're wrong, Dad. This is me, winning." Another plunge, and I tilt my weapon until it's driving up into his ribcage, piercing his black fucking heart.

The anger fades from his face as he falls limp between Nikolai and Alexei.

They let him slump to the ground.

"Nice job." Ben smiles and pulls out a couple of cigars.

"Good shooting. Thank you." I clap him on the shoulder, then hold out my bloody hand for Sven to shake. "You guys came at the right time."

"Thank Drago. He had us on standby and told us to wait after they left." Sven pushes his hair back, and takes one of the smokes from Ben.

The formidable twins high five each other, then turn back towards the forest.

I know I should go back to Ana.

But all I can do is stare down at the lifeless body of my father.

Nikolai does the same.

All the turmoil. So much loss, and pain.

Because of him.

Nikolai's face darkens, and he pulls back one leg, launching a hard kick into Ivan's ribs.

Then another.

He keeps swinging his boot until ribs break.

"I hate you so much!" He screams at the dead man.

My stoic statue of a brother, broken to screams by our father.

"Come here." I tug on his arm, and he clutches me in a hard embrace. "We did it. We survived him. And now we'll prove him wrong by being better men than he ever was."

Nikolai pulls away, his jaw working with a nod. "Damn right," he grunts. "Go get Ana. We need to get the hell out of here."

CHAPTER 63

ANASTASIA

"Ana! I need help with Jax!" Alexei cries out from the living room.

Tugging Galena with me, we hurry through the hall to find Alexei dropping a bloody Jax onto the couch.

"Hold this here. I'll be back as soon as Mikhail is done with Ivan." He grins.

"Wait, is Mikhail okay?" I hold up my hand.

I need to know.

"Yep, he has Ivan caught. Time for fun, now." He cackles as he races away.

He caught Ivan.

When I heard the bullets, I was so terrified.

"Jax? Can you hear me?" I press my palms where Alexei had pointed.

Jax is so pale, it scares me.

"Hmm?" He cracks one dark eye, and grimaces. "Yea, sis, I'm here." The corner of his lip turns up. "Hurts like a bitch."

His cool hand covers mine.

"Jax?" I can feel tears burning to fall. "I'm lucky I got you." Biting my lip doesn't stop it from trembling.

I hate this life of chaos. I just want everyone I love to be safe and healthy.

"You got me forever." His eyes roll back into his head when he tries to open them. "I'm just so damn tired. I'm glad Hades is here."

His hand goes limp, but his breathing is even.

"Come on, big brother, stay with me." My forehead falls to my wrist as I silently plead with him to not let go.

"Is Jax gonna be okay?" Galena glances between him and the body of Zoya still lying on the floor in the corner.

"Yea, sweetie. He will be." I sniffle back my tears. I need to be strong for her, even if I don't believe my own words.

A roar comes from outside, and I know it can only be from my husband.

Oh no. Is he hurt?

Within a moment, heavy footsteps echo on the porch, and Mikhail comes striding into the room, directly for me.

He pulls me into a crushing hug. "Ana, I was so worried."

"I'm fine, but please, Jax…" I can't finish as a sob rips out of my throat.

He looks down at my unconscious brother. "I'll do everything I can for him." His lips touch my forehead before he disappears outside.

Alexei follows him in. "I'll make sure he lives long enough for Sofia to yell at him."

Mikhail reaches out and pulls Galena close. "Let's go home."

CHAPTER 64

MIKHAIL

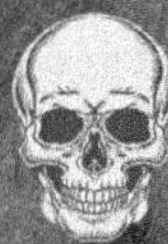

With Galena heading home with Niki, I hold on tight to Ana's hand leading her back home with Hades following by her side.

I owe that dog. Even if she did make him into a big softie for her, he did exactly what he was meant to.

He saved our family. If she wants him to be a pet and sleep in our damn bed, that dog can have whatever he wants.

As the door closes, I spin to face her, without uttering a word, I wrap my arms around her and she does the same and we just stand there.

Letting time pass by in silence, holding onto each other.

I nearly lost her.

I would have lost my whole life if it wasn't for Tatiana.

"I'm so sorry, Ana," I whisper into the top of her head.

"Sorry? It wasn't your fault. It was hers."

I swallow the lump in my throat. I allowed that monster into my home, around my family. Risking my life to save hers.

I don't regret that as I have Galena to think about.

Yet, Zoya was seconds away from destroying my world.

"Are you okay?" I ask Ana, even though it was Hades who killed Zoya, Ana gave the command. I don't want that on her conscience.

She tips her head back to look at me, her eyes watering.

"Am I fucked up that I don't feel bad? I hated her. She took you away from me and could have killed our baby. I'm glad she's dead. And if it wasn't Hades, I would have done it myself."

I smile down at her, pushing her hair away from her face. I press my lips against hers.

"I'm proud of you, iskorka. You saved me and our little boy. Thank you."

Running my hands over her shoulders and down her side, I cup her ass, pressing her firmly against me.

"But from now on, you stay out of danger. I cannot lose you, Ana."

She purses her lips, deep in thought.

"You gotta be more careful too, Miki. I am not living life without you."

"Deal. Now, how does a shower sound?" I whisper in her ear, feeling her shiver against me.

"I'll clean you if you clean me?" She bats her lashes.

"Every. Fucking. Inch."

She lets out a scream as I bundle her in my arms and rush us up the stairs, kicking open the bathroom door, I set her down and turn on the waterfall shower.

"Strip." I tell her, but as I turn to face her, she's already naked on the top half. Rolling my bottom lip between my teeth, I admire her body as she pushes off her leggings and black panties.

"Beautiful." I blow her a kiss and whip off my own clothes, kicking them away from me across the tiles.

I grab her hand and lead her into the shower, the hot spray beating over us as I press her against the wall, slamming my hand on the tiles and my other hand around her throat as I kiss her.

She moans in my mouth and I trail more kisses along her jaw, working my way down her neck.

I keep going, leaving a trail of them between her breasts and placing a long kiss on her growing belly bump.

As I get down onto one knee, I take her calf and rest it on my thigh, then dive my head in her pussy, spreading her open with my fingers.

"I fucking love you."

As I look up, she drags her fingers through my curls with a grin and pushes my head back against her pussy.

"More, Miki. Sir. Please." Each word a breathy moan.

Her back arches and her hips rock against my face. Sliding two fingers inside of her soaking pussy, she bucks against me.

"I love you," she breathes out.

Sucking on her clit, I pull my head back, still thrusting into her with my hand.

"Eyes on me, baby."

They snap open, full of hunger and pierce into my soul.

"Marry me, again, iskorka. This time, a real ceremony."

I curl my fingers, hitting her sweet spot and she cries out.

"If you come on my tongue, I'll take that as a 'yes'."

I feast on her like I've been starved, getting her soaking until her body is shaking around me.

"Say yes, pretty girl. Come for me."

She screams out my name, yanking my hair so hard it burns my scalp and she rides out her orgasm all over my face. As soon as she's finished, I'm on my feet, lifting her up so she can wrap her legs around me.

"Yes, Miki. I'll marry you again."

She tugs me closer by my neck and kisses the life out of me.

"Good. You didn't really have a choice. My wife. Always"

CHAPTER 65

ANASTASIA

Two Weeks Later...

"ARE YOU READY, SIS?" Jax asks.

I clutch my black rose bouquet tighter, its velvety petals cool against my skin, as he links his arm through mine.

"More than ready."

"Do you want to switch sides? Is your shoulder okay?" I ask, looking up at him.

He looks like our dad.

My heart sinks, a heavy weight in my chest, as I realize neither of my parents are here.

"I'll live. What's with the face?"

I frown and he chuckles, clicking his tongue bar against his teeth.

"I put on the same one when I'm upset. We're more similar than we think."

He smiles down at me, and I realize how lucky I am.

I found my brother. We have a big family that loves us.

We might both have been lost in this world, but we were found by the most incredible people.

"You seem pretty happy with life now?" I ask softly.

Mikhail told me about Jax's history and my heart broke for him. I'm glad he had Sofia to drag him out of the darkness.

"It's always going to be there in the background, that sadness that creeps in. But I am happy. My family keeps me out of chaos, and now you. It's kinda perfect, isn't it?"

A single tear tracks down my cheek, leaving a cool trail that he gently wipes it away with his thumb.

"It is perfect. And we get to watch our kids grow up together."

"Shh. That little man might have a cousin the same age as him."

My mouth falls open, and I squeal with excitement, wrapping my arms around him.

"Congratulations, bro. This is going to be amazing. Watching our kids have the childhood we wished for."

I pull back and re-link my arm through his.

"Here's to a beautiful life of chaos, sis."

"To chaos." I smile back at him. "Let's get me married, again."

He nods, tugging down on his suit jacket as we head towards the entrance.

"I never thought I'd see the day Miki falls in love."

A burst of laughter escapes my lips.

"I don't think he did either. I tricked him with my spells."

"Can you mix up a spell to get him off my ass? I'm exhausted."

With a dramatic roll of my eyes, and a tug at his arm, I pull him toward the main chamber, the handle cool beneath my hand.

"I'll see what I can do."

As the heavy wooden doors creak open, revealing the

dimly lit gothic church, a wave of emotion threatens to overwhelm me.

Black and white roses climb every surface, their thorny stems intertwined, creating a dramatic display.

Only the first three rows are filled with people. Close family and friends, the ones we trust and love.

Not that I take notice of those people. My eyes lock onto my husband. Even in the mask, he's the most attractive man I have ever seen.

I can see by the creases and the way his dark eyes speak to me. He's smiling.

I blow him a kiss, a silent, playful gesture, as I step into the room.

He might already be my husband, but this is the real deal. The wedding we both deserve, one for love, not for convenience.

Although, even all those months ago, we loved each other.

This was always meant to be. It was written in the stars for us.

CHAPTER 66

MIKHAIL

Song- Sleeptoken Eulicid

It's time to leave the broken version of me behind.

My wife deserves better.

My family deserve more.

Ana has given me the strength to not need to hide. Everything I need is right in this room.

The people who love me for who I am, scars included.

My past and my future combined.

I don't need this mask anymore. That part of my life is over.

Even though the nerves pit in my stomach, I remember the day I revealed my true self to Ana. She didn't flinch or run away. She accepted me, every single broken inch of me.

And I know my family will do that too.

Jax squeezes her shoulder as he returns to Sofia and his kids. I promptly return my focus to my stunning wife.

The dress, a masterpiece of form-fitting fabric, showcases her curves and her little bump, sending my heart racing.

Elegant yet sexy. Her curls fall around her face, and those lips. Deep red, my favorite.

The scent of the dark roses fills the air as I take them from her, pulling her into my embrace.

"You look breathtaking, iskorka. Absolutely perfect in every way."

She blushes as I press a soft kiss to her cheek.

"You look so handsome in that black suit, Miki."

With a playful wink, and a final glance, I pull away.

I nod to Nikolai and hold out the bouquet. With a grunt, he rises, takes them from me, and gives them to Galena, whose face breaks into a broad smile as he sits back down. I know that is the best place for her now. Nikolai and Mila will make sure she is safe and loved and she has Elena to keep her company.

Lacing my fingers through Ana's, I feel the softness of her skin against mine as I reach up with my other hand, to grab the knot of my balaclava. Her eyes go wide, then crinkle at the corners as she smiles, her nod a silent affirmation.

"I've got you, Miki. It's time."

Taking a deep breath, I can hear the blood pounding in my ears as I untie it and tug it away from my face. I don't know why I expect gasps in horror. But they don't come.

Nothing. Just silence as if nothing out of the ordinary has happened.

"Everyone in this room loves you, Miki. We don't see the scars, we just see you."

Fuck. That hits me like a spear through the chest.

"I love you, pretty girl." I twirl her thumb with my own, for comfort more than anything. I need her by my side.

As I bravely look to the small selection of friends and family here, my eyes lock with Lara's glassy blue ones. She sniffles but gives me the biggest smile. I know this will mean a lot to her. She always tells me she misses seeing my face.

Nikolai gives me a nod. We may not use many words for each other, but the love is there.

Enzo, Jax, Ben, Sven and Drago are all pretty unphased. And then there's Alexei, grinning at me with his silver tooth like a kid in a candy shop.

He gives me a thumbs up and Lara nudges his side with her elbow.

"What? He did a good job?" Alexei whines to Lara.

We would all be lost without our donkey, Alexei. I'm surprised he didn't bring his flamingos, Sheila and Bruce and whatever the hell they called the baby one.

With a shaky exhale, I feel the chill of the air as Ana's reassuring grip tightens on my hand.

Frankie clears his throat from the third row back and we lock eyes. A silent gesture of his approval. Me and him have been through enough over the years for him to be here. I trust him and his guys.

Revealing myself wasn't that bad.

I finally am free from my past. Now that my father is dead and I finally have his blood on my hands.

I can move on, with my iskorka.

Till death do us part. No where to hide. No reason to run.

I get to spend the rest of my days loving the woman who danced with my demons and cut away my chains.

The minister greets us all and I hear it, but I'm too busy admiring my wife.

"Mikhail, do you have your ring?" the old man asks, looking down at my empty finger.

I shake my head.

"Miki, what?" Ana whispers.

Instead, I reach into my pocket, the familiar weight of my blade comforting, and flip it open with a satisfying click.

"Rings can be lost. I want something forever."

I take Ana's soft hands, feeling the warmth of her skin, and place the cool, smooth knife in them.

"Have you lost your damn mind?" She blinks rapidly at me.

I dare not look at Lara and Nikolai.

"I hate my scars. They fuel my hatred. They make me cold. Who I need to be to survive. But this scar. This one will be my reminder that not everything in this world is evil. That not every mark I have is a punishment. This one represents my devotion to you. This one I will look at on my finger every day and smile. I won't hide it, I'll show it off to the world because it represents that I'm yours, for life."

Tears well in her eyes as she looks down at the blade and then into my eyes. I know she can read how serious I am about this.

"Aww, Miki. That's so cute. What do you want me to do?"

The sweat on my palms feels clammy as I pat down my suit jacket.

"Your initial, please, baby."

She nods, looking at my hand as I hold it out flat in front of her.

"What if I do it really shit? I've never done this before?"

I shrug, my fingers brushing lightly against her skin as I stroke her arm.

"I don't care what it looks like. It's about you marking me as yours. That's all I want, iskorka. Claim me."

Her hand trembles slightly, the blade glinting dangerously close to my ring finger, and then the metallic scent of blood fills the air.

She looks up at me for reassurance.

"Green, baby," I whisper.

I don't really feel it, it's a clean cut. She gets it done quickly. The minister clears his throat next to us. Pulling out the bandage from my pocket, Ana helps me wrap it up, laughing to herself as she does.

"You are something else, Mr. Volkov," she mutters.

"Well, I'm all yours, pretty girl. Even got the mark to prove it." I wink at her, making her blush.

Damn, I can't wait to get my hands on her later.

The rest passes in a blur. We wanted this short and simple. No long vow exchanges. That isn't for anyone else. We have written vows to read to each other at home later.

"You may now kiss the—"

I don't let him finish. I grab ahold of her, my hand encircling her throat as I pour all my love into the kiss.

"I love you, wife."

I slam one last kiss on her lips.

With a gentle swipe of her thumb, she removes the lipstick stain on my mouth, the touch lingering for a moment.

"I love you, big man. More than you could ever know."

She places her dainty hand in mine, and I lead us out of the church. I'm lucky I didn't go up in flames.

We all somehow survived that one. Maybe we aren't so bad after all.

The next room is cozy, with worn couches and the faint smell of old books. Alexei has arranged an entire wedding reception in his backyard for us. We just have to wait for whatever extravagant transport to arrive.

Bursting through the door, Lara immediately engulfs Ana in a hug, murmuring a hushed reassurance in her ear before her gaze finds me, a mixture of anxiety and determination in her eyes.

"I'm proud of you, big bro. The scars are a reminder of your strength, that we are all still alive because of your sacrifice. Always remember that and how much we love you."

I pull my sister tightly against me, the dampness of her tears a heavy weight against my chest.

She's been through a lot, and recently, I've never seen her happier. Thanks to Alexei.

"No one can tear the Volkov's apart, sis," I whisper to her.

A blonde server, her hair catching the light, glides into the room from the left entrance, carrying a tray laden with flutes of chilled champagne. Everyone rushes over, the sound of their feet pounding on the floor mixing with the kids' giggles as they bounce on the couches. I take a moment to wrap my arm around Ana's shoulder.

I pick up one of the elegant glasses, then start to thank her, but the server shuffles away, pulling down her hat. She glances up long enough for me to lock eyes for a split second. I come face to face with a ghost, a woman who's a master of disguise.

Tatiana.

Spinning around to get Enzo's attention, but when I turn back she's vanished.

"Miki, what the hell?" Ana looks up, confusion on her features.

I kiss the side of her head.

"Nothing to worry about."

I hope.

If she wanted us dead, we would be. She's after something else. Or someone else. Enzo will figure it out. My father's warning rings in my ears. If that old bastard feared her, I should too.

"Hey, Miki. My feet hurt," I tell him as he pulls me onto his lap.

Dancing all night with Lara, Sofia and Mila has made my ankles swell. Luckily, my dress hides it. I need a break. Alexei sure as hell knows how to throw a party.

Mikhail grasps my calves and gently lifts my legs onto his lap, sliding my dress up. He unbuckles my heels one by one, the metallic click echoing softly in the quiet room. They land with a thud on the plush cushions of the couch.

"You looked like you were having fun there, baby." He kisses my cheek.

"It was amazing. Do you want a dance?"

He shakes his head and smiles, flashing his perfect white teeth.

Niki's smile is bright, his eyes crinkling at the corners. I can tell it means a lot seeing his brother's face again.

"I only dance for one pretty girl," Mikhail whispers in my ear and butterflies erupt in my belly.

"Like, strip? Or like in Russia?"

"Both."

I stroke the back of my hand along his cheek.

"Sheila, get back here!" Alexei shrieks, getting our attention. I laugh as I see him chasing a flamingo through the garden and Lara following closely behind.

"Welcome to the family," Mikhail chuckles, watching the scene with amusement.

Enzo props himself down with a glass of whiskey on the couch opposite, swirling the ice cubes round.

"I need to speak to you tomorrow," Mikhail tells him in a low voice.

Enzo nods, almost looking defeated.

"Is he okay? If it's important you can go now." I whisper in Mikhail's ear.

"I'll speak to him tomorrow. Tonight is about you."

I watch as Frankie and Zara join Enzo on the couch. That seems to perk him up as he chats to Frankie in what I assume is Italian.

Everyone here is relaxed and happy. Which means, it's our time to leave.

"Shall we go back to the room? This momma is tired now. Unless you want to stay with everyone? I don't mind waiting."

He silences me with a passionate kiss, the taste of him a heady mix of spice and something wild.

"You are most important to me, Ana. My life is about you and our little baby boy."

Tears well up in my eyes. Damn hormones.

"And we have to consummate our marriage again." He winks as he pulls back.

I shift my weight on his lap, and he lets out a low groan. I know why. I can feel his cock pulsing against me.

"Shall we?" I grin.

"We shall. Immediately."

I slide off his lap, and as he stands, the warmth of his chest radiates against mine as he scoops me into his arms.

Luckily, it's only a short drive back from Alexei's. We didn't want to leave Hades, and it's too risky going away while I'm pregnant.

We'd rather spend the night in our home.

We rush through the front door, and he steals my breath away with a kiss.

"I want you so badly, Ana." He keeps kissing me.

I tilt my head back to give him better access to my neck.

He presses me tightly against him, sucking and biting with intense passion.

"Use your words. Tell me what you want." He licks all the way up my throat and I can't help but moan.

"Your mouth on me."

As he groans, his warm breath tickles my skin as he works on unzipping my wedding dress.

"Where? Be more specific."

"I want your mouth on my pussy."

He gives me the confidence to want to explore everything but also to use my words and tell him what I need.

He set off a sexual demon in me, and he loves trying to tame it.

"Beg for it."

Once the zipper is all the way down, he pulls it off my body to a pool around my feet.

My nipples harden with the cool breeze and he wastes no time in taking one in his mouth as I brush my hands through his hair.

"Shouldn't you be begging to taste my pussy, big man. I thought I was your favorite meal."

His hand slips under my white lace panties and I open my

legs as much as I can with my ankles caught inside this dress on the floor.

He slides his fingers in, smothering me in kisses.

"Hear how wet you are?"

"For you," I tell him.

He grabs my hand and rushes us through to the living room. As he spins to face me, his eyes hungry, he rips off his tie and undoes his top button.

"Heels stay on, panties off." His deep voice has me pulling them off in record time.

He sits himself on the floor in front of the couch and leans back.

"Sit on my face then, pretty girl."

Can't argue with that.

My heels click on the marble as I reach him. Lifting one leg over, I rest my knees either side of his head on the couch and grab the headrest. Wrapping his arms around me, he grips my thighs tight.

"Sit. All the fucking way. I want that delicious cunt smothering me."

I push down as he groans, licking my soaking pussy.

"So good, Miki." I rock my hips, grinding on his face.

My back arches as he sucks on my clit and spanks my ass.

"Fuck," I whisper, squeezing my eyes shut, letting myself feel every bit of pleasure he's giving me.

I jolt up as his fingers slide inside me, the sounds of my wetness filling the room.

"Oh. My. God." My mouth drops open and I pant until my lungs burn.

His fingers hit so deep my legs tremble and I grip the couch tighter, bucking on his face with screams of pure ecstasy erupt through me.

"Sir. Please. Let me come."

"Mmmm, give me it. Soak my face."

I cry out in release. My body tenses as he licks me all the way through it. He doesn't let up, so I ride the blissful wave.

As he slows down the pace, I lift my ass up, allowing him to move from under me.

He flips me round to face him, grabbing me by the throat to pull me up to him, and crashes his soft lips against mine.

"Bedroom. Now. I gotta be inside you. Fucking desperate for you."

I nod, and he lifts me into his arms.

CHAPTER 68

MIKHAIL

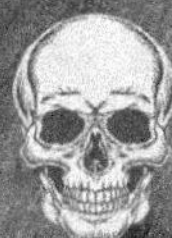

Song- when he holds you close, Omido

I'VE NEVER STRIPPED SO FAST in my life.

My perfect girl is spread out naked on the bed and I am desperate to sink inside her.

Claim my wife.

Climbing on the bed, I crawl to her and settle between her thighs, letting my cock press against her pussy.

"Ready to give me another one?"

I push the tip in and she lets a breathy moan fall from her lips.

"I-I don't know if I can. That was intense."

She smiles up at me, and I nip her lip. Grabbing her waist, I roll onto my back and she's straddling me.

"Baby, you don't have a choice. Ride my cock, pretty girl." I give her a smirk.

"Seeing as you asked so nicely." She blushes, raising herself up and sinking down on my cock.

"Fuck, you feel so good," I groan.

Using my grip, I assist her, lifting her up and pushing her down. She does that perfect pelvis roll at the same time that sends me feral.

"So good. Shit. Miki. I think I love your dick."

She throws her head back in pleasure and her hips grind on their own accord.

"That's it baby, ride me. Use me."

I pinch her clit and lightly grab her throat. I can feel she's close.

"Open your mouth."

She does as I say. I slide two fingers in.

"Suck. Get them nice and wet."

Her warm mouth coats them. I spread open her ass cheeks and slide my index finger in her ass slowly.

"Breathe, pretty girl."

I watch her reaction, her eyes fluttering closed, the moans that fall from her lips have my cock ready to explode.

When I push in a touch more, she bites down on her lip.

"Such a good girl," I praise as my finger goes all the way in.

"I need to come, Miki. Sir. Please."

Fuck. I need to come too.

"Give it to me. Now!"

With a few final thrusts up, her screams fill the room, and I call out her name at the top of my lungs as my own release takes over. I let her milk every last drop of me with her tight cunt.

"Fuck baby. Come here." I pull her into my chest letting my cock twitch inside her warmth.

"I love you, Ana. So much."

"I love you, big man. Mine forever." She leans up and kisses me.

Her hands tangle in my hair as she deepens the kiss.

"I'm getting hard again," I whisper against her lips.

"You're always hard around me, and I'm always wet. Soul mates." She winks.

"Mmm." I nip her bottom lip. "True. And I fucking live for it."

CHAPTER 69
ANASTASIA

Song- Devil Eyes, Luke Muzzic

I LET OUT a moan as he swipes his finger along my pussy. I can feel his cock growing inside me.

"I want another one." I tell him, and he kisses me harder.

"You think you can handle me?" He sucks on my bottom lip.

"You know I can, big man."

He carefully rolls me over onto my back and spreads open my legs.

"I want you filled in both holes."

He drags me to the edge of the bed. I groan when he pulls out of me, leaving my pussy aching to be filled again.

"W-what do you mean?"

I sit up on my elbows and watch him pull open the drawer, pulling out my small red vibrator and lube.

I can't stop looking at his enormous cock as he squirts the lube on the toy.

Scooting forward, I sit on the edge of the bed and grab his

thick thighs, dragging him closer to me so his dick is in my face.

"Want something, iskorka?" He smirks at me.

I look up at him through my lashes.

"Cleaning you up before round two."

"That's right, my dirty girl. Put that mouth to work."

Leaning forward the best I can with my growing belly, I take him in my mouth.

The way he moans out my name has me squirming on the mattress.

I lick him clean, digging my nails into his legs. Just as his thighs tighten, he pulls my head back.

"I want to come in your ass."

Fuck. That sets me on fire.

"Bend over, butt in the air, pretty girl."

I shuffle to my feet and get in position, crossing my arms on the bed.

His hands stroke over my cheeks.

"What a beautiful view," he says and taps his palm on my sensitive skin.

Every touch ignites a new fire for him. I might be his spark, but he is the one who sets me alight.

"Take a nice deep breath for me."

I do as he says, sucking in as much air as I can.

"Good girl, now breathe out."

I exhale and hear the vibrator buzz to life.

I keep my breathing steady as I feel it press against my back entrance. It makes me jump forward when the cool plastic is pushed slowly inside.

"Good fucking girl." His deep voice relaxes me. He slides his fingers inside my pussy, distracting me from the intrusion in my ass.

The deeper it goes, after the initial sting fades, I start to relax and close my eyes, focusing on the feeling.

"Color?"

"Green." I breathe out.

With slow thrusts, he matches the speed of the vibrator with his fingers in my pussy.

"Oh my god," I cry out, clenching my fists.

"Hold it in, baby." He slaps my ass.

Fuck.

He removes his fingers and grabs my ass. Biting down on my forearm, I brace myself as his cock pushes against my pussy.

"Fuck, Ana. Fuck," he hisses.

"More, Sir," I plead.

"Whatever you need." A growl erupts from his chest as he slams into me, over and over.

I'm so close to the edge. Vibrations shoot through my body, which is uncontrollably shaking.

"Miki."

"Almost baby," he groans, dragging his fingers through my hair and pulling my head back. "I wanna hear my wife scream for me."

Just as I'm about to explode, he pulls the vibrator out of my ass, and his cock presses against there. Then his fingers fill my back up, his thumb expertly circling my clit.

A primal scream rips through me as he sets me off. Stars fill my vision and his warm come covers my ass, his fingers so deep, hitting that sweet spot that has me gushing down my legs.

"Holy fucking shit."

I can't breathe. Everything is fuzzy. Slumping my head in my arms, just about holding my legs up. The next thing I know, a warm cloth is being gently rubbed over my sensitive skin.

"God, I love you, Ana."

"Hmm." I smile, turning my head to the side.

"I love you," I whisper. I don't have any energy left in me.

Once he's done, he helps me stand, wrapping his arms around me.

"Can I have a break before the next one?"

He chuckles, nodding in amusement. "Even I need a fucking break."

Nuzzling my head against my chest, I relax listening to the strong beat of his heart.

That belongs to me, just as mine belongs to him.

My monster.

Mine to love for the rest of my life.

CHAPTER 70

MIKHAIL

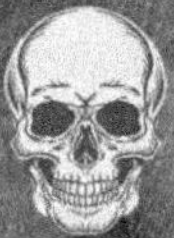

Song- Atlantic, Sleep Token

I've never felt so at peace in my life. Running my hand over a sleeping Ana's little bump.

Everything has fallen into place.

Not just for me, but for all my family.

Jax has Sofia and his kids, Niki and Mila are living in their crazy bubble, and she hasn't stabbed him in a while, and Lara and Alexei are happier than ever with their flamingos and skydiving.

And me.

I have a wife and a son on the way. Something I never imagined in my future. I never believed I deserved this.

The scarred monster.

But she saw through me, she was fated to be mine. No one could love me as fiercely as her. She has given me the confidence to be a better version of myself.

I'll always be a monster. It's bred into me. Never to her. Just for her and my family when I need to.

This woman saw my flaws and loved me deeper because of them.

She snores softly against my chest. I stroke her dark hair away from her face and tuck the blonde streak behind her ear.

"You're perfect, pretty girl," I whisper.

I could sit and watch her all night. She has me hypnotized. Not just by her beauty, but by her pure soul.

She smiles and rubs her face against my chest.

As the rain beats against the window, I grin, thinking about that night in Russia.

I think that's the night I realized I love her. That I could never let her go again.

"Hey, iskorka?" I whisper.

"Hmm?" Her eyes flutter open as I stroke her cheek.

"It's raining outside."

She lifts her head and rubs her eyes.

"It never rains here, does it?" She holds back a yawn.

"Hardly ever, baby."

When she sits up, I push myself off the bed and hold my hand out to her.

She raises a perfectly sculpted eyebrow, and I wink back, a playful glint in my eye.

"A pretty girl once asked me to dance in the rain with her and look up at the stars."

"Did she now?"

The warmth of her hand in mine sends a jolt through me as I nod.

"And did you do it?" she asks, chewing the inside of her mouth.

"I danced with her. Yes. But I didn't look up at the stars. I didn't need to."

She tilts her head, her dark hair falling around her face, as I lift her to her feet, looking down at her small form.

"And why is that?"

"Because the spark I needed to bring me back to life was standing right in front of me. With her big, blue eyes piercing into the depths of my soul. Turns out, she was the missing piece in my life that I'd been searching for. She is my soulmate. My first true only love."

"So I was right?" She gives me a wide grin and my heart flutters.

Fuck. I love her so much.

"You were right, baby. I knew it then, I know it now. Entangled with me, forever."

My hands run over her stomach and tears fall down her cheeks.

"I have one more question for you,"

"What's that, big man?"

I wipe the droplets away, pressing a kiss to her forehead.

"Will you do me the honor of dancing in the rain with me, pretty girl?"

I grip both sides of her face and press my nose to hers.

"I'd love to dance in the rain with you, handsome."

I press my lips against hers, and she strokes the scars on my cheek. Sliding my left hand down her body, I rest it over her bump, feeling my little man kick my palm.

Closing my eyes, I relish in this perfect moment.

It's like time stands still.

I almost wish I could stay here forever.

As I pull away, her glassy blue eyes meet mine, and I'm lost for words.

"Come on." I swipe my sweater from the side of the couch and help her put it on before leading her outside.

The rain beats down over us. The cold water can't even tame my fire for her.

I spin her round like a ballerina and then tug her flush

against me, holding her close as we sway in the gentle drizzle.

There isn't a soul on this planet I could love more than this woman in my arms right now.

Our children, yes.

But without her, our future wouldn't exist.

I'd still be living in the depths of my own hell, letting the scars of my past taint my future.

She clawed her way in. She took my heart in her hands and she claimed it as hers.

Anastasia Volkov saved me when I didn't even realize I needed to be saved.

And I will repay her for the rest of my life.

I will worship and adore her.

Fuck, I'll even bark for her.

And I will forever be owned by my pretty girl.

I was right when I gave her the nickname "iskorka". The woman that sparked me back to life.

Love is about letting them claim your soul and your heart.

True love is finding someone who will dance in the rain with you, and love your imperfections when you can't yourself.

"I will always dance in the rain with you, pretty girl."

The End.

EPILOGUE

ANASTASIA

"You can do this, baby. One more push."

Mikhail's deep voice calms me as he wipes the sweat from my forehead.

Another wave of contractions cripples me. I squeeze his hand harder than I've ever gripped anything in my life.

The pain is so fucking bad. I can't see straight.

"Take a deep breath in and push, Ana. We have to get him out on the next one."

Fuck. This feels like it's been going on for days.

"I can't take anymore."

"Now Ana!" The midwife calls out from the end of the bed. The room is filled with beeping and I close my eyes, letting a scream rip through my lungs and I push with everything I have left in me.

It takes everything out of me as I sag back against the bed.

Newborn cries fill the room. I look up and smile.

"You did it, pretty girl." Miki presses a kiss to my head and squeezes my limp hand.

The smiling midwife brings him over and places him down on my bare chest.

"I'm so proud of you," he croaks out and that brings tears into my eyes as I look down at our little boy.

A mass of dark chocolate hair, long thick lashes and a perfect little button nose.

"He's so perfect, Miki," I gush. I can't stop smiling, it almost makes the pain bearable.

"Just like his momma, then."

Miki leans down and kisses the top of Misha's head.

"You've given me the greatest gift, Ana. And the best possible life." He nuzzles his face against mine.

In this moment, having my new little family cuddled against me, I close my eyes and enjoy the calm.

This is everything I could have ever dreamt of. My heart is so full of love and joy, I will never forget this.

Every single bit of pain was worth it.

And just like he promised all those months ago, he held my hand through all of it.

"Hey, big man. Can you help me?" I throw my legs over the edge of the bed.

Everything aches so damn much.

Mikhail has been incredible with Misha. He told me I had to get my rest. Miki holds Misha on his chest. His huge hand nearly spanning our baby's whole body.

He walks over and holds out his arm, getting me to my feet.

"I hate being this weak." I tell him.

It's annoying me, I want to get up and help out. I want to

just go home. But they have to monitor my iron levels and blood pressure.

I'm hoping to leave today, two days is quite enough in this bright white room.

"The doctor came while you were napping, he said you're both clear to go."

I tip my head back, relief washing over me.

"Oh, thank God."

He wraps his arm around my waist and cuddles me against him. I stroke the side of a sound asleep Misha.

"My god, you look so hot being a daddy." I look up at him.

"Hmm. You can call me daddy all you want, pretty girl." He winks.

It's going to be a long six weeks.

"Daddy Miki." I slide my hand up his chest.

"Has quite the ring to it, maybe we can try it out."

He leans down and captures my lips.

"You mean when we can make another one of these beautiful creations?" He smirks.

My eyes nearly pop out of their sockets.

And then he chuckles and my blood pressure lowers.

"I'll give you a year."

"I can deal with that. See if I can give you a little girl to run circles around you."

He rests his head on top of mine.

"A mini version of you would be perfect, Ana."

EPILOGUE

MIKHAIL

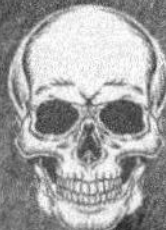

One Month Later…

"Alexei, it's fine. Stop panicking!" I pat him on the shoulder trying to stop him running round. It's exhausting me just watching him.

Probably the lack of sleep. Misha has a good set of lungs on him.

"It's Misha's baby shower, Miki, and the cake is not here yet."

"Nikolai is fixing it. Everyone is on their way and your house looks like a circus threw up in here."

I glance over at Lara clapping at the flamingos to get them outside.

Galena is a bit scared of the birds.

"Hey, big man." A glowing Ana walks over, cradling our little boy in her arms.

She is incredible. We've been in our own little bubble for a month.

I'm enjoying this family man life.

Jax and a heavily pregnant Sofia walk through the door,

Maeve running straight for Alexei, and Maverick in Jax's arms grinning at all the balloons.

"Daddy! Pop!" He claps his hands.

"Anyone for vodka?" Enzo comes in from the kitchen with an enormous bottle. His eyes are red, he looks like he's slept worse than me this month.

He's been quiet.

"It's 11am, Enzo."

"Wait till 12." Alexei smirks, not realizing Lara is right beside him until she taps his arm.

"We have a flight to catch later, Sladkiy."

Wrapping my arm around Ana's shoulder, I press her tight against my side just as Nikolai and his clan make their loud entrance.

Elena and Galena are giggling, heading straight for Maeve. With a huff, Nikolai drops the white box on the dining table.

"Fucking hell, Niki. The cake!" Alexei rushes over throwing the lid behind his back. He looks up and glares at Niki.

"You're lucky." He wiggles his finger.

Niki leans against me. "Can I punch him? He's been a pain in the ass all week worrying about this party."

"No. Brother. He's done us proud."

"Fine," he grunts, walking past me and stopping in front of Ana.

"Can I have a cuddle with my nephew?"

"Of course." Ana carefully hands a scrunched up Misha into Nikolai's arms. He starts lightly bouncing on his feet. I watch his eyes land on Enzo knocking back a shot.

Niki nods to me at the back door.

"I'll be back in a second." I kiss Ana and stride over to Enzo, grabbing him by the collar and dragging him outside.

"Talk."

He slumps down on the seat and pulls out a packet of cigarettes. Nikolai takes a big step back.

"I got so close to finding out the truth and then poof." He mimics an explosion with his hands. "Gone. Again."

I frown looking at Nikolai, he seems just as lost as I am with his riddle.

"Who?" I question.

Enzo sparks his lighter and takes a long drag.

"The ghost from my past. The reason I am who I am today. The woman who carved my damn heart out of her chest."

"Give us a name and we can help you."

Enzo cackles, his blue eyes burning into mine.

"No one can help me. If I'm right, I could be walking into my own death. That might put me out of this misery."

I press the bridge of my nose.

We cannot lose Enzo. And he sure as hell is not going to war in this state.

"There isn't anyone we can't find, Enzo. You know that."

He shakes his head, laughing to himself.

"There is. You know damn well there is. I'm ready to tear our worlds apart, Miki. Be prepared."

Oh fuck.

You are invited to decadence. Where you must step into hell to get a taste of heaven.

INFERNO is coming soon.

Mr. Declan Quinn, the 21st Century Willy Wonka of Dark Desires.

This is an Irish Mafia, Willy Wonka inspired retelling with a BDSM game of survival twist.

Releasing April 1st on Amazon and Kindle Unlimited.

PRE ORDER HERE: https://mybook.to/5oqz

There is more in the Beneath Universe. The mystery surrounding Enzo is about to be solved in the Beneath The Ruin duet, in 2025. Want another clue as to who his FMC is?

Download the bonus scene here:

https://BookHip.com/NXNQSDD

His duet will be releasing in Summer 2025. Starting with Surrender (book one) and Salvation (book two)

You can pre- order it here: https://mybook.to/k00FBr

HAVE YOU READ THE FIRST BOOK IN THE SERIES, CHAOS YET?

A brother's wife, biker, boxer and a vibrating tongue piercing, you're welcome.

It is available on Amazon and Kindle Unlimited.

READ IT HERE-https://mybook.to/qyAgjg

You can complete the series:

CAGED: Book 2 (Nikolai and Mila) A Single dad, bodyguard x spy, enemies to lovers mafia romance. https://mybook.to/TGXqvJA

CRAVE: Book 3 (Alexei and Lara) A best friends to lovers mafia romance. https://mybook.to/LNT6

MORE BY LUNA MASON

Beneath The Mask is Luna Mason's first series, in the same universe as Beneath The Secrets. If you haven't had a chance to read the series, they are all now live on Kindle Unlimited.

Distance, book one, Keller and Sienna- https://books2read.com/u/mgPk2X

Detonate, book two, Grayson and Maddie- https://mybook.to/3tlYU

Devoted, book three, Luca and Rosa- https://books2read.com/u/brB0xA

Detained, book four, Frankie and Zara- https://mybook.to/PfoRNy

Roman Petrov, a marriage of convenience novella, part of the Petrov Family Anthology will be releasing July 12th 2024. You can pre-order ROMAN here: https://mybook.to/I5APQd

ABOUT THE AUTHOR

Luna Mason is an Amazon top #12 and international best-selling author. She lives in the UK and if she isn't writing her filthy men, you'll find her with her head in a spicy book.

To be the first to find out her upcoming titles you can subscribe to her newsletter here:

Luna Mason's Newsletter

You can join the author's reader group (Luna Mason's Mafia Queens) to get exclusive

teasers, and be the first to know about current projects and release dates.

https://facebook.com/groups/614207510510756/

SOCIAL MEDIA LINKS:

http://www.instagram.com/authorlunamason

https://facebook.com/groups/614207510510756/

https://www.tiktok.com/@authorlunamason